SILK

SILK

LINDA CHAIKIN

BETHANY HOUSE PUBLISHERS
MINNEAPOLIS, MINNESOTA 55438

Published by Bethany House Publishers
A Ministry of Bethany Fellowship, Inc.
6820 Auto Club Road, Minneapolis, Minnesota 55438

Printed in the United States of America

Library of Congress Cataloging-in-Publication Data

Chaikin, Linda.   Silk/ Linda Chaikin.
         p.   cm.

      1. British—India—History—18th century—Fiction.
I. Title.
PS3553.H2427X54   1993
813'.54—dc20   92–46506
ISBN 1–55661–248–6   CIP

This first book of *Silk*
is dedicated to
Sharon Madison,
along with the words of Psalm 20:1–5.

LINDA CHAIKIN is a full-time writer and has two books published in the Christian market. She graduated from Multnomah School of the Bible and is working on a degree with Moody Bible Institute. She and her husband, Steve, are involved with a church-planting mission among Hindus in Kerala, India. They make their home in San Jose, California.

Prologue

KINGSCOTE SILK PLANTATION, NORTHEAST INDIA

JUNE 1793

The gilded clock in the Long Gallery of the Kendall mansion chimed the hour of ten. Through the open verandah the familiar jungle sounds from the Kingscote Plantation drifted on the humid air into Coral's bedroom. The screech of a night bird pierced the darkness, followed by an eerie cackle. Leaves and vines rustled, and if she fed her imagination, she could distinguish the low grumble of a Bengal tiger.

Dressed in a white peignoir, Coral, newly turned sixteen, left her bedroom and hurried down the hall. Her deep green eyes shining with excitement in the candlelight, and her golden hair falling about her shoulders, she descended the winding mahogany staircase intending to speak with her mother about the following morning's event.

Coral paused in the shadows at the sound of low, anxious voices in the gallery below.

Clutching her candle as close as she dared, Coral peered over the banister into the Great Hall. She was greeted by the sight of her stalwart father, Sir Hampton Kendall, standing near the door in a boot-length riding cloak. Her mother retrieved his tricorn hat from off the table as he belted on his scabbard.

Whatever would goad her father to ride out at this hour?

His deep voice reached her on the stairs. "Major Jace Buckley best be sending some of his sepoys to track this tiger, or the commissioner will hear my complaint. A half-dozen kills along the river alone! Aye, the brute's the worst man-eater seen in many a year."

"Must you ride to the outpost tonight?" Coral's mother questioned him. "Tomorrow's ceremony means so much to Coral. This will be her first time out of sickbed in months."

"Aye, I'm not forgetting that, Liza."

"She expects you to be there. She is already disappointed her sisters are still in Calcutta."

Her father's voice lowered, and Coral strained to catch his words. ". . . is it wise? The ritual could provoke the ghazis . . ."

"On Kingscote?"

"To be certain, this is not the raja's palace at Sibsagar, and yet . . ."

"We've always respected their beliefs, as they have ours."

"Tales of abductions, of druggings permanently affecting the mind, are not exaggerations. First converts from among their own are oft times murdered by the ghazis. It is their way of discouraging any from abandoning the caste system."

"Surely you do not think anything so dark could happen here?"

"With the maharaja asking the East India Company for military help against Burma, I discount nothing. Major Buckley arrived a few weeks ago, and more sepoys are on the way from the Calcutta garrison. Resentment over the Company grows."

"But it was the maharaja who sent emissaries to Calcutta asking for help."

"Aye, yet not all in the royal family are pleased with his move."

"They fear another annexation by England?"

"This time the province of Assam. Distrust of the Company's motives in sending troops cannot benefit Kingscote. And a Christian baptism of a Hindu taking place here will only increase the tension among the workers."

Her mother's voice lowered: "You are right about mounting tension. Even Rajiv wonders if he did the correct thing in giving Jemani permission. If we hadn't promised—"

"You spoke to him?"

"He came by this afternoon hoping to talk to you. He told me you promised him your support. Your presence as the *burra-sahib* of Kingscote would lend credibility before the other workers."

He groaned. "Ah, Liza, I did promise him . . . little Coral talked me into it. But that was before the drums of war beat so loudly."

Elizabeth Kendall laughed with soft affection and rested her forehead against his strong arm. "And you tell me I am too lenient with her."

"Are we both not spoiling her? Yet this long struggle with her illness . . ." Her father sighed. "But there is little I can do about keeping my promise now. This ugly matter of the tiger must be taken care of. The beast will soon be stalking Kingscote if we do not stop him! With twenty new children arriving to work in the silk hatcheries, the tiger must be killed."

He laid his hands on her shoulders and kissed her forehead. "Explain the matter to Coral."

"Yes, but what of Rajiv?"

He frowned. "I will stop by the bungalow before I leave. Another warning is wise. Should anything happen, I do not want these hands of mine tainted with their blood."

"Hampton! Do not say that. May God give us peace."

"Aye, and you and Coral best be getting to your prayers as soon as possible."

"You will encourage him?" she asked as he embraced her.

"I will," came his rugged voice. "I already vowed to stand with him. But—I am not comfortable with this. I was against this Christian ritual from the moment Coral came to me with it."

"I know, dear, but it is not as if we are sounding a trumpet before us. It will only be the four of us at the river."

He sighed.

"Darling, we did promise," she insisted. "Coral has been so ill . . . and this is the one bright moment she has known in a year. It is not as though she deliberately pressed Jemani to be baptized."

"I know, Liza, I know. But the words of those books have been burned into Coral's soul. I dare say they've kindled thoughts of bold exploits."

She hesitated. "Yes, the books . . . I sent for them from the shop in London. . . . Men like Brainerd and Wesley are worthy of study. And she enjoys them so."

"Goodly men, all. But this past year, with naught else to do but read and study them, she has changed from the girl we raised."

"She is joyful now, whereas in the past she was melancholy."

"It is only that she is so young to have brought the Indian girl to faith in the Blessed Christ. And she worries me a little." He frowned. "Will she ever want to mind the matter of marriage and children?"

"Of course she will. Give her time, dear."

"Does she not spend too much time with the workers? If she is lacking friends, perhaps it is time to send her to school in London."

"You sound so European!" Elizabeth chided in a teasing voice. "It was you who laughed at my colonial attitude when I arrived here as your bride, so naive of India. But Coral was born here! She feels none of that. Is it any wonder she has developed this kinship with the land and its people?"

"Aye, and I am proud of her. She is naught like her sisters. But is it not time she also meet the lords and ladies at Roxbury House in London? Her sister Kathleen is enough trouble . . . worming her way out of marrying her honorable Scottish cousin! Coral should be married soon—"

"Oh, Hampton, she is much too frail! Please, you promised me we would wait!"

He swiftly embraced her, his strong hand awkwardly patting her lustrous dark hair. "Now, now, my sweet dove, do not be upset . . . we will wait . . ."

There was a moment of silence, then Elizabeth's voice came again: "Hampton? About Jemani . . . you must admit that she is worthy of Coral's friendship. She is an excellent teacher of the Hindi language. And with Coral leading her into the Christian belief, it is not so surprising the two have formed a bond."

"And what is wrong with her two blood sisters?"

"You know very well Kathleen and Marianna are still in Calcutta. Besides, they do not share the same interests Coral has developed."

"In that, she is like you," came his tender voice. "I will not begrudge her the faith that makes you so strong."

They held each other until Elizabeth spoke. "But I do wonder sometimes about Jemani."

"In what way, Liza?"

"She is so gracious, so intelligent for being an untouchable." Elizabeth's voice lowered. "The other day she was reading Indian poetry to Coral."

"Is that so surprising?"

Elizabeth's voice remained quiet: "It was written in Sanskrit."

"Sanskrit! Now how would she be knowing the language of the ruling caste of brahmins?"

"I don't know, Hampton, I have often wondered. . . . Did Rajiv ever explain who their families were?"

"Nay. They were hungry and exhausted when I found them by the river. Jemani ill and expecting the child. Rajiv mentioned Rajasthan. They wandered here, looking for work, he said. I saw no reason to pry. Are you asking me to?"

"No, no, not now. I would not wish to alarm them by your questions. They risk enough already."

"Whatever Rajasthan meant in their past, it will not matter to Kingscote. If trouble confronts us, it will come from the meddling of the East India Company in Assam! I blame my brother-in-law for it. Sir Hugo is at Jorhat now. And I have little doubt he is promising the maharaja protection from Burma."

"Let us not discuss Hugo. . . . I would delay the baptism until you return, dear, but in Jemani's condition I think it best we do not. The baby is due in eight weeks."

He sighed. "Do as you will, Liza. I shall return as quickly as I can settle matters about the tiger with Major Buckley."

"Isn't he Colonel Warbeck's son?"

"Aye, and a friend of our son. Buckley's a good-looking devil, a rogue and a gentleman all in one. Good blood, too, and a strong wit. I suspect he'd produce me some strong grandsons—"

"Hampton!"

Coral had not moved from the shadows on the staircase, nor did she now. Her legs felt weak from being confined to bed for so many months with tropical fever. With one hand gripping the banister, and the other holding tightly to the candle-holder, she watched her father bend to kiss her mother goodbye, then leave by way of the heavy wooden door. Coral's excitement died like an extinguished flame. *Ghazis . . .*

Unwilling that her mother know she had overheard, she rose and silently retraced her steps up the stairway to her bedroom. A movement below in the shadows of the open library door caught her eye. Without a sound, the door shut. Someone else had been listening. *One of the house servants?*

She waited until her mother had left the Great Hall for the kitchen to give the nightly orders to the *kansamah;* then, bolstering her courage, Coral went quietly down the stairs and crossed the marble floor to the library door. Taking hold of the door latch, she opened it wide.

The library was in semidarkness. She stood in the doorway with the light from the hall behind her, still holding her candle. Books lined the walls from floor to ceiling and filled her nostrils with the rich smell of leather. During her year of illness these precious books had been her only friends.

"Who is in here?"

Silence greeted her, and so did a breath of the hot, muggy night air coming in through the split-cane window shades. Coral stood there for a moment longer, then went to close the window. She peered out into the garden, but saw no one. Had she imagined seeing the door shut? Was her ongoing fever playing tricks with her mind again? She pulled the window shut and latched it.

Exiting the library, she slowly climbed the staircase, pausing at each landing to glance back.

Once in her room, Coral stood in the shadows, her gaze fixed on the small whitish flame of her candle. She tried to shake off the feeling of unease, but the words of her father burned within her mind:

The first converts from among their own are oft times murdered by the ghazis.

Had not her mother said there were no fanatics on Kingscote?

Coral knew the Hindu caste system was strictly adhered to, and there were times when there was trouble in the village. But the Hindus that were part of Coral's world—men and women like Natine, Mera, Rosa, and a host of others—were all people whom she had known and grown up with as a part of her life on Kingscote. They were always friendly to her, and she held a deep affection for them. But it was true that her beliefs and theirs had not yet collided. Would Jemani's baptism change all this?

Some of her first memories were of her gray-haired *ayah*, Mera, rocking her in a split-cane chair in the nursery, humming some ancient Indian song while Coral's older sister, Kathleen, played with wooden blocks on the ishafan rug. Mera had been their ayah until the birth of Marianna and the arrival of the younger Burmese woman, Jan-Lee. Coral's childhood memories were all pleasant, like the many times she and her sisters had crept into the kitchen to beg sweet *barfis*—milk cakes made with coconut—from Rosa. While her brows would scowl down at them, Rosa's dark eyes were always full of mirth.

No ... these dear people were not the Indian fanatics known as ghazis. She would never believe that they could act in violence. Yet what did she truly know about their ancient religion? Except for the Hindu festivals when the juggernauts—huge, extravagantly decorated temple boxes—were dragged through the streets, she knew little.

In spite of Coral's efforts to dismiss her unease, her father's words brought a prickle to her skin. It was true that permission for Jemani's baptism had been nearly impossible to obtain from Rajiv.

Coral smiled to herself as she recalled how Jemani had retained her demeanor when arriving last week for the daily language lesson. No sooner were they alone, than she rushed to Coral with the news that her husband Rajiv had changed his mind. After three months of firm refusal, Rajiv finally agreed to permit his wife's baptism in the holy river before the baby was born. They had thrown their arms about each other and laughed when Jemani's extended womb hindered the embrace.

"You were right! Our God has heard my prayer!" Jemani then lowered her voice to a whisper. "Do not say a word to anyone, but Rajiv is also showing interest in the Christian teaching. Last night as we lay in our bed, he asked me important questions about the Christ of your Book."

Thinking back over that moment of spiritual joy brought Coral new resolve. No, she had not been wrong in showing Jemani the gift that Grandmother Victoria Roxbury had sent to her on the Christmas of 1791. The Bible was bound with embossed leather, the pages edged in gold, and Coral's name had been inscribed on the cover leaf along with the Roxbury coat of arms.

What had happened to Jemani after that was more an act of God than a plan instigated by Coral. She had asked Jemani to transcribe some of the verses in the gospel of Saint John into Hindi. And within five months, after much secret discussion between them, Jemani had declared that she wanted to become a Christian.

Now, as Coral lay in the dark, sleep remained elusive. She convinced herself the reason was that her father had ridden to the military outpost at Jorhat while a man-eating tiger was roaming the jungle. Watching the mosquito net that encircled her bed flutter lazily in the light breeze, Coral soon found herself drifting off.

By morning, the ghosts of the night before had evaporated with the sweltering Indian heat. At the still waters of the glittering Brahmaputra River, Coral slipped the ankle-length tunic over the head of the lovely young Indian woman, and let it fall into place.

Jemani smiled, her warm brown eyes shining and a tinge of rose showing beneath her copper skin.

"Rajiv will come with the memsahib," she told Coral, speaking of Elizabeth Kendall. Jemani glanced through the mango trees in the direction of the dirt road and her gaze took on a far-distant look. "My Rajiv is a prince. There is no one better among men. He shall be a goodly father."

Coral strained to hear the *ghari* coming down the narrow road. Instead she heard the familiar cackle of mynah birds in the branches. To ease the building tension, she tried to coax a smile from Jemani. "You are right about not wanting to wait. If we delayed any longer, instead of an oversized tunic, you would need to don a *shamianah*," she said, speaking of a large Indian tent.

Jemani gave a nervous giggle, then sobered, running her palms over her protruding womb. "Both I and my child will be baptized together. Rajiv knew I wanted this."

Coral picked up the skirts of the simple muslin dress that she had donned for the wet and muddy occasion and hurried toward the bank, feeling the dried elephant grass brush her pantaloons. She stooped, letting the warm water trickle through her fingers. Her gaze scanned the river. There were no crocodiles, nor any sign of the one-horned black rhino. A few disinterested monkeys swung through the green branches along the bank, and fruit bats enjoyed the mangoes.

"The temperature is fine," Coral called over her shoulder. "Mother said the water will not hurt your condition."

"The memsahib is wise. I feel at peace knowing she will deliver my son."

"Son?" teased Coral. "My, but you are in a positive mood. I will take a girl any day."

She expected to hear another laugh, and when there was silence, Coral turned her head to discover the reason. Jemani had walked toward her, her dark eyes searching Coral's face.

"If my baby is a girl, Rajiv and I will name her Coral. Son or daughter, you will protect my child?"

Coral stared up at her. The idea that any child would need protection on the Kendall silk plantation brought immediate anxiety. A realization of her own responsibility over Jemani's public confession deepened Coral's resolve to protect her friend.

"Say you will, Coral." Jemani stooped down beside her, anxiously searching her eyes.

Coral rested a hand on her shoulder. "The Kendall family has produced silk on this land for nearly a hundred years. Our men have fought soldiers from Rangoon and warriors from Sikkim. Neither my father nor my brothers will run away from danger, Jemani. And neither will I."

"Your father is honorable, and brave."

Coral felt a rush of pride. "Yes, he is all that. And he will not permit hostility toward you and Rajiv as long as you live on Kingscote. Your baby will be safe."

Coral felt Jemani take hold of her hand and place the palm against her womb. She whispered intently: "You and the memsahib are my only friends. Now the true Holy Man—Jesus—has washed me clean. He has done what the holy Ganges cannot do. Today my heart can laugh and sing. For the first time I do not fear death, for a thousand rebirths do not await me, rather eternal life. But there are things you do not know, Coral. Things I cannot—must not—tell you."

Coral felt uncomfortable. *What things?* she wanted to ask, but Jemani continued. "Is not memsahib a godmother to your cousin in Calcutta?"

Coral thought of her spoiled cousin Belinda Roxbury. Her two sisters were visiting her now.

"Yes, and my aunt and uncle are my godparents. Why do you ask?"

Jemani's expression was intense. "And this you do in the church?"

"Yes . . . I suppose you might say that."

Jemani drew in a breath. "I know we are different. You are from England and I—"

"I too was born in India," Coral interrupted.

"Yes, that is so. Then please, will you consider becoming godmother to my child?"

Coral stared at her, wondering if she had heard correctly.

"Rajiv told me to ask you before the baptism."

Coral felt her throat constrict. She had never seen Jemani this earnest before. For Coral to make such a promise without her parents' permission was unthinkable, and yet . . . she felt a gentle pressure from within that bid her to risk something of herself, since Jemani was risking so much.

Coral looked into the trusting eyes of her friend and found that it was easy for her emotions to let the request take root in her soul. During the year of her illness, she had lain in bed listening to her mother reading from the autobiography of the great colonial missionary to the American Indians, David Brainerd. His dedication to Christ, and his love for the people he served, had often brought tears to her eyes, and it was easy to imagine herself following in his steps.

Her sister Kathleen insisted that Coral felt too deeply, and reacted impulsively, but Coral could not help herself. Strong emotion came easily. And now, the urgent request made by her first convert lit a small flame in her heart. As she stared into Jemani's dark eyes, she could feel the heartbeat of the child touching her palm.

21

"Yes, Jemani."

Jemani's eyes glistened. "You are more than a friend. You are as close to me as my sister was."

"Was?"

"She is dead."

Coral stared at her, but the creak of ghari wheels and the plod of horse hooves on the road caused Jemani to loosen Coral's hand, and she stood, drawing Coral up with her.

Coral squinted beneath her raised hand. "It is my mother, and your husband is with her."

With a pleased cry, Jemani hurried to meet him.

Coral watched as the dark, handsome Rajiv stepped from the ghari and assisted her mother down to the ground.

Elizabeth Kendall, carrying her Bible, greeted Jemani with a palm to her cheek, then walked to Coral. "I am proud of you, dear."

Coral slipped her arm about her mother's slim waist.

Minutes later, Coral stood on the bank, holding the blanket and a cloth to dry with. Her heart thumped as she watched her mother leading Jemani by the arm into the river. A quick glance at Rajiv showed an immobile face. What was churning within his mind Coral could only guess. She looked back to see Jemani standing before her mother, nearly waist deep in the water. Coral squeezed back her tears.

Thank you, God, for this privilege. I thought my life was wasting away on a sickbed. Yet out of my weakness, you have brought life everlasting.

She heard her mother speaking, and the words came enriched with new meaning to Coral.

"Jemani, you have taken Jesus the Son of God to be your Savior and Lord. And because you have confessed your new faith, I now baptize you in the name of the Father, the Son, and the Holy Ghost. Amen."

A gentle swoosh filled the hot morning. Water rippled, and Jemani came up sopping wet, her ebony hair sticking to the sides of her face. Elizabeth opened her arms, and Jemani stepped into them.

Coral watched them standing there in an embrace that transcended nationality.

Yes, Jemani had been right. They were truly sisters.

Rajiv broke the emotional intensity. He stepped into the river, reaching out both hands to help the two women back onto dry ground, and then holding his wife, he murmured something in Hindi. She smiled up at him, and he brushed his fingers across her cheeks, wiping away the tears. He kissed his fingers, then touched Jemani's lips. Coral turned away from the intimate scene.

Coral heard a sound behind her, coming from the thick jungle growth. A sweeping glance along the fringe of trees revealed nothing. *The wind?* she wondered. *Perhaps a bird or a monkey.*

She was turning back toward the river when the unmistakable flash of a white *puggari* disappeared into the thick green. Someone had been crouching behind the bushes. Watching. Someone who did not want to be seen. No doubt he had only been curious, and yet fearful to show himself, not wanting to associate with the condemned act.

Just then, several overripe figs plopped to the dirt from the branch above Coral's head. She looked up into the gnarled tree, shading her eyes. Eight-year-old Yanna straddled the limb, her black pigtails swinging. The girl swung down and landed gracefully on sandaled feet.

Coral let out a nervous breath. "Yanna, were you up there all that time?"

Yanna ran toward her, wearing dusty white. She murmured in Hindi: "Burra-sahib warn me to stay away. But Jemani is my friend."

The title of burra-sahib—the "great man"—was used on Kingscote for Sir Hampton Kendall. But her father was away at the military outpost in Jorhat. Had he spoken to the child before he left late last night, or was Yanna speaking of someone else?

Her mother's voice interrupted her thoughts.

"Coral, come along dear, we must get back."

"Yes, Mother, I'm coming."

"You too, Yanna," called Elizabeth. "You can ride on the driver's seat with Rajiv."

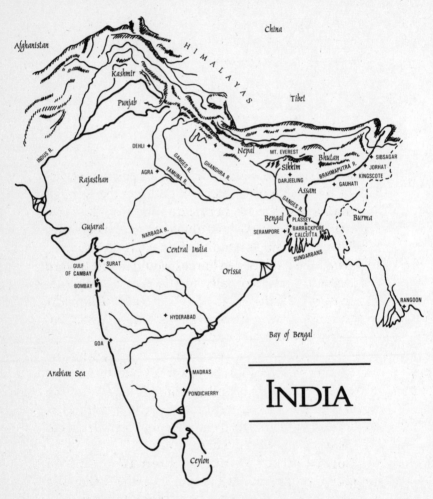

Afghanistan

China

H I M A L A Y A S

Kashmir

Tibet

Punjab

INDUS R.

DEHLI

Nepal

MT. EVEREST

Sikkim

Bhutan

SIBSAGAR

JORHAT

GANGES R.

GHANGHRA R.

DARJEELING

BRAHMAPUTRA R.

KINGSCOTE

Rajasthan

AGRA

YAMUNA R.

Assam

GAUHATI

GANGES R.

Bengal

PLASSEY

Burma

Gujarat

NARBADA R.

SERAMPORE

BARRACKPORE

CALCUTTA

Central India

GULF

OF CAMBAY

SURAT

Orissa

SUNDARBANS

BOMBAY

HYDERABAD

Bay of Bengal

GOA

Arabian Sea

MADRAS

PONDICHERRY

INDIA

RANGOON

Ceylon

INDIAN   OCEAN

1

Coral stared anxiously from her bedroom verandah at the jungle perimeter surrounding the Kendall silk plantation. Silence permeated the rosy dusk. No elephant feet raised the dust along the road where they usually carried huge bundles of raw silk to the river. In season, the flat wooden barges would set off toward the Ganges, and eventually to the port of Calcutta, where ships belonging to the East India Company would sail for the ports of the silk-hungry West: Venice, Cadiz, Lyons, and London.

Coral's eyes were riveted on the road, where the twilight seeped through the branches of intertwining trees. There were no sounds coming from the Indian workers in the huts, nor from the newly arrived children being trained to feed chopped mulberry leaves to the silkworms in the hatcheries.

Coral tensed. Thinking about the children brought her concerns back to Jemani and the dilemma confronting her. Rajiv was missing! Jemani, distraught by the news, had gone into premature labor. If she gave birth now, the baby would be born six weeks early.

Her hands tightened on the wrought-iron railing. Perhaps the news that Jemani's husband was missing would prove to be nothing serious, and he would return unharmed. But even if he did, the crisis now facing Coral would remain.

Unaware of Rajiv's disappearance and its effect on Jemani, Coral's mother had left before dawn to deliver medicine to the nearby village. With the tiger scare holding Kingscote captive, her father had accompanied her, bringing several armed workers with him. Even her two sisters were away; not that they would be much help, she thought dourly. Kathleen would balk at the idea of delivering a baby, and Marianna would swoon!

Unless her mother returned soon, she would need to deliver the baby alone. Coral's heart gave a nervous flutter. . . . Suppose she forgot something important? Suppose she froze at the sights and sounds of Jemani's suffering?

No, she must be strong. She had promised Jemani that she would not forsake her. Coral took in a deep breath and tried to relax, but her efforts brought no relief. Her heart thudded. She had previously accompanied her mother to assist during the birthing process of other workers on Kingscote, but never had she delivered a baby by herself. She closed her eyes and tried to remember everything her mother did, but anxiety left gaps in her memory.

If it had not been for my prolonged struggle with tropical fever, I would not be facing this emergency, she thought. How simple matters would be if she were with her sisters in Calcutta visiting her aunt and cousin, with nothing more important to do than attend a round of elegant balls and picnics in the escort of young British officers.

Of course! she thought. She could turn to Jan-Lee! The Burmese woman who had been her devoted ayah could deliver the baby. She whirled to leave the verandah, but stopped. Her delicate brows came together. No, she could not! Jan-Lee would not be in any condition to aid her as midwife, since she had given birth to her own child only days ago.

Frightened, Coral stared out across the sloping lawn that led to the low banks of the Brahmaputra. The eastern sun deepened into shades of orange above the river, and thread-legged cranes gathered to drink and lift their eyes to the distant clouds.

If only her mother would arrive in the boat! Not a whisper of wind stirred her flaxen tresses that were plaited in thick braids at the nape of her neck. She was dressed as one would expect on a plantation that produced some of the finest silk in the East—in a cool and loose-fitting silk tunic—a practical style of dress bearing little resemblance to the yards of skirts, crinolines, and hoops that she would be expected to wear at Roxbury House when she arrived in London to visit her grandmother.

The leaves on the trees were painted with dust, and her mother's garden of purple bougainvillea lay withered and thirsty in the sun's heat. Coral had lived through many dry seasons where all life was poised with expectation, waiting for the first grumble of thunder, the first fat drops of water to splat against the powdery dust. The insatiable thirst of the giant land awaited brief fulfillment in the flood that would wash all things clean and fill the rivers. At the moment, Coral's prayer broke like an India flood upon her soul:

Lord, please help Mother get here in time!

Cutting through the afternoon stillness, frantic voices shouted from the direction of the river, followed by the trumpeting of an elephant.

Coral shaded her eyes, hoping that her prayer only moments before had indeed been answered.

Coral stared toward the *ghat*, where stone steps led down to the small boats. Two white-clad barge workers, called *manjis*, ran toward the mansion. Another rode the back of a gray elephant, its ears flapping like tents.

Natine, who was her father's *kotwal* over the other servants on Kingscote, left the front porch to meet them on the lawn. He stood with dignity in a white puggari and a long blue shirt over white baggy trousers. The manjis spoke rapidly in Hindi, but Coral could not hear what they were saying. They seemed overly excited for the mere arrival of her mother. *Something is wrong.*

Natine hurried back up the lawn toward the house, and Coral grasped the railing and leaned over.

"Natine! What is it? News from my mother and father?"

The turbaned head lifted in her direction. His walnut-skinned face was grave. "No, miss-sahiba. They are still in the village."

Her father had returned a week earlier from the British outpost near Jorhat. Only yesterday, he had warned them that it was a Royal Bengal tiger—ten feet long, male, aggressive, and white-ruffed. Tigers, of course, were not unusual around Kingscote, and Coral had seen many. This one, however, was a maneater. Since her father had ridden to the outpost, the tiger had attacked two fishermen, mauling one and eating the other. The tiger proved to be cunning, avoiding the traps, terrorizing the village, and now holding Kingscote captive.

"What did the manjis say? Is it the tiger?"

"Major Buckley sent a message: The tiger is on Kingscote. He says the workers must be on guard. The women and children are not to venture out."

Her father had already told her that a patrol belonging to the 21st Light Cavalry in command of the native *sowars* had been on the lookout for days.

Her stomach muscles tightened. She had no choice but to disobey the major's orders. Did Natine know about Jemani, that she must deliver the baby? She guessed that he did, but his expression had not softened.

From the kitchen below, she heard the pleasant sounds of dinner being prepared. Mera's voice floated up to her on the verandah, rebuking the two Indian children who had done something wrong. Faithful, loving Mera . . . but there was no use ordering her to assist in the delivery; the head female servant of the household would vow that she preferred death to breaking caste with an untouchable.

"Any news about Rajiv?" she called down.

Natine hesitated. "Not yet. With the news of the tiger, I must call off the search."

He turned away and began to issue orders to the two workers. Coral felt queasy. *Where is Jemani's husband?*

She remained at the rail looking down. The workers listened to Natine as though he were the burra-sahib. Recently, she had become aware of how all the *nauker-log* jumped to obey his commands. Natine was both respected and feared. She had once

31

asked her father about Natine's background, and discovered that he was of the *rajputs* from Moghul country in Rajasthan, central India. The rajputs were said to be born in the warrior caste of the Hindu system, only one rank below the priestly *brahmins*. One thing was certain; Natine did not permit the nauker-log to forget.

A distant rumble reverberated. She tensed. The tiger? No—she blinked as a brilliant flash of dry lightning zigzagged across the murky sky, heralding the monsoon. The sullen grumble echoed its warning as movement drew her eyes in the direction of the silk workers' huts. Yanna raced across the dusty field toward the house, her willowlike body lost in the flapping white sari. Coral's heart began to pound. No. . . .

She had sent Yanna to stay with Jemani early that morning after the news of Rajiv's disappearance, and she knew the child was bringing her the words she did not want to hear.

Yanna stood barefoot in the dust. "Missy Coral! Missy Coral! Must bring memsahib and come quick!"

Coral's hands turned clammy. Her own calm voice surprised her. She leaned over the rail. "Wait for me, Yanna. I will be down in a minute!"

The girl nodded, her small hand clamped across her mouth, her round dark eyes frightened.

Natine was still standing below in the stone courtyard adjacent to the lawn. She noted the rigid shoulders that shouted his resentment over her involvement. Except for his common garb, he could have passed for some Moghul king from the glorious Indian past, disdainful of the English influence. She called out, ignoring his displeasure: "Natine! I will need

Mera to help me. Call her at once."

For a moment he remained immobile, like a deaf mute staring up at her. At last, he brought his fingers together at his forehead in *namaste*. He went up the porch steps into the house and headed toward the back of the mansion.

Coral whirled, ran from the bedroom verandah, and snatched up her mother's medical bag that waited by the door. She lifted her tunic and rushed down the flight of stairs, ignoring the weakness in her knees. Whether it was due to fear or illness, she could not be certain. She paused at the bottom and caught her breath, feeling her heart thumping. With dignity that far surpassed her sixteen years, she walked past silent servants who pretended to know nothing of the emergency. In the hall, she stopped and looked toward the back of the house. "Natine? Mera!"

The mansion walled her in with silence. From outside she could hear the distant shouts of *mahouts* riding away on their elephants to warn the silk workers of the tiger.

Had Natine delivered her message? "Mera!" She set the bag down and ran back into the kitchen. Only the male kansamah was there, his brown hands dusted white with flour. He looked up, the usually good-natured face impassive.

"Harish! Where is Mera?"

"I do not know, Miss Coral."

"Where is Natine?"

"He went to warn the workers of the tiger."

So. Natine had ignored her instructions. Well, there was nothing to be done about it now. She spun around and hurried out.

On the verandah steps, she paused to look out

across the wide lawn toward the river, still hoping to see the barge bringing her mother.

The white-clad manjis, leaving their work on the Kendall boats, ran along the bank shouting to the other fishermen to take heed.

"Tyger! Tyger!"

"Kahbahdar! Tyger! Kahbahdar! Tyger!"

Coral dared not think about the ten-foot Bengal tiger. She hurried after Yanna, who ran ahead across the field in the direction of the road, dust rising beneath her soles. Every so often Yanna stopped to cast an anxious glance over her shoulder to make sure Coral was following.

What will I do when I get there? thought Coral, feeling the sweat trickle down her ribs. With her mother's bag in hand, she hurried on. "Lord, please be with me. . . ."

Again she tried to remember everything her mother had taught her about delivering a baby. Months of illness left her gasping as she ran behind Yanna, the dirt encasing itself inside her slippers. Fatigue assailed her. Her brain spun dizzily.

Yanna waited near the road. Here they would cut across the shadowy acres of mulberry trees to the whitewashed hut.

"Wait," Coral cried breathlessly, forced to pause beneath an arch of trees. She leaned against the trunk trying to catch her breath. There was no wind, insects droned, the jungle smelled hot and dry, and the sounds of the tropics were magnified in the stillness: "Monsoon, monsoon," they seemed to murmur.

Yanna stood watching Coral, her large dark eyes tense. She impatiently brushed the gnats from her cheek.

A sound coming from farther down the road caused Coral to straighten, and she gazed down the avenue of trees. Horse hooves raised the distant dust, followed by a faint jangle of metal.

"Soldiers, Missy." Yanna ran back and stood shyly behind Coral's skirt.

Relieved, Coral stepped into the road. Her older brother, Michael, would be riding with them.

A small patrol belonging to the regiment of the 21st Bengal Light Cavalry rode around the bend, and encountering Coral, reined in their horses. She caught a flash of dusty black and silver uniforms from the six British soldiers and two officers. Behind rode a dozen Indian sowars, who drew up on sweating horses and waited.

Coral's eyes scanned the faces of the British soldiers, looking for Michael, but he was not among them. Inadvertently she met the confronting gaze of the officer in command. His physical good looks were indisputable. He was strongly built and wore the uniform well. His hair was very dark; his eyes, a penetrating bluish black beneath dark lashes. His chiseled features, streaked with dust and sweat, betrayed that he had ridden hard for some distance.

Unsmiling, his gaze swept Coral with eyes that revealed nothing. He rested his gloved hands on the saddle in front of him.

"Miss, I sent orders that no women or children were to venture out."

His tone was official, immediately putting her on the defense. Coral's lips closed mutely.

"I suppose you are one of the Kendall daughters?" His voice suggested that he already knew who she was, and that he expected a confrontation with this spoiled silk heiress, who would add to his frustration after a disagreeable day of tiger tracking.

Coral considered herself anything but spoiled, and said too sedately: "I am Miss Coral Kendall, if that is the intent of your question, Captain."

"Major," he corrected with a faint smile. "Major Jace Buckley."

Coral's emotions retreated behind a dignified shield. She did not trust men who were either too good-looking or too self-confident.

She felt unusually stiff, and tore her eyes away, giving a touch to her thick braids. She saw an older man with a reddish gray beard and heavy brows and felt more comfortable. There was something familiar about him. She had seen him before, but where?

"Now, lassie, to be sure, we be knowin' who ye are," he said with a thick Scottish brogue. "Did ye not get the warnin'? The tiger's been spotted nearby. Ye best not be aboot."

She raised her arm and pointed in the direction of the silkworm hatchery centered in the large mulberry orchards. "I'm not going far. I have urgent business to attend to." She paused for emphasis. "My father *owns* Kingscote."

The uniformed captain smiled kindly. "Aye, lassie, and I be knowin' Sir Hampton Kendall well. 'Tis a fact I'll be workin' for him soon. The name is Seward."

Seward. . . . The name had a pleasant ring to it, and she placed it in her memory. Before her father's marriage to her mother, Lady Elizabeth Roxbury of London, he had sailed to China for trade in tea, jade, silk, and porcelain. That segment of his adventurous life he no longer talked about, for her mother would gently interrupt and change the subject, but Coral recalled that the name Seward was part of that history.

"I believe my father has mentioned you."

Seward grinned. "Aye, lassie. And ye be the prettiest picture of a Kendall that could be!"

Coral was afraid she would blush and glanced back toward the major, who impatiently flapped his reins against his gloved palm.

"I doubt if Sir Hampton would want you wandering around without an escort, Miss Kendall," came his bland interruption. "Is your father about? I have business with him."

"He has gone to the village with my mother. My brother was said to be riding with you, Major. Would you know where Michael Kendall is?"

He did not answer. Captain Seward turned in his saddle to look at him. "Well, Major?"

Coral picked up the tension in their exchanged glances but waited silently for an answer.

The major responded with the lift of a gloved hand, and while his voice was polite, he gave the impression that Seward was to keep silent. His eyes fixed on the child Yanna, then came back to Coral.

"Miss Kendall, I am sorry to report a death on Kingscote. I believe he is one of your father's workers. Michael is seeing to him now."

The major's words came as a sickening blow. Instinctively Coral knew that it was Rajiv. In a gesture of protection she drew Yanna against her skirt.

"The tiger?" she asked, but even as she inquired, she read something unpleasant in his eyes.

"It has not yet been determined." He appeared to take note of the fact that she had drawn the child close to her, and he studied her face. "As Seward said, the

37

tiger was spotted close by. I will have one of my men escort you and the child back to the house. I am sorry, but that is an order."

Coral's frustration mounted. She shook her head. "You do not understand." She picked up her mother's medical bag and said delicately: "Ahh . . . a friend of mine is about to . . . to deliver." She wanted to add, *Possibly the wife of the man you found*, but aware that Yanna clung to her, she did not. Before the long night was over, she must tell Jemani that Rajiv was dead.

Had his death been an accident? A tight feeling restricted her throat. More than ever she felt responsible for Jemani. Did Rajiv's death have anything to do with her baptism?

Major Buckley did not seem the slightest bit bothered about the delicacy of childbearing, although the situation did seem to provoke a spark of irritation.

"She is about to have a baby?"

Coral glanced toward the trees, brushing a stray strand of hair from her throat. "Yes, excuse me, I must hurry."

"Then you will need an escort, Miss Kendall. Where is your friend?"

"Not far." She pointed. "In one of the huts."

He gave her a slanted look. "Those are the silk workers' huts."

Did he think that because she was the daughter of Sir Hampton Kendall that she had no friends among the Indians?

She was about to reply when behind her, coming from the direction of the mansion, the clop of hooves interrupted. Coral whirled with expectation, and with a rush of relief saw her mother driving the pony trap.

Her dark hair was smoothed back into neat braids coiled at the nape of her neck, and she wore a modest muslin working-dress, now splotched with perspiration. Even so, her mother retained an elegance not easily masked. Coral knew that hidden from view near her feet was the rifle her mother always brought with her.

Coral gathered up her skirt and ran to meet her. "Mother!"

Elizabeth Kendall stopped the wagon and reached both arms to clasp her daughter.

"I was afraid you would not come," breathed Coral, taking solace in the familiar fragrance of her mother's sachet. The quiet brown eyes and the gentle touch of her mother's palm to the side of her face told Coral that all was once again in order.

"You were brave to come alone, Coral. But you should not be out of bed."

Coral basked in her mother's compliment. "I had to. It is Jemani! She went into labor!"

Elizabeth frowned. "Yes, Mera told me. Did she fall?"

"No, oh, Mother!" she lowered her voice. "It is Rajiv! He was reported missing last night, and now—"

"What! Last night? But I was not told before I left this morning with your father."

"Natine did not mention it until breakfast. By then you and Papa had already gone! Jemani went into labor, and now the soldiers seem to think that—"

"Oh no! Does Jemani know he is missing?"

"Yes, but it is worse than that. The major has found the body of one of the workers. Michael's looking into the matter now. Mother . . . suppose. . . ?"

Elizabeth's face drained of color, and Coral felt her

mother's fingers tighten about her arm.

Major Buckley had maneuvered his horse up to the side of the wagon, and Coral noted that now he was the precise military gentleman.

"Madam, I regret to report a death. I believe your son may know who he is."

Elizabeth's questioning gaze met his and she gave a guarded glance in Yanna's direction.

"Your fears are justified. Your son is taking care of matters now. I will have Captain Seward notify Sir Hampton."

Her mother sat for a moment in the wagon, stunned, and Coral's thoughts rushed to Jemani. She would have no husband to help raise her child.

"I understand a baby is due. I will have several of the sowars escort you."

"Yes, yes, thank you, Major Buckley. You are very thoughtful."

"Shall I escort your daughter back to the house?"

Coral felt a prickle of exasperation. Now why did he press the matter of her returning to the house?

Elizabeth looked preoccupied with troubling thoughts. "Yes. Perhaps that is best." She turned to Coral. "Dear, maybe you should return with the major."

Coral took hold of her mother's arm. "But I promised Jemani. After what has happened I cannot just go back to my room and wait. Mother, you must let me help, please!"

Elizabeth scanned her daughter's face worriedly. "Are you feeling strong enough? You look a trifle pale, Coral. . . ." Quickly she felt her forehead for a new outbreak of fever. Her dark brows came together. "You know you should not be out of bed. It is much too soon."

"I cannot abandon Jemani at a time like this. It was I who encouraged her baptism, and now Rajiv—"

Coral stopped. Her eyes averted to Major Buckley. He sat listening and watching her, apparently without the slightest qualm at doing so.

Coral managed to retain a practiced dignity that could equal her mother's. "Mother, I feel well enough. Jemani expects me to be there. I would never forgive myself if I were not."

"At least use my *chunni* over your head. The sun is still hot." Elizabeth helped Coral into the wagon and turned toward Yanna, who was already seated in the back. "Yanna dear, hand Missy Coral my chunni. It is in the basket. . . . By the way, Major, will you tell my husband to come for us in the morning? And do stay the night. My husband will see to your comfort."

Major Buckley touched his hat and turned his horse back toward the road. "Your hospitality is received gratefully."

Coral felt his gaze, but stared ahead, her back straight.

The wagon surged forward, and Coral held both hands on the seat as she bounced from side to side.

"The major is the son of Colonel Warbeck in Calcutta?"

"What, dear? Oh . . . yes, Jace Buckley is adopted."

Colonel Warbeck was not familiar to Coral, although she was acquainted with some of the military in the East India Company. Her uncle—Sir Hugo Roxbury, who was married to her mother's younger sister Margaret—was a high official in the civilian service to the governor-general at Calcutta.

41

"You do not know Colonel Warbeck, but your aunt Margaret knew him when she was a young girl in London. . . . The colonel's a rigid man, very much the soldier, I am told. His son, on the other hand, is somewhat of an adventurer."

"The major is adopted? What happened to his parents?"

"I am not certain anyone knows. I've heard everything from his father having been a corsair, to his mother being a lady in London. One must never listen to gossip. Evidently he was already an orphan when the colonel found him. Somewhere near Darjeeling, I believe. He had been taken into the home of a guru."

A guru! Then was he raised a Hindu? Coral glanced over her shoulder past the two sowars who were riding a discreet distance behind to guard them. The major was talking to Seward. There was a noticeable air of earthiness about Major Buckley that contradicted any notion of mysticism. As Seward turned his horse to ride, the major looked in her direction. Quickly, Coral jerked her head away.

If he were brought up by a guru, then he would possess a clear insight into Hinduism. Was this Eastern religion important to him?

Elizabeth Kendall touched the pony lightly with her whip, and Coral steadied herself as the trap jostled forward across the dusty field. In the distance, the whitewashed huts stood against a darkening backdrop of thick jungle. Chattering monkeys and shrieking birds permeated the branches of the trees above their heads.

"Rajiv's death complicates everything," murmured her mother. "Say nothing to Jemani until the child is born."

Coral nodded. "You do not think it had anything to do with the baptism?"

"The major and your father will discover what has happened." She reached over and squeezed Coral's arm. "Do not feel badly. You did well in instructing Jemani in the Scriptures."

Coral felt anything but victorious. *What about Rajiv?* The hopeless question kept repeating itself in her mind. Yesterday he walked the earth, with a wife and their first child on the way, a man with hopes, with the potential of knowing God. Now, he was dead. It was over. Like a tiny flash of light streaking across the Indian sky. Gone. *Jemani! How can I tell you?*

2

Night was upon them. A shudder of thunder shook the hut. The small earthenware oil lamps cast shadows on the walls of the low, square room, with its floor of smooth-plastered mud and cow dung. Jemani gripped the cloth tightly, biting into it, as Elizabeth Kendall murmured words of courage.

Coral's wrists ached from wringing cotton cloths to swathe the perspiration from Jemani's body. "Get fresh water," she told Yanna.

The child struggled to the door with the earthen gurra, then paused to look back, her round eyes luminous as the thunder growled.

"Hurry, Yanna, be brave."

Coral knelt beside Jemani and gently washed the sweat from her face and throat. Her skin had taken on a puffiness, and dark circles showed beneath her eyes as her suffering continued into the night. Coral did not show her feelings of alarm over childbirth, but inside she cringed. She had witnessed the anguish before, but seeing Jemani suffer so made it more real.

How many times had her mother gone through this? Five times—no! How could she have forgotten even for a moment the death of baby Ranek who had died after only forty-eight hours? That was six months ago. . . . A worried glance at her mother showed that signs of frailty due to that difficult birth were still evident.

The room was empty except for the birthing stool that Jemani was lying on. Her mother had it brought to the hut a week before. It had armrests, a slanting back, and a cutout seat. Elizabeth sat on a low stool, and Coral sat at Jemani's left. Despite the suffocating heat, a fire blazed in the open hearth, where Yanna kept the water boiling.

Coral was exhausted, and her clothing stuck to her skin. Far worse was the frustrating task of trying to keep flies away. When Yanna wasn't busy watching the fire or going for water, Coral had her stand behind Jemani swishing the two large chik fans shaped like elephant ears. Now and then, Coral would get a burst of the refreshing breeze.

Next to her mother was a low rattan table containing yards of white cloth. For the first time, Coral caught a glimpse of the baby clothes that would dress Jemani's new infant. With a blink, she recognized them as having belonged to Ranek Kendall. He had worn them during his brief hours on earth. Her eyes darted to her mother's face, haggard with heat and weariness. Nothing of her mother's generosity truly surprised Coral. Not even her willingness to use the expensive embroidered blanket and infant gown that had been sent by Grandmother Victoria from London. The colorful Roxbury family insignia clashed in the meager hut with its walls blackened by woodsmoke.

A muffled cry brought Coral's attention back to Jemani. She cooled her face with the cloth, her touch reassuring. Coral glimpsed the baby's head, and both excitement and fear welled up inside her. "Soon now, Jemani, go ahead and yell. As loud as you want!"

Sweat mingled with Jemani's tears, and anguish furrowed her young brow. "Coral . . ." Jemani's ragged whisper came. "Not good . . . I . . ."

"Soon, Jemani, soon," and she glanced at her mother. Something new and startling in her mother's face frightened her, and she wondered if she had the right to reassure her. She wanted to cry out, *What is it? What's wrong, Mother?*

Jemani's body tensed in a final push to free the tiny newborn.

"The baby is alive," came Elizabeth's quick voice. "It is a boy, Jemani! He looks healthy!"

Coral watched her mother working quickly now with brown cord, a boiled knife, and an odd assortment of ointments, bottles, jars, and cloths.

Jemani was crying softly, and Coral dribbled water across her cracked and bleeding lips, and smiled down at her bravely, although she suspected that her friend could not see her. "Did you hear, Jemani? A strong, healthy boy! You see? God did hear our prayers! What will you name him?"

"Coral . . ." Jemani's whisper came so weakly that Coral brought her ear close to lips that barely moved. "My baby . . . is not crying . . . he must cry . . ."

Yes, why isn't he crying? Coral wondered with growing alarm. Her mother had said the baby was alive. She watched her mother washing the tiny pink infant in a pewter bowl of wine.

Again Coral tried to smile, wiping Jemani's face, even as perspiration wet her own. "He will."

Jemani's voice was scarcely above a whisper—"My Rajiv . . . any news?"

Coral glanced anxiously at her mother, but Elizabeth shook her head.

All at once Coral heard the infant suck in a breath, sneeze, then let out a hearty wail! Coral laughed and leaned toward Jemani. "Did you hear that? All India is awakened. You will have your hands busy with that one."

But a closer look at Jemani's face wiped the smile from Coral. She was turning a sick-white, with blue splotches beneath her eyes. The wails of the newborn filled the hut, mingling with the thunder. Jemani's lips formed words, but her voice was too weak for Coral to hear. Coral's frightened eyes darted to her mother. Elizabeth's words sliced through the stillness: "Quick, take the baby, Coral."

Coral took the bundle and placed it next to Jemani's side. When she turned back toward her mother, she saw an expression that caused her to freeze. Fear clamped about her insides like iron fingers. Her eyes dropped to the blanket beneath Jemani, and widened. She wanted to gasp, but choked it back, her throat constricted. She stood rigid, staring at the growing pool of bright red blood. Slowly it grew larger in spite of her mother's tireless efforts to stop it. Her mother kept massaging and kneading Jemani's womb, her own face wet with perspiration, her lips moving in silent prayer.

Coral could not move. Yanna let out a tortured sob.

"Outside, Yanna!" Elizabeth choked, but the child stood there, two small hands pressed against her mouth choking back sobs.

"Coral! Put her outside!"

Coral's legs moved as heavily as though weighted down with lead. She stooped, struggled to pick Yanna up, and brought her to the door.

She stepped out into the blackness. A gust of wind struck against her, causing her to lose her breath. Her braids at the back of her neck came undone, and her tunic whipped about her. Lightning stabbed the sky. Yanna clung to her like a frightened cat.

Unexpectedly a man stepped from the night, but she could not see his face.

"Yes?" The calmness of Major Buckley's voice shocked her back to her senses. She pushed the child into his arms, and her voice was muffled in the wind.

"Take her, please! I must get back!"

He must have understood what was happening from the anguish in her voice, for he said something comforting to Yanna, who willingly clung to his neck, sobbing.

Coral turned back, slamming the door against the wind. One look at her mother's face told her what was happening. Helpless, Coral watched her trying to stop the bleeding. Stained cloths were tossed aside one by one as she reached for yet another.

Coral's eyes rimmed with tears. Her throat cramped. She sank back against the door, feeling the wind push against it. *Not Jemani too, Lord! Do not take her, please . . . do not take her. Not with the baby just born. Not with Rajiv gone too.*

But she knew that Jemani was dying, and her mother could do little to save her.

"Coral! Quick! She's asking for you."

Coral rushed to her side and knelt, throwing aside her own fears. "I am here, Jemani," she said, surprised that her voice could sound so calm, so strong. She must not let her know how frightened she was.

"Jemani?" she took her hand. How cold and clammy she felt! She held it between her own, as though by holding tightly she could hold on to her life.

"... member ... you ... promised ... won't ... change mind ... won't forget ..."

"I remember. I will not change my mind."

"... so weak ... cannot face ... leaving me ... do not go ... afraid ..."

Coral swallowed against the ache in her throat. Hot tears blurred her vision. "Remember the words we read in Hindi? Say them with me in your mind."

Coral struggled to utter the words of Psalm 23 aloud, and slowly the little room was enveloped in a sweet hush. Elizabeth Kendall's voice joined in as she knelt beside Jemani, resting a hand on the young woman's damp hair.

"Yea, though I walk through the valley of the shadow of death, I will fear no evil for thou art with me ..."

"... with me ..." came Jemani's murmur. "With—"

No longer was her face frantic, no longer fearful. Jemani grew quiet. The promise of Scripture came on wings of pleasant breezes, as clear as sunlight shining on crystal water.

"Jesus," whispered Jemani, so sweetly that Coral's breath paused. She watched Jemani's lips move softly into a sigh. "Jesus ..."

Coral felt Jemani's fingers, heard her whispering, "Take ... my son. His godmother—you promised—no ... untouchable ..."

Coral glanced desperately into her mother's face searching for permission. Elizabeth's face was wet; she hesitated, shutting her eyes and helplessly shaking her head as though tortured by decision. "Dear God in heaven! Whatever shall I do?"

"Mother," rasped Coral, pleading. "Mother, please!" Coral's heart felt as though it would burst, and she choked: "This is partly my fault—I—I am the one responsible for what has happened! The baptism, Rajiv—"

She could not go on and laid her wet face on Jemani's chest. She felt Jemani's fingers weakly touch her hair.

"Coral—"

"You may promise," came Elizabeth's whisper.

Coral lifted her face. "Yes, Jemani, yes! I promise."

The young mother let out a soft sigh. The room was wrapped in silence.

Coral shut her eyes, one hand holding Jemani's, the other resting on the baby next to her. She caressed the blanket, feeling the softness of the expensive silk edging from Roxbury House in London and the gentle breathing movements of the baby beneath her hand.

The pressure of Jemani's fingers grew weaker, fading away, until at last Coral felt it no more. She stared down at Jemani's still face, and Coral's expression set with determination. "I promise," she whispered again.

3

The red embers in the hearth were out. Streaks of grayish dawn were breaking in the eastern sky, and outside the hut the first large drops of water made contact with the dust.

The door stood ajar, letting in the damp smell of earth and trees, and the monsoon broke into its full fury. Piercing zigzags of light did a war dance across the sky, and the rains came gushing forth turning dust into mud, the mud into small running streams. Kingscote rejoiced, and the jungle came to life. Coral sat without moving, drained of emotion. She watched her mother wrap the newborn more carefully in the blanket for the wet ride back to the mansion.

Her mother walked toward her with the infant in her arms, and their eyes met in wordless understanding. *She too wants this baby,* thought Coral. *Will he fill a void left by Ranek?*

Coral smiled weakly as her mother's fingers played in her mussed blonde hair. For a moment neither spoke, and Coral rested the side of her face against her mother's breast.

"I feel so ancient."

Elizabeth continued stroking her daughter's hair in silent understanding.

Coral lifted her head and scanned her mother's wearied face, searching for answers. Reality came rushing in like a flood.

"What will Father say?"

Elizabeth looked toward the open door as though expecting to find the rugged form of Sir Hampton standing there. The rain hammered so loudly on the small roof that Coral wanted to place her palms over her ears.

Elizabeth was quiet. She raised her hand to push back a wisp of dark brown hair. "I do not know."

Coral knew her father to be a rugged but tender man. There was not the slightest doubt in her mind that after twenty years, he was still deeply in love with her mother. She had seen the way he looked at her at the dinner table after a long, tiring day, and could not mistake the devotion in his gray-green eyes. If anyone could win over the heart of Hampton, it would be her mother.

Elizabeth moved the blanket aside to peer at the baby. The silence lengthened. When she spoke, her voice was a whisper. "He will say . . . it was a fair thing to do, Liza, but an unwise decision where Kingscote is concerned. Especially after Rajiv's death."

Coral shivered, although the monsoon did not cool the air. The hot, dry, dusty weather was now hot, humid, and muggy. She murmured hopefully, "Maybe his death was an accident. Maybe it had nothing to do with Jemani's baptism."

But one look at her mother's expression did little to reinforce her words.

"Your father will know more today," Elizabeth said simply.

Coral took Jemani's son into her arms and wondered about the future. "And *then* what will Father say?"

Elizabeth managed a smile. "Then he will say, 'What did you name the lad?' "

Coral felt so completely relieved, yet so exhausted, she laughed and wept at once.

"Gem," Coral said after a moment. "That is his name. Like a jewel, he is the one bright glimmer in all that has happened, born the night of the monsoon, when the earth is quenched and satisfied."

"We will indeed call him Gem. And we shall raise him to serve the Lord of the monsoon, that he may bring new life to his people."

Coral looked toward the open doorway, hearing the crunch of boots. Major Jace Buckley stood there, his hat pulled low to keep the rain out of his eyes. His gaze took in the scene in one glance, then focused on the infant in Coral's arms. His expression remained unreadable, and his resonant voice was directed to Elizabeth.

"You no longer need worry about the tiger, Mrs. Kendall."

Elizabeth gave a deep sigh of relief. "You trapped the beast?"

"I had to shoot him," he stated.

"Yes . . . of course. Thank God it cannot harm anyone else."

Coral busied herself with the infant, refusing to comment, unwilling to meet the gaze of the intriguing officer.

"Yanna is back at the house," he told Coral.

She was obliged to look up at him. "Thank you."

"I left her in the kitchen."

"Yes . . ."

"You have our gratitude, Major," said Elizabeth. She walked toward him. "I am afraid I will need someone to tend to the burial. Your sowars will most likely refuse."

He showed little expression, giving Coral the impression that he knew the Indian mind well. "Seward and I will see to it," he said.

"Thank you."

"There is a ghari waiting to bring you back. Better leave now before the road turns into a riverbed."

"You have been very helpful," she said tiredly. "However, I will stay until after the burial. Has the body of the worker been identified yet?"

"It is Rajiv."

Coral held the baby a little tighter. "How did he die, Major?"

She noted a hard glitter to his eyes. "A dagger through his heart."

A dagger! Coral felt sick. Then his death was not an accident as she had hoped! But who would do such a dreadful thing to Rajiv? Ghazis? Oh, surely not! Not on Kingscote. Someone from the village, she thought . . . yes, that was it. *It has to be.*

Her mother's face was drained of color, and she turned toward Coral as though anxious for her to be safe at the house. "Major Buckley will see you to the ghari, Coral. The baby will need to eat soon. Bring him to Jan-Lee."

"Yes, Mother." Coral lifted the blanket protectively about Gem and walked past Major Buckley into the downpour. The rain was warm on her face and felt sweetly refreshing.

The silk workers were standing in the rain, smiling and celebrating, although furtive glances were cast in her direction by the women. She felt them staring

at the bundle in her arms. Coral held him close, looking from face to face, almost challenging any of them
to raise a word of opposition. Children played in the
mud, squealing. And from the jungle came the distant
sound of an elephant trumpeting his delight.

Major Buckley's voice interrupted the moment.
"Boy or girl?"

"A boy."

"What did you name him?"

Her eyes rushed to his, and for a moment she was
confronted by flecks of hard black within deep blue.

"Gem." And without completely understanding
her feelings of determination, or what motivated her
to say so, she added, "Gem Ranek—after a baby
brother who died some months ago."

He did not reply at first. "A worthy name," he said
smoothly.

"So I thought, Major."

The ghari waited with the door open.

"Your brother has said you've been ill with fever.
Better get inside. You are dripping wet."

She brushed aside the damp hair that clung to her
throat, and allowed him to assist her across the oozing
mud. He handed her into the ghari, and Coral settled
her wet tunic about her, holding Gem.

Before the major closed the door, he paused. "I
commend you for your courage."

Her eyes reluctantly met his steady gaze as she
responded, "I have never considered myself especially
brave."

"While we are alone, I would like to say something."

She glanced at him cautiously. "Yes?"

"You have me mystified."

"Indeed? I cannot imagine why."

"A silk heiress . . . a white colonial lady taking a servant's baby . . . an Indian baby . . . which makes me wonder if you know what you are doing."

Coral stiffened but made no reply.

She studied him as he stood there, oblivious to the downpour, in a rather arrogant stance. Here was a young man with strong opinions, a man who did not fear voicing them.

"I am sorry that I mystify you," she said lightly.

A dark brow shot up. "May I ask why Jemani and Rajiv's baby should mean anything to you? There must be a hundred other babies about Kingscote."

She busied herself with Gem's blanket. "Not a hundred babies, Major. Perhaps ten or twenty."

He smiled a little. "Granted. Ten to twenty . . . but why *this* baby?"

"For a number of important reasons. I did not consider Jemani a servant. We were friends. During the months of my illness, I was confined to my room—I doubt if a man of your background would understand how lonely and boring prolonged illness can become."

He watched her thoughtfully.

"Jemani taught me Hindi, and I taught her the teachings of the Christian church. Now she is gone . . . and Rajiv is dead. And her child has no friends here among the Indians on Kingscote. I promised her I would protect her baby . . . a godparent, you might say."

He was silent, and Coral felt her face turning warm. There was no sound but the splat of rain hitting the roof of the ghari.

"You will, of course, find an Indian family to take him," he said.

Why is he so interested? she wondered. "No. I intend to keep him."

"I was afraid you would say that." His gaze was sober. "You are making a mistake."

Her lips parted slightly over his temerity, but he went on easily. "I suggest that if you pursue this idea, you will invite trouble. More than you realize."

She was alert. "Why do you say that? What do you mean? And what concern is it of yours?"

"Just this. I knew Rajiv well."

"Oh?" Her breath went out of her all at once. "You knew him? When? Certainly not since he came to Kingscote?"

"No, but I knew he was working here for your father. I've known Rajiv in the past."

His tone was evasive. Was he trying to keep his own past in shadows?

"I know who his family is. They will not want this child raised a Christian."

Coral tensed, and as though expecting him to take Gem from her arms she leaned back a little, holding the baby close to her shoulder. "You are wrong, Major Buckley. Rajiv had no family. Neither did Jemani. They wandered here months ago, escaping a famine in Rajasthan. Rajiv worked with the elephants—he was very good—"

"Yes, he was," came the calm interruption. "Rajiv was a fighter. He led them into battle. We fought together once."

"Truly? You seem to have quite a past of your own, Major."

"Which has nothing to do with our discussion."

She rushed on—"And Jemani came to the house as my personal tutor in the Hindi language. My mother baptized her only a few weeks ago."

"And partly because of that baptism, Rajiv is dead."

Coral wanted to flinch. "You do not know that. You said yourself you had no idea who killed him!"

"No." His jaw set. "Otherwise I would do something about it. But I have a good guess. Whoever put that dagger in his heart knew exactly what he was doing. It was a ritual killing."

Coral felt a pang of nausea.

His voice softened. "I am sorry to be blunt, but it's important you understand what you are getting involved in. I believe someone sent for Rajiv. Someone he trusted. And he went, only to find that trust misplaced."

She recalled what her mother had said about Major Jace Buckley being raised by a guru. Her father had also commented that he was a rogue and a gentleman all in one. Could she trust him? Was he relentless in his attitude because he opposed converting Hindus to what the Indians called a *European* religion?

"Rajiv's uncle is a Raj."

Coral grew still.

"You understand the implications?"

Coral was astounded by his words. "Yes." Her voice was quiet and dull. *But it cannot be true*, she thought.

"Royalty," she stated aloud. "I do not believe it is possible."

"I have heard that the Raj disowned his nephew because he married an untouchable. For a loyal Hindu to break caste is worse than death. Others besides Rajiv have been put to death for doing it."

She whispered: "You think he was killed because he married Jemani?"

"I have no proof of the maharaja's involvement. It may have been someone else in the royal family. Yet I've seen these types of killings before. The Raj rejected his nephew, but if it comes to his attention that Rajiv has a son, and that son is now a ward of an English family who intends to raise him a Christian—well, Miss Kendall, you see my reasoning."

Coral shuddered at the thought of turning Gem over to vindictive relatives. They might throw him to the crocodiles as a sacrifice.

"Jemani entrusted her son to *me*. It was her dying wish. Had she wanted Gem given to Rajiv's family, she would have told me."

His expression was now bland. "You might consider that she had something to hide. Something she never explained to you, even though, as you say, you were friends."

Reluctantly she recalled Jemani's words at the river. *There are things you do not know . . . things I cannot—must not, tell you.*

But Coral would not discuss this with the major. Instead, she said firmly, "I do not believe it. What could she have to hide? Had Rajiv lived long enough, he, too, would have committed Gem to me. They would want him to be raised a Christian, and I intend to see that he is. He is mine now," she stated. "I will not give him up easily."

Even at a time of sobriety and warning, the major could show unlikely amusement, as if her determination alerted his curiosity. He smiled. "The depth of your conviction surprises me. How old are you?"

She blushed. He could be too blunt. She was tempted to exchange years with Kathleen, but instead spoke the truth. "Sixteen."

He looked exasperated. "Sixteen! You are hardly more than a child!"

Child!

"Major! You forget yourself. I am not a child."

"Maybe. In my opinion—"

"You are somewhat aggressive in sharing your opinions, Major."

"In my opinion, Miss Kendall, you are too young to get into this kind of dilemma. Therefore, it is my duty to inform your father of the Raj."

She sucked in her breath, and for a moment she visualized her plans in ruin.

"Sir, you will not frighten me," she whispered.

"I am not trying to frighten you, but warn you."

"Gem is *mine!*"

A brow lifted. He looked her up and down. "I am certain a silk heiress can have anything she wants—"

Coral felt her cheeks turning warm. The man was arrogant!

"—but an Indian baby who is the grandnephew of the maharaja? It may prove costly to you . . . *and* to your father's silk plantation."

His suggestion disturbed her more than she was willing to show. "I know exactly what I am doing."

"Do you?"

"Yes." Her eyes refused to yield.

His narrowed a little. The rain ran down the brim of his hat. After a moment he gave a little nod of his head.

"As you wish. But remember that I warned you."

Coral shivered, not knowing if it was from her wet clothing, or the warning in his voice. He started to turn away, and she stretched out a hand in a pleading gesture. "Wait—"

Suddenly she felt bone tired, her emotions spent. He must have noticed. He seemed to notice everything, she thought, troubled.

"I am sorry if I sounded rude," he said. "But I

dislike the idea of a young girl ending up with a broken heart."

Coral gazed down at the baby. How could this infant warming her embrace ever bring her a broken heart?

"Please . . . say nothing to Sir Hampton. I—I am not the only one who wants him," she found herself explaining quietly. "My baby brother died six months ago . . . he was only two days old. My mother . . ." she stopped, feeling as though she were betraying her mother's privacy.

His expression was inscrutable, and she could not tell if his thoughts on the matter had wavered or not. Before she could say anything more, her mother came out of the hut, covering her head with a sari.

"Go on without me, Coral," she called. "Major Buckley is kind enough to see that I give Jemani a Christian burial. Tell your father I will be home soon. We will talk then."

"Yes, Mother."

Coral's eyes swerved back to Major Buckley's, and her dark lashes narrowed a little. "I do not suppose you would change your mind? I suppose you will tell her everything . . . and frighten her."

He folded his arms across his chest. "Neither of you seem to frighten easily," he said flatly.

"She will not believe you any more than I do."

Coral turned her head away as a sowar walked up and saluted the major. There followed a quick exchange in Hindi.

The major spoke fluently, a result of being brought up by the Indian guru, Coral decided. She caught something about Captain Seward reporting back to him at once. The sowar saluted and climbed inside the ghari.

Without another word exchanged between her and the major, he shut the door. A moment later the vehicle moved off toward the Kendall house, the wheels churning through the reddish-brown mud.

Coral turned in her seat to look out the window at the driving rain. Her mother stood next to the major, a fragile figure beside his rugged build. A small black book was in her hand. Coral then glanced across the seat at the sowar. His deep brown face was impassive, his eyes straight ahead. She wondered what he thought of the Christian burial of Jemani, and of the Indian infant in her arms that would be carried inside the Kendall mansion and taken upstairs to the English nursery.

4

Coral awoke from her nap with a start. Rajiv and Jemani were dead . . . and she had taken responsibility of Gem.

Neither her father nor her brother Michael had come to the dinner table earlier that evening. Along with the major, they were still looking into the matter of Rajiv's death. The workers were being questioned about what they might have seen or heard, and her father had talked to Natine alone in the library. Evidently no one knew anything, and Rajiv's death remained unsolved. What effect this might have on the Kendall relationship with the Indian workers was unclear. In the past it had always been pleasant; the men and women who worked for her father were loyal servants. But the ugly death of Rajiv cast a foreboding shadow . . . and now his son slept in the Kendall nursery.

Coral sat up, hearing her father and mother speaking in the hallway. Prompted by her mother's pleading voice, Coral slipped from her four-poster bed and went to the door.

What if Major Buckley had spoken of the maharaja to her father? And what if he refused to let them care for Gem? What would become of the tiny infant? She already knew well enough that no one on Kingscote would raise him. And if he were sent to this unnamed royal family, there was a chance Gem would be slain. Coral had no weapon or resource but prayer.

She rebuked herself for listening to her parents' conversation in the hallway, but having caught the baby's name she could not resist. She stood by the door listening, her heart thudding. Her father's voice was clear:

"The Roxburys will not look upon this easily. I fear Sir Hugo is right. Mutiny is ever a shadow hovering over Kingscote."

"Yet you always told me it was part of the risk of being a *feringhi* in India. And the child will never take the place of your blood grandchildren. As he matures, we can send him away to school in London. If we hesitate to stand by our friends, what will the Hindus think of the church?"

"Now, Liza, I've no thought of abandoning the lad. But I confess to being worried about Coral. You know better than the rest of us that she isn't well. She is only sixteen! She will be going to London soon. How can she mother a child?"

"Coral is more mature than you give her credit for. She is more studious than her sisters. And . . . she wishes to stay at Kingscote instead of going to finishing school in London."

"Aye! Not go to London with her sisters!"

"Now, Hampton! At first I said no, that you would not allow it, but darling, perhaps it is not so terrible an idea. She is hardly strong enough for a five-month voyage. Do let her stay at home with Gem until he is three," she pleaded. "After that, she can journey to

Roxbury House. Gem will be old enough to travel with her, and we'll place him in a good school."

"Whist! Three more years? What of a husband?"

"Hampton . . . she is so lovely. She will have no difficulty . . . and remember your promise. It will give her time to grow stronger. And—well, Coral has suggested she does not wish to marry soon, and—"

"Oh she has, has she?"

"There is time for all that. Girls do not marry as early as they did when we were young. Belinda is all of seventeen, and Margaret and Hugo are quite patient."

He gave a grunt. "Do I not have Kingscote to think of? I need strong heirs, and I am hoping to have many of them. With young Alex interested in music, and Michael restless and wanting to travel, what will Kingscote do if both my sons turn their backs on silk?"

"They will not disappoint you. And yet, shall our sons and daughters be traded in marriage for good blood?"

"Blood, I am not worried about, but grandsons, I am. Coral needs to go to London to get a husband. That young nephew of Sir Hugo's . . . what was his name? Hugo boasts enough of him! The chap has pestered me on the subject for the last two years!"

"Ethan," she explained. "Doctor Ethan Boswell. And I must say, I'm inclined to think he is the correct choice when the time comes. Margaret too has written of Ethan. He is young and gifted. Uncompromising in his interest in tropical diseases. And more importantly, Ethan is Christian. And I'm assured he is willing to wait several years, since he is aware that Coral is ill."

"A physician will make a fitting husband." He gave a laugh. "I dare say she may need one close at hand.

Perhaps we should arrange for her betrothal now."

"Oh, Hampton! Do be serious! Give them both time to meet and become friends. In the meantime, dear, she can pursue her education here. Her interest in languages continues, and there is much I can teach her. Although," she said thoughtfully, "I do think we should insist on at least a year at Lady Anne's Finishing School with her sisters. Hampton—about the child. Jemani died believing we would see to her baby, that he grows up in the church. I shall never forgive myself if I do not see the vow through. And Coral feels as strongly."

"But Coral is so young. Can she handle this?"

"Are you not forgetting me? I will do everything I can to help with the child. The infant is so beautiful."

His voice grew husky with sudden emotion. "So maybe it is you, my love, and not our little Coral who is determined to keep him? Then why did you not say so in the first place?"

Elizabeth's voice rushed on. "I have already spoken to Jan-Lee. She has agreed to nurse him with her own Emerald."

"Oh, Liza, Liza my love, you know well enough that I would do anything to please you. When we first married, I was even willing to turn Kingscote over to Hugo and return to London with you to live the life of a lord. Forbid! It was you who wished to stay, who came to love Kingscote as I. Yes, if you want this Indian baby, then you may have him. And when he is old enough, I shall pay for his schooling in London. But are you certain it is not our own son you have on your heart, and the Indian baby only reminds you of him?"

Elizabeth's voice broke—"God gave me Ranek for such a short time . . . and we will never have another child—"

Inside her room, Coral closed her eyes and leaned against the door, her throat constricting. She knew how her mother ached with loneliness. When did empty arms ever get used to losing a child?

"Liza . . ." Hampton's voice came as a broken whisper.

There was silence.

"Liza, let the child stay . . . and if one day we are sorry for this act, so be it. Let the Good Master who waters Kingscote look to our path."

Coral's heart felt as if it would burst. She could not contain herself and flung open the bedroom door, throwing her arms about her father's strong neck. Her cheeks were wet. "Oh, Papa, Papa, thank you. I will make you proud of him, you will see."

Hampton's gray-green eyes glistened. "What is this?" he pretended to be stern. "Listening behind closed doors? I'd expect as much from Kathleen, but you?"

She laughed up at him. "Dear Papa, I love you."

Elizabeth smiled up at her husband, and her eyes shone with pride. She rested her cheek against his forearm.

"You will both have to stand with me against the outcry certain to come from the Roxburys. Sir Hugo will have a dark expression over this."

"We will stand with you no matter what the rest of the family says," Coral stated.

"Grandmother Victoria will listen to reason," said Elizabeth of her mother. "I will write her at once. Knowing Mother, she will threaten to swoon over an Indian child in the family, but she will soon relent."

"Sounds like war," he said with a wince. "Then so be it. Is not justice and mercy on our side? Kingscote has survived a hundred years, and by God's grace it will continue."

"Why, Papa, you sound like a parson," laughed Coral.

He cleared his throat. "Seward would disagree, having known my nefarious past." He brightened. "Did I tell you? He soon will be out of the military. He's coming to work for me here at Kingscote. I cannot think of a man I can trust more than Seward!"

Unexpectedly he called out to his Indian servant, his voice in good humor. "Natine! What do you mean standing there in the shadows on the stairs? Find Seward and Major Buckley! We shall celebrate with a toast to the future!"

Natine stepped forward, his dark eyes remote. He salaamed. "Celebrate, burra-sahib?"

"Tonight marks the birth of Gem and his entrance into the Kendall household. No, do not look like a croaking toad, my old friend. We will hear no omens of ill news from you." He turned back to Elizabeth. "Who knows? Maybe I will get myself an heir after all." He gave a laugh. "An Indian godchild as committed to silk as I am."

Natine stood masked in shadows. He turned away, turban held high, and went down the stairs.

From the room that joined her own, Coral heard the wail of the infant and hurried back to find Jan-Lee lifting him from the cradle. Holding her own child in one arm and Gem in the other, she sat down in the rattan rocker, and Coral drew near, kneeling beside her.

"One day I will see you rewarded for your kindness, Jan-Lee."

The Burmese woman wore an impenetrable face,

and her dark eyes were solemn. Rain beat against the windows.

"Jemani is gone . . . her husband too. It is sad. I will do my best for you, Miss Coral."

Coral laid a hand on the shoulder of her childhood ayah. "It is not the end for Rajiv and Jemani. It is the beginning. And the beginning for Gem. To the living belong the promises of this life. I want to see that Gem has opportunity to grow up strong, with an education in London, to become all that he can be. It is in my power, the power of the Kendall family, to do this, and we will."

"Your heart is kind, child. But not everyone understands this kindness. Some misunderstand. As if you deliberately step into the Indian flower bed, and crush. For your sake, Miss Coral, walk with light feet."

"I shall try, Jan-Lee."

They listened to the raging monsoon, and the contentment of both infants feeding. One, the daughter of Jan-Lee, an oriental servant; the other to become Coral's godchild, perhaps one of the many future inheritors in the wealthy and powerful silk dynasty that reached from India to London.

5

Recalling Major Buckley's remark that she was little more than a child, Coral chose a blue silk frock that she felt added a touch of maturity to her years. She brushed her hair until it shone like burnished gold, then she drew it back into a neat chignon.

Pausing on the octagonal stairway, she looked below. Golden lamplight flooded down upon the square entrance hall and showered upon the polished red-stone floor. At the bottom of the staircase, and to her left, was the ballroom, with its double crystal chandeliers that her mother had shipped from Vienna and the heavy wood furniture with muted-rose velvet cushions. There would be no dancing tonight, so Natine had ordered the servants to leave the plush ivory-colored Afghan rugs on the polished marble floor. Elizabeth's prized paintings from the Roxbury London collection graced the pale walls, including a recent painting of Coral with her pet elephant, *Rani*. There was another painting of her older sister, Kathleen, in a white French lace ball dress, and one of her baby sister, Marianna, with her strawberry hair still in

childhood braids, seated in a garden of yellow prim-
roses.

Coral came quickly down the stairs as strains of
Mozart began to fill the house. She walked to the arch-
way that led into the ballroom and saw Alex seated
before the keyboard, master of his music. His fingers
danced across the keys, while every fiber of his lean
body consumed the drama of his music. His dark
handsomeness hinted of poetic moodiness, with eyes
that flashed an internal storm. The familiar shock of
dark hair fell across his forehead, and like his character, it forever resisted any attempt toward manage-
ment.

The guests in the ballroom were attentive as his
personalized music style crashed with the violence of
lightning and thunder, held its emotional peak for several moments, then eased like a sigh into ocean waves
playing across the sand. . . .

Coral glanced across the room until she saw Major
Jace Buckley. He was not watching Alex, but her. She
turned her head away.

The music ceased. The room was still. Then exuberant applause broke out.

Alex stood, smiled almost shyly, then walked toward Michael and Major Buckley.

A minute later as conversation resumed, her father's strong voice could be heard above the crowd, and
she caught glimpses of her mother overseeing the silver trays of refreshment, while a dignified Natine
watched the other servants. One mistake, one slip of
etiquette in their well-trained behavior meant that he
would delegate them to less important jobs in the
kitchen.

There were several other young men in uniform
with Major Buckley, and Captain Seward was there

enjoying a discourse with her father. Michael was speaking with the major, while Alex, newly arrived from his musical studies in Austria, only listened, as though drained by his music.

Coral noted that the major appeared at ease in fashionable surroundings. He was no longer dusty or sweat-stained, and he wore a clean riding cloak. He was assessing the painting on the wall of Coral with her elephant. Rani was kneeling in a circus stunt that she had taught her.

"Coral, come here, I want you to meet Jace."

Michael's voice interrupted her thoughts as her older brother walked toward her, grinning, his arm outstretched.

So Michael was on a first-name basis with him. Had Major Buckley told him that he believed Gem was related to a maharaja?

Her brother showed no concern, however, as he took her arm and led her in the major's direction.

Michael was gifted, as were all the Kendall children, with physical attractiveness. His hair was not as dark as Alex's, and bore the Roxbury tinge of red when seen in the light, and he was strongly built like his father. Unlike Alex who hated the sun, Michael had always thrived outdoors, on adventure—a trait not at all appreciated by his father. Perhaps Michael's cravings for risk would not have been frowned upon had those ambitions been centered on Kingscote silk.

"This is my sister Coral," he was saying to Major Buckley, his strong arm wrapping around her shoulders.

"We've met. Good evening, Miss Kendall."

She could hardly believe that the languid tone and the disarming smile belonged to the same arrogant man who had earlier confronted her about Gem.

"Good evening, Major," she said precisely.

Michael laughed. "Call him Jace. He is not the hardheaded officer he appears. He's more suited for an Indian tunic, buckskin trousers, and a seacap."

Coral smiled politely, but the thought of calling him Jace made her uneasy. She was relieved when the major gestured his glass toward the painting, changing the subject.

"Your elephant?"

"Yes. She is called Rani, a true queen. She was only a baby when I got her."

He murmured smoothly: "The mother was killed, and you adopted her?"

"Yes, she—" Coral hesitated. Her eyes swerved to meet his, her cheeks turning warm. She found a hint of a smile on his lips. He turned back to the painting and seemed to study it with a good deal more interest than was genuine.

"I enjoy collecting orphaned animals," she said with a hint of challenge.

"I commend you. It is not every woman who enjoys the excitement of wild and dangerous pets. I've collected a few myself."

"Indeed?" she sipped her refreshment. "A cobra?"

She was aware that Michael and Alex turned to look at her, surprised by her tone, but she ignored them.

Major Buckley did not appear to be the slightest bit offended and fixed her with a disconcerting smile.

"Actually, a cheetah. . . . I still have her. If I get mauled one day I'll have no one to blame but myself."

Coral glanced away to the painting on the wall, swishing her peacock-feather fan. "A cheetah, you say? How interesting, Major. I collect them."

A dark brow went up.

"Miniatures, that is," she said. "I am searching for one carved in ebony stone. I understand they are rare and hard to come by."

"They are. But they can be found in the right place. You need to know where to look. I will keep your interest in mind in my travels."

What kind of travels had he involved himself in? Aside from the vague description given of him by her mother and father, she knew nothing of Jace Buckley. How had Michael met him?

"You are a collector of rare menagerie?" she asked.

"Only to sell. I've a man in London who collects. I would like to see your collection sometime."

"You travel to exotic locations a good deal, Major?"

"Recently this uniform has kept me on a leash. All that will change soon."

Coral became aware of a rather curious expression worn by her brothers. Michael in particular seemed to enjoy watching Major Buckley.

"I suspect you have Rani eating out of your hand," Major Buckley told her.

"She is outrageously spoiled," agreed Coral. "She wouldn't have posed for me had I not bribed her with more time in the river . . ." She touched her chignon. "Actually, I like things to be free and wild."

"Not a typical Kendall as you can see," said Michael with a smile. "Coral's the only one in the family who would approve of our treks into the Himalayas."

"Have you two known each other long?" she asked.

"For several years. Michael and I met in Darjeeling. Your brother saved my life in an avalanche."

"If I recall correctly, old friend, it was the other way around," Michael countered. "Do not be so generous, Jace." His smile vanished. "Cowardice is not your cup of tea."

"An avalanche!" repeated Coral. "Michael, you never mentioned it."

Michael glanced toward his father, who was in conversation with Seward, and said in a low voice, "You are jesting, of course. You know Father. Any talk of a near-fatal accident, and there would be further opposition to my expeditions."

"A grand idea," quipped Alex dryly, sipping chilled pineapple juice. "What you see in ice, wind, and jagged peaks, I shall never fathom." He grimaced. "Grant me the intoxicating summers on Vienna's Danube any day."

"Ah, I might agree with that. Having felt the wings of death brush against me is quite enough for the present. Jace and I are turning civilized." His expression took on an intensity that Coral had seldom remembered seeing on Michael. "We are entering into a partnership in a tea plantation in Sikkim—perhaps the hill of Darjeeling."

Coral attempted to keep herself from catching her breath in surprise. *Michael and Jace—partners?*

"A tea plantation," mused Alex. "Father will be disappointed."

Michael sobered. "I hope to provoke a bit of excitement in his blood. Jace and I have our plans made. But I will need Father's good graces."

Alex smiled at Major Buckley. "In other words, Michael will need a loan to buy the land from the Raja of Sikkim." He turned his smile on Michael. "I wish you luck, dear brother. You will need it."

Michael pretended to throw a punch at his shoulder. "That, and a brother's moral support to help convince him. You and your music have more persuasive power over Father than anything I could ever do."

Alex's smile disappeared. "My good favor will increase if you provoke Father's displeasure again. He will not like it if you take to sea with the major next year." He added with rueful tone—"Since I am the younger son of the famed Sir Hampton Kendall, I might be able to get by with studying music in Vienna. But you know too well how he has his mind set on you taking over the silk production one day."

"Perhaps we will join the two plantations into one grand enterprise," said Michael lightly. "Silk and Darjeeling tea! What more could the English want?"

"England may smile, but you are forgetting Jace," said Alex. "Half the tea plantation will be his. He may have something to say about merging with the Kendalls."

"Ah, yes, let us toast the famous name of Buckley! Good Queen Bess would have rejoiced to have such a seadog in her service," said Michael, and turned to Jace. "Success, my adventurous friend! Let us salute the fastest clipper yet to sail the seas!"

A tea plantation in Darjeeling, thought Coral, intrigued, but uncertain whether or not she liked the idea of her brother being partners with Jace Buckley. His friendship with Michael meant she would come into future contact with him. The thought brought with it unease, since he shared her secret about Gem. Yet she found herself wanting to earn his admiration. She waited for an opportunity to display her knowledge of Darjeeling, unable to forget that he had called her a child.

"Why Darjeeling, Major?" she asked casually. "If I remember correctly, my father said there was fighting in Sikkim." And to show herself quite grown-up and informed of military matters, she added: "Gurkhas from Nepal, are they not?"

Major Buckley's expression showed both surprise and admiration. "Yes, they gained some territory, but fortunately, the Raja of Sikkim was able to turn them back with the help of Bhutan and China. Fighting goes on, but the area we are interested in is reasonably quiet."

"But whoever heard of tea growing in Darjeeling? I thought it came from China."

"It does. But an Indian friend of mine is certain it grows wild in Darjeeling. I believe he is right. However, we have not found it yet. We plan another expedition soon."

"Did you say *wild* tea?" asked Alex with apparent disbelief.

"A wild tea bush most likely suggests it was first smuggled in from China," said Major Buckley. He smiled slightly. "Perhaps our first 'Indian' tea shares something of a common history with the first silk cocoons brought into Assam."

"Forbid," jested Alex throwing up a slim hand. "Do not let our father hear you say that. He is adamant that silk is native to Assam."

"As well it might be," said Michael. "But do not forget our illustrious but notorious great-grandfather James Kendall settled here after he left Burma and China."

"What?" mocked Alex good-naturedly. "You nurture suspicions he carried silk caterpillars with him? Let us toast the grand memory of Princess Mei Lin Chang!"

Coral was not thinking of silk but of Alex's remark about Michael going to sea with Major Buckley. Her father would not be pleased. There was no secret about the disagreement between Sir Hampton and his two sons over the future of the vast enterprise of Kingscote. Alex had been permitted to his serious study of music in Austria only because he had lapsed into severe depression when first forbidden. Mother and Grandmother Victoria Roxbury in London had convinced their father to permit Alex to pursue his passion. However, Michael, as the firstborn, was another matter.

She hoped her voice did not sound too cautious, "Then you have not told Father of your interest in a tea plantation?"

Michael winced. "After tracking the tiger for two days, I am not in any mood to take on a wounded bear. But I admit Father seems in a good mood tonight." He looked across the room in Hampton's direction. Devotion to his father, despite differences, showed in his dark eyes. "It looks as if the thought of a new baby in the house has been well received. Mother looks radiant too. Perhaps Gem will become the needed balm for the loss of Ranek."

"And his disappointment in his own sons," added Alex.

Michael leaned over and planted a kiss on Coral's cheek. "Congratulations on Gem. Rajiv and Jemani would be pleased if they knew."

As Michael's lips brushed her cheek, Coral's eyes went to Major Buckley, searching for reaction to the remarks about Gem. She noticed that he did not seem to be attentive, but preoccupied by other thoughts as he gazed across the room. She turned her head and saw Natine standing unobtrusively near a window, as much of a fixture in the ballroom as one of the paintings.

Coral's thoughts drifted back to Michael. He had never mentioned Jace Buckley before, and aside from the incident in the Himalayas, she wondered how they had met. Evidently they were trusted friends, since both men were willing to risk partnership. Michael had many friends who were considered to be adventurers, who belonged to another side of his life—a life that he did not bring home to Kingscote.

Major Buckley sampled a dessert of fresh mango and coconut, sprinkled with sugar. She wondered what was meant about Michael going to sea with him, but hesitated to ask, not wishing to show herself too curious about his ventures. Somehow she suspected the major of having too many.

She picked up a small glass of pineapple juice, the cut crystal glimmering.

"Then you are not of a mind to pursue your career in the military, Major Buckley?"

He set his plate down and his eyes followed an Indian who was now offering hot tea and Arabic coffee. Coral motioned for the boy to come.

"As a matter of fact, I will be out of uniform in a few months," he said.

"You sound pleased."

He smiled. "Delighted."

The major took a cup of coffee from the outstretched silver tray and dismissed the boy.

No doubt the military had curtailed his freedom. She thought of what her mother had told her about his upbringing.

"Colonel Warbeck must be disappointed. Usually fathers wish their sons to carry on the family interests."

"Most fathers do," put in Michael, and again glanced toward Sir Hampton. "Excuse me a moment."

He left them, walking in the direction of Sir Hampton and Captain Seward.

"When do you intend to start the tea plantation?" she asked.

"Michael will start without me. I will be away from India for some time. There is the small matter of money before I am able to buy in. I will be taking my clipper to sea. If Michael fails to convince your father, then he will join me. We intend to sail to Macau for tea and jade."

Alex chuckled. "Michael gets nauseous riding an elephant. He will prove little help on board your clipper."

Coral sipped her cool refreshment. "You own a ship?"

"I am buying the *Madras* from the Company. She's at berth in Calcutta right now, anxiously waiting for me to discard my uniform."

"From China, where will you go?" Coral asked.

"Oh, Cadiz, Portugal, other places, then London."

As he spoke of his plans in hauling cargo from China, his restlessness was apparent. Underneath his present facade of discipline, Coral saw a young man without bonds or ties, and she could almost feel the energy straining against its leash.

East India men were away at sea for two years at a time, and sometimes longer. She surmised that he was out to become independent and successful while enjoying the freedom of his own ship. An adventurous sea captain was a man to stay away from, she decided, friend of Michael's or not.

Natine appeared behind them carrying a letter. "A message for you, Major-sahib."

Coral could tell nothing of the contents of the message from the major's expression, but he seemed preoccupied. A moment later he folded the paper and placed it in his jacket. "I must leave tonight."

"Trouble?" Alex asked.

"Another skirmish with Burma near Manipur. Your father, I believe, has also had trouble recently."

Alex sighed. "Kingscote has had trouble with Burma for as far back as any of us can remember. We hire mercenaries to fight with us. Thankfully, matters usually calm down after a skirmish or two."

"I'm wanted back at the outpost."

He turned toward Coral. "If you will excuse me, Miss Kendall, Alex."

She watched as he exchanged polite farewells with her parents, explaining his need to return. He said something to Michael who laughed loudly, then glanced in her direction. Annoyed, she swished her fan to cool her face. In the company of Seward and several other military men, Major Buckley took his hat and gloves from Natine and followed him from the ballroom into the hall.

Coral waited a discreet moment, then slipped away unnoticed.

She found Major Buckley by the front door, alone with Natine. From Natine's expression, she surmised that he did not feel comfortable in the major's presence. Seeing Coral standing behind them, he salaamed and walked away.

Major Buckley turned toward her, and for a moment neither of them spoke. The pelting rain crashed against the window, drowning their silence.

"You did not say anything to my father about Gem."

He gave no direct reply as he slipped on his gloves.

"Why did you remain silent?" she asked.

"Take into consideration what I told you earlier."

"I have. My decision remains the same."

"I thought it would. Then I will leave you to set your own course."

Her voice was soft, hopeful: "Then . . . you are not going to voice your suspicions?"

"Do not ask me why I decided not to speak. I haven't the dimmest notion." He gazed down at her. "Maybe it is the shine in your eyes. Maybe it is your mother's laughter tonight . . . maybe it is the hope I have for the boy. Rajiv was a friend. His son is an orphan, and maybe I'm sentimental. Always a mistake. But with the chance to grow up in the Kendall household as a godchild of Miss Coral Kendall—I find myself hoping it works out for Gem, and you. Perhaps I've decided to believe in the laughter I heard tonight." His lips turned into something of a smile. "You, of course, do believe in impossible dreams?"

Impossible dreams . . . was that what the future held for Gem?

She was touched by his unexpected warmth. "Yes . . . and thank you."

"Do not thank me. I have the distinct feeling I am not helping you at all."

"Oh, but you are."

"I doubt that. In fact, if I had an ounce of good sense I would speak to your father at once."

"But you will not."

He studied her, then reached to open the door. "No. But my silence makes me partly responsible for the future—and that too is a mistake." His gaze became distant. "Goodbye."

He opened the door to step out into the torrent of rain.

A few minutes later, when the sound of horses' hooves had died away, Coral lifted her skirts and made her way up the wide stairway toward the upstairs hall.

Gem was waiting.

85

6

The Madras, *Diamond Point Harbor, Calcutta*
December 1793

Jace Buckley whistled as he shed his black and silver jacket, shako, and military sabretache. He slipped into the worn buckskin breeches, and rubbed his smooth chin; in a short time he would have a beard. He imagined the colonel's blue eyes turning into icy daggers should he see him looking—not like his disciplined son, but like the illegitimate offspring of the notorious Captain Jarred Buckley.

In the Great Cabin aboard the clipper *Madras,* he was no longer Major of the 21st Light Cavalry, but an independent sea captain on his way to buying his own ship. An interloper, as the Company called them.

Jace's lips thinned into a tight line. Interlopers were better known as China traders. They had betrayed his father, leaving him on the beach of Whampoa in a storm to face angry warlords while they escaped on junks.

Jace stared at the coffee mug in his hand. It had belonged to his father. . . .

Even to this day, he could relive every second of that scene on the beach with the waves crashing in around him, the cold black water tasting of brine, and in his imagination, of blood.

As a boy of eleven, he had clutched to the sharp rocks where he hid, and he could see his father tied hand and foot on the beach, the waves crashing against the shore.

Jace felt his stomach churn with the vivid memory. He could see the Chinese warlord in black, hear the angry words shouted in Chinese, see the curved blade smash against his father's throat, beheading him. As he watched the waves suck back the head, he turned away to vomit, betraying his presence.

Jace Buckley's years as a child-slave to opium dealers began that day. It wasn't until he was in Whampoa at age fourteen that he had managed to escape.

Jace had survived by a strong will—although Seward insisted it was by divine providence. Seward also had a notion that pain over the past prevented Jace from risking emotional involvement with others.

He had escaped China through the caravan route over the Old Silk Road through the Himalayas. In India he was befriended by a guru named Gokul. When the British army sent a patrol into central India to put down a quarrel between ruling Marathi factions, Jace had been discovered by then Captain John Sebastian Warbeck.

Warbeck, who had never married (Jace knew it was because of losing Lady Margaret Roxbury to her family's choice, cousin Hugo), had brought him back to the Company headquarters in Calcutta and, in process of time, had "civilized" him, as the colonel put it.

Jace was sent to the respected military academy

in London, and upon his graduation, had emerged as the cool and restrained young son of the colonel. Jace had returned to military life in Calcutta, out of respect for what the colonel had tried to do for him, and taken his place in the East India Company as expected.

For the first few years, in order to honor the colonel, Jace served the Company well in India—he even won an award for bravery and was eventually promoted to the rank of major. But Jace yearned for freedom and often found himself at odds with the interests he was meant to serve.

The East India Company and the military worked closely together, for the Company was more than trade—it had become part of the British government. The military's purpose was to support Britain's interests in India, interests with which Jace often found fault.

Jace now had his freedom . . . but the disagreement between him and the colonel had gone so badly that the colonel had lost his usually restrained temper and ordered Jace out of the house.

Jace's rugged features flushed in anger at the memory. In a gesture of subconscious rebellion, he belted on the scabbard holding the sword that had belonged to his privateer father. Jace then snatched up the urn and sniffed the brew . . . if his kansamah had watered down the Arabian coffee again, he would throw him into the harbor. He had warned him twice. A good soaking would do him good. He poured a mug and tasted it. Ah, just the way he liked it: strong and scalding. Jace turned to the small golden langur monkey. "What do you say, Goldfish, are you ready to adopt a life at sea?"

The monkey clapped its palms together, then contentedly munched on sections of coconut. Jace had intentionally given the monkey a name to fit its new life aboard ship.

Jace looked over at Gokul. The old Indian merchant who had befriended him as a youth folded each article of the uniform as carefully as he counted his rupees at the end of a thieve's day at the bazaar. He flecked off a piece of dust. "Ah, sahib, it had its glory." He breathed on the brass buttons, then rubbed them against his sleeve.

Jace lifted a brow. "Sorry, old man. I do not share a glimmer of your sentiment." He then mocked a groan of ecstasy as he slipped into a leather jerkin and calf-length boots. He stretched his muscles.

Gokul chuckled. "Ah, the cheetah, he is free again!"

Apparently caught up in the excitement of the upcoming voyage, Gokul rolled his dark eyes toward the cabin ceiling, holding the sabretache to his protruding belly. "The sea! The wind!"

"Aye, we'll second that," bellowed Seward, ducking through the cabin door, with Michael Kendall just behind, carrying his bags.

Michael dropped them and stood feet apart, hands on hips, looking about the Great Cabin with interest. Just beyond was the Round Room.

"My first voyage to China," said Michael. "You will end up making a seadog out of me yet, Jace."

Jace tossed him and Seward tin mugs, and Gokul poured.

"To freedom," he said with a smile.

Michael laughed. "And the *Madras!*"

"And we best not forget the good clipper's captain," added Seward with a grin. He walked up and grabbed Jace's shoulder with a hearty hand. "There be none better but Jarred Buckley himself—" and he added swiftly, "Christ rest his soul! May the ship's first cargo of tea and porcelain bring ye a step closer to payin' her off."

"Do not forget our Darjeeling project, sahibs," urged Gokul.

A banana skin slapped against Gokul's belly and landed at his sandals. The others laughed when the monkey escaped from the cabin, leaving Gokul muttering with indignation.

———

The *Madras* set sail from the Bay of Bengal for the Dutch East Indies, taking on spices at Sumatra, Java, and Bali. Aside from some minor disagreements with the Dutch, they continued on their voyage to Singapore, where they harbored for two weeks, then entered the waters of the South China Sea two months after leaving Calcutta.

In February, while nearing the China coast, they made their first contact with foul weather when a typhoon struck. Jace brought the ship to safe harbor at Macau, and they arrived at Canton two weeks later.

The wharves were a babble of ethnic singsong dialects, mingled with the stringent odors of sweaty bodies, stale fish, and feathered ducks—head and webbed feet intact—strung up to dry.

Seward insisted upon going to Heavenly Jade Garden, an open-air bazaar where throngs of peasants gathered in the cool of evening to shop, eat, socialize, and enjoy the traveling magicians.

As always, the Garden was teeming with people. Tiny shops competed for space in the crowded bazaar, their colorful paper lanterns glowing in the darkness. Ornamented arches and floating paper dragons of red and yellow created a ceiling of color.

There were many coolie kitchens in Heavenly Jade Garden, each one sending forth pungent smells of Chinese cooking. Memories of his boyhood came flooding back. Jace felt both anger and pain. He had thought he would be able to handle the sights and sounds of the only face of China he had known, but as it all came rushing back he felt trapped.

Jace found himself amid a throng of people: acrobats, magicians, Flower Drum Song singers, and calligraphers. Men sat puffing from water pipes and drinking tea; still others cracked watermelon seeds between their teeth. Owners of shops, trying to lure in customers, hustled about the ancient boulevard in skull-caps, some had pigtails, others had their heads partially shaven, their silk gowns often threadbare. Jace recognized the brightly dressed minority races from the northwest provinces of China and Mongolia in embroidered red and blue jackets.

He watched Seward striding ahead unintimidated by the foreign culture, his sharp eye sizing up the various coolie kitchens for the evening meal. Jace remembered Michael, and looked behind him. He had stopped to watch an acrobatic family with a black and white Panda bear on a leash.

Jace waited for him, hands on hips. From the empty expression Michael wore, Jace assumed that he had ceased to take in the sights, smells, and the high pitch of the Chinese language. He was about to walk back and take him by the arm when Michael's expression turned to one of amazement.

Now what? thought Jace wearily, and lowered his hat. Michael jerked his head toward him, gesturing at Jace across the Garden. Not wanting to involve himself, Jace scowled and gestured for him to follow, but Michael threw up both hands and again beckoned him to come. Jace sighed, glancing ahead to see where Seward was. His rugged frame was easily spotted among the peasants going into a coolie kitchen.

Jace began making his way back through the crowd to Michael. It took him a minute to get there, for someone was setting off firecrackers, and the sparks and trails of smoke had evoked a crowd. As Jace walked up, Michael grabbed his shoulder.

"I say! Look over there—the man in black is about to lop off an old man's head!"

Jace felt a sickening reminder of the past. Michael's words did not surprise him. Cruelty to slaves and the indifference of the ruling class he knew by experience only too well. The last thing he wanted to do was to look in the direction where Michael pointed. But Michael was persistent. "Is it real? A circus, perhaps?"

Reluctantly, Jace turned in the direction of a myriad of gleaming lanterns strung over an arch constructed of stone blocks, named inappropriately for this particular occasion the Plum Blossom Gate of Good Fortune.

Masking the revulsion he felt inside, he studied what he knew to be a Chinese merchant of some authority, for he was dressed in a black satin jacket that reached to his knees. In his hand he carried a long sword gleaming as fiercely as his black eyes. He glowered down at a wizened old Chinese man with silver pigtails.

"The Manchus are a minority from northeast China," Jace explained. "They've conquered and ruled the Hans for some two hundred years. The old one must be a Han, his master a Manchu. Obviously he is a slave who has annoyed him." His voice revealed none of the kindled emotions churning inside.

Michael whipped his head around to stare at Jace. "Annoyed? Will he be permitted to cut off his head because he is *annoyed*?"

Jace had never told Michael about his father being beheaded on the beach at Whampoa. He could not explain to him how he felt now at seeing the cruelty repeated. Nausea swept over him. He must get away as swiftly as he could. Jace masked his feelings and met Michael's gaze.

"The old one is probably one of a thousand others across China who has died this day for angering some imperial magistrate, or even a merchant of peasant blood. Those who die are the lowliest of slaves. And whoever owns them may do as they wish, including lopping off their heads."

Michael stared at the ongoing scene. Jace looked at the old man sprawled on his face, begging. Jace gave Michael a prod in the opposite direction. Seward was waiting in the coolie kitchen, probably wondering what had happened to them. Besides, he could not stomach seeing the old man losing his head—

"Sha!" shouted the ruler.

Jace hesitated, knowing enough of the language to understand the death threat.

"Most worthless dog! Most vermin-infested piece of flesh! Where is the stone? Find it now in the dust! Creep and crawl and sift with your fingers till you find it or I shall chop you into a hundred pieces for the cauldron! The eye—where is the eye?

"Sha!" The Manchu swung his sword, whipping it over the old man to terrorize him, slicing at his threadbare gown. With a yell, he grabbed the pigtail as though to lop it off, but struck the dust instead. He leaped from his stair, shouting again, landing firmly on two muscled legs. "The stone! Find it!"

The old man was crawling frantically about, sifting handfuls of dust between his thin trembling fingers.

The scene was mostly ignored by the crowd, who hurried about their business with passive faces, too afraid themselves to notice. Hawkers continued pitching their wares—perhaps with louder voices—mule carts plodded by a little faster, and beggars limped away.

Jace unexpectedly found himself pushing his way through the crowd until he stood facing the rich shop owner. The merchant held a miniature black cheetah in his hand, and one of the emerald eyes was missing. Jace was surprised to hear his own voice, calm, almost disinterested, as though he did not care in the least what was happening.

"The cheetah with the missing eye . . . how much?"

The angry man turned to him. "It was worth much until this dog dropped it! The emerald is lost!" He calmed suddenly and bowed. "But I have others to show you. Please! Step inside my despicable and humble shop!"

Jace exchanged bows and said tonelessly: "I seek a cheetah with one eye, Most Honorable Sir."

"One eye?"

"One eye. Two eyes will not do. I will buy this one, or I shall resume my journey through the Heavenly Jade Garden a disappointed wretch."

The merchant's countenance swiftly altered. He gave another bow and murmured: "Step inside my worthless shop. The cheetah with one eye will be yours."

"I shall pay handsomely, but only if this inferior, miserable dog also becomes my property."

Jace withdrew a small leather pouch from inside his tunic and emptied gold coins into the merchant's palm. They glimmered in the lantern light, and the merchant ogled. Even the peasant-slave turned his white head to stare at the dancing glitter.

I must be a sentimental fool, thought Jace, and clamped his jaw as the merchant laid aside his sword to count the coins.

"The one-eyed cheetah and the old dog are mine," said Jace.

The merchant bowed deeply. "The cheetah and the old dog are yours, Most Honorable Sir."

Michael stood with an expression of disbelief. Jace accepted the ebony cheetah, then gestured for him to bring the old man. Jace walked away. Michael and the old slave followed.

They had not gone far when the old one rushed past Jace, stopped a short distance in front of him, and fell to the ground.

"Honorable Master! I am Yeh Jin-Soo, your miserable, wretched dog."

Jace said quietly: "Get up, friend Jin-Soo, you are safe now. You will call me Captain. I hope you don't get seasick. We are on our way to London."

The old one was struck speechless. He stared at him. Then rose to his feet, his thin black kimono dusty. He brushed it with dignity, bowed gravely, then walked behind to follow.

Jace looked askance at the cheetah with one eye, then shoved it inside his tunic. Michael burst out laughing, threw an arm about his shoulder, and they walked on.

They found Seward seated in a coolie kitchen. Jace sat to join him, and although he had no notion of what he was eating, Seward confidently boasted: "It be simmerin' for a day or two in a cauldron. Makes for flavor and tenderness."

Jace was now in a good mood and hungry. He ate while Seward went on to educate Michael on the correct way to eat among the peasants. "To show satisfaction, ye need to be makin' loud slurpin' sounds, smack yer lips, and snap yer chopsticks like so."

During the following days, the *Madras* was loaded with its cargo of tea and prized Chinese wares. A short time later, the crew set sail from Canton, confident about the next leg of the voyage to the port of London. After a year of prosperous and adventurous expeditions, they returned once again to the Indian waters of the Bay of Bengal.

Calcutta remained as Jace had left it, but perhaps even more crowded, with the East India Company thriving. English families had arrived to meet their husbands serving the Company and to take up residence at Fort William.

It was now February 1795, and Jace had not seen Michael in several weeks. Sir Hampton Kendall had arrived from Kingscote to meet with Roxbury about a family matter, and Michael was staying at his uncle's residence near Government-House.

Anxious to return to the shipping business that would secure their tea plantation, Jace had left the bungalow he shared with Seward in the infamous Chowringhee area of Calcutta, and had gone to the East India Company to discover what opportunities were available in shipping. He found nothing that interested him. He could do better as a privateer. As he left the office and crossed the wharf, he heard a loud shout in a familiar voice.

"Buckley! Wait up! I've splendid news!"

It was Michael, riding by in a carriage with Sir Hugo Roxbury's daughter, Belinda. As the driver brought the horses to a stop, Michael jumped out and came toward Jace at a run. He was dressed immaculately, bearing no resemblance to his appearance during his year aboard the *Madras*. He was again a Kendall, an heir to a silk dynasty. Jace looked at Belinda Roxbury. She stared at him, smiling demurely, her lashes lowering.

"The benediction from heaven is upon us!" said Michael.

Jace was skeptical and gave him a slanted look from under his hat.

Michael said victoriously, "You will see I am right. My father is looking to haul a cargo of silk to Cadiz. He asks to meet with you on the ship this afternoon."

A voyage to Spain alerted Jace's interest, for he also had a friend in Cadiz whom he wished to see again, an Arab merchant who handled expensive Moorish heirlooms. Jace had bought items from Hakeem before, and he was looking for the mate to a pair of ivory elephants that the director of the Company in London wanted.

He took paper and pen from his tunic to calculate the profit they would most likely clear from the voyage. It turned out to be nearly double what the Company had just offered him for a run to the Spice Islands.

"Is your father willing to contract with privateers?"

"He is now." Michael pulled Jace out of his cousin's hearing. "Last night he and Roxbury argued over the Company. My uncle's been after him to make a pact with the East India Company to protect Kingscote from Burma, but my father will have none of it. He prefers to do things his way. Independence is in his blood. First thing this morning he told me he'd decided to hire interlopers."

Jace respected Kendall for standing his ground against Roxbury. Partly because he resented the Indiamen for monopolizing shipping. This new knowledge sparked his curiosity about the relationship between the Kendalls and Sir Hugo Roxbury.

"Your father has always hired mercenaries to fight for Kingscote. Why is Roxbury pressuring him to sign a pact with the Company?"

Michael frowned. "The disagreement between them is not new. Even as a boy I remember my father complaining of Hugo's manipulations. The Roxburys of London own a percentage of Kingscote, just as the Kendalls do a portion of the Silk House in London. But Hugo's share in the actual plantation doubled when he married my mother's sister and also inherited her share."

No wonder Roxbury wanted Kingscote under East India Company jurisdiction. Since he was a high official he would benefit from the decisions made, just as he would gain by a marriage between his daughter Belinda and Michael. Sir Hampton had a strong contender for the silk enterprise in his brother-in-law, Sir Hugo. Jace already knew that Michael was interested in his cousin Belinda.

"This is our opportunity, Jace. My father has spoken well of you."

———

That afternoon, Sir Hampton arrived on the *Madras* with Michael. Jace was pleased to see that the disagreement between him and his son over his sailing to China was over. Kendall stood with a hefty arm about Michael's shoulders.

"I admit to having a bit more on my mind where you're concerned, Buckley, than the *Madras* taking on Kingscote silk."

Jace was instantly cautious. He was not certain that he liked the sound of Kendall's voice. "Oh? And what could that be?" But Sir Hampton did not appear anxious to explain. He roamed the Great Cabin, pausing now and then as though recalling pleasant memories of a ship. Kendall picked up the cheetah with one emerald eye.

"Roxbury will return to Kingscote with me, and Michael too," he was saying. "There is to be a family gathering of some importance. It concerns my middle daughter, Coral. I believe you met her when you were a major in the military."

Jace said nothing. He watched Sir Hampton inspect the cheetah.

"What will you take for this?"

Jace thought of Jin-Soo. "It is not for sale."

"A shame. My daughter collects wildlife miniatures."

"Yes. She told me."

"She would like this one."

"It has a missing eye. Even at that I paid an exorbitant price!"

Michael smiled and said to his father, "An interesting tale about that cheetah; I'll explain later. It has become our mascot."

"Mr. Kendall, surely a cheetah for your daughter is not what brought you to my ship."

Sir Hampton smiled. "No. Clever workmanship, though," he said of the miniature. "If you do change your mind, I would like to buy it." He set it down on the desk and turned to fix Jace with his full attention.

Jace leaned back against his desk, his features unreadable. He was determined that Kendall would not rummage through his mind.

"I want to hire you and your ship to bring my silk to Spain. Did Michael explain?"

"He did. And I'm interested."

"Good. As I said, there is something else, Buckley. There is to be an official church ceremony on Kingscote. I came to Calcutta, not only on business, but to bring back the Anglican minister from St. John's. My daughter is adopting Gem as her son. Did Michael tell you? He'll be a new member of the Kendall family. Since Coral is not well enough to make the tedious journey to Calcutta, the bishop has kindly agreed to travel to Kingscote."

Jace wondered if he had heard correctly. The Kendall daughter was *adopting* Gem? And Sir Hampton seemed quite willing to allow her to do so. Had he forgotten what happened to Rajiv? But how could Jace fault Kendall when neither he nor the rest of the family knew the background on Gem? That was due, not only to Coral's silence, but his own. Jace could hardly accuse Sir Hampton of recklessness for allowing Coral to make the child her son—and his heir. A look in Michael's direction showed no concern either. Both were oblivious to the risks involved.

"If you wish to hire the *Madras* to sail to Cadiz, well enough. However, I do not see how else I can be of help to you."

Sir Hampton kept his sharp gaze on Jace. "Both Michael and Seward tell me you are experienced in silk from your years in China."

Jace had not told Michael he had learned silk as a child-slave to the emperor, and he wondered what grand picture Michael might have painted of his years in China to Sir Hampton.

"I would like you to return to Kingscote with me," Hampton said, and he must have seen Jace's surprise, for he added with a chuckle, "Only for a brief duration, Buckley. I need an experienced man to oversee the loading from the hatcheries. I usually do it myself, but I shall be absorbed with the family events surrounding Gem's adoption. I've spoken to Seward, and he insists you are most qualified with hatchery work."

Kendall pulled a five-hundred-pound note from inside his vest, and laid it on the scarred desk. Jace became aware of Michael's look, urging him to accept.

"Another note will follow, upon safe delivery of the silk to Cadiz," Sir Hampton said. "What do you say, Captain Buckley, do we have a bargain?"

Michael coughed. Jace glanced at him. *Darjeeling*, Michael's expression prodded.

"Your offer is hard to resist, Sir Hampton," said Jace.

Sir Hampton laid a heavy hand on his shoulder. "I know a strong captain when I see one. Michael has every confidence in you, and so do I. I have not forgotten your help on Kingscote. You are the manner of man I can trust." He held out his hand. "Then we have us a bargain, Buckley. Say we leave Sunday after the services at St. John's?"

Jace took his hand. "A bargain, Sir Hampton."

"Good. Michael will fill you in on the details. We will need to travel more slowly because of the women. Lady Margaret and her daughter Belinda will accompany us."

Jace watched Sir Hampton and Michael walk to the cabin door, but there was more on his mind.

"About your daughter's adoption of the child,"

Jace said, keeping his voice casual. "This must be quite a celebration for the Roxbury side of the family as well."

A flicker of annoyance showed in Sir Hampton's bronzed face. He masked it swiftly enough and smiled. "Roxbury protested as we expected. But his and Margaret's decision to come to Kingscote to attend the family affair is a healthy sign that he will soon mellow."

Jace did not judge Sir Hugo Roxbury to be a man who mellowed. Showing none of his thoughts, however, Jace went on casually, "Your daughter must be quite pleased."

"Aye, she is indeed." His rugged face softened. "My daughter adores Gem, and so does Mrs. Kendall. And I would be remiss, if I failed to include myself." He gave a brief chuckle, and straightened his hat. "The rascal has won me over without a bit of difficulty."

Jace said pointedly: "I hope his charm equally woos Sir Hugo."

If Kendall caught his insinuation, he chose not to show it. He turned away. "Gem will make a fine Kendall grandson. A strong heir." He gave a swat to Michael's shoulder and pretended to scowl. "With you as slow as your sisters to marry, I best be thanking the good God above for a grandson."

Michael responded with a laugh. "I promise not to disappoint you. As soon as Jace and I buy our tea plantation, I shall consider Cousin Belinda."

"Tea!" came the lightly mocking voice. And he turned to Jace with a helpless expression. "What is wrong with silk, I ask? Tea, bah! 'Tis a curse to swallow the stuff!"

"Jace will agree with you on that much."

"As for your cousin Belinda, she has her eyes on your brother Alex."

"Alex! What does she see in *him*?" he asked fiercely.

"Now, now, enough of your envy. Come, Hugo is waiting for us at Government-House and pacing the floor, to be sure. An odious fellow—but do not tell your mother I said so."

After their footsteps died away, Jace murmured under his breath, "Adoption!"

Absently picking up the cheetah, Jace rubbed his thumb over the smooth carving. From what he knew of Roxbury, he was a ruthless seeker of power in the politics of India. What if he prowled around, asking questions about the boy's parents? If he discovered the child was the grandnephew of a maharaja, there would be harsh political consequences for Kingscote.

I should have spoken to Kendall the night of the monsoon, he thought, and felt a rise of irritation with himself. Why did he allow a sweet, young face with pleading eyes to come between him and wisdom?

7

Although a week had passed since his arrival, Jace had not yet seen Coral. The group's arrival at Kingscote had been met with little fanfare, as the family was immersed in preparations for the adoption ceremony. There was to be music, numerous religious rituals, a gala picnic on the front green with huge amounts of food, and a British military band from Jorhat. News of the elaborate preparations disturbed him, and Jace told himself that he must speak to Coral without further delay.

Upon casual inquiry of her whereabouts to Michael, Jace was informed that Coral was confined to her bedchamber, recovering from a recent attack of fever.

"Uncle Hugo wants her to go to London to seek medical treatment from Ethan," Michael added.

"A physician?"

"Yes, and a cousin. They say he specializes in tropical diseases."

"A Roxbury cousin, no doubt."

"Yes. Hugo's nephew."

Jace assumed that Michael had mentioned his

own presence on Kingscote, and that Coral would find little cheer in knowing that the one who shared her dark secret was here.

When another day went by, and their paths did not meet, he decided he would risk sending her a message by way of the child named Yanna, asking to speak to her alone. If she was strong enough to attend the ceremony, then she could take a ghari to meet him at the hatcheries where he was working.

Jace wrote what he hoped would force her to meet with him:

> *I must see you alone about Gem.*
>
> *Captain J. Buckley*

Coral's reply was swift in coming. Yanna giggled as she brought the message to him, then turned and ran away to a group of other giggling girls.

> *I will come down to the river the morning the elephants haul the silk to the barges.*
>
> *Miss C. Kendall*

Satisfied, Jace went back to work on the river, overseeing the Indian workers preparing the flat-bottom barges for the trip downriver to Guwahati.

———

It was the morning the children working in the hatcheries most anticipated. At least twenty elephants were loaded with bundles of silk cocoons for the circus-like trek down to the river's edge. The manjis would unload the bundles onto the barges for the journey to Guwahati. After the elephants were unloaded, their reward was to be washed and humored by children carrying brushes made of boar bristles. No one on Kingscote was certain who enjoyed the ritual more: the elephants, or the host of orphan children.

The great gray beasts were now coming from the direction of the hatcheries in the mulberry orchard. The first elephant in the long line came around the corner of the dusty road, followed by a host of others trumpeting and flapping their ears. The shouting children, carrying their coveted brushes and rags, ran to the side nearest the thick trees, well out of range of the heavy lumbering feet. The experienced *mahouts* sat low on the elephants' necks, directing them with an ankus. Behind them were the bundles of silk cocoons that the *Madras* would bring to Spain.

Jace stood near the wide gray waters of the Brahmaputra, but his attention was arrested away from the caravan and toward the Kendall mansion. In the carriageway, a two-horse ghari was wending its way down to the river. Once near the road, the ghari-wallah stopped, climbed down from the seat, and came around to open the door.

Jace saw Coral seated alone with a baby boy, who was about a year and a half old. The boy was squealing with excitement and pointing, while she kept a firm hand around his waist to keep him from escaping her lap. The child was the picture of affluence, obviously the object of Coral's doting affection. Gem was a striking child, his handsome features and brown eyes full of innocence and delight.

The scene intensified Jace's dilemma. He watched as the toddler squirmed with joy at each elephant lumbering along the road. Gem threw his arms around her neck, and Coral pointed to where the elephants slowly lowered themselves knees first into the shallow banks for their wash. Their trunks thankfully sucked up the water to squirt over their backs, sometimes spraying the boys attending them. Gem's laughter mingled with theirs.

Coral laughed too, and the musical sound drifted to where Jace stood. His eyes narrowed. She, too, was the image of affluence, and he convinced himself that he did not notice how time had enhanced her attractive appearance. She wore festoons of blue silk, and a straw hat trimmed with white lace covered her blonde tresses.

Jace jerked his hat lower and strode across the road toward the ghari. He stopped in the dust, feeling the heat, his eyes confronting the freshness of her sun-touched beauty. Coral's ability to make an impact on his emotional armor irritated him.

For a moment, she appeared to be so occupied with Gem that he thought she was oblivious to his presence. He rested his hands on his hips, staring at her from beneath his hat. Would she even recognize him without his uniform? At least he had shaved off his beard before he arrived.

"Miss Kendall," Jace said in a voice that was altogether too formal.

Her green eyes, fringed thickly with lashes, met his. The color in her cheeks told him she was not as indifferent to his presence as she made out to be.

"What a pleasant surprise to see you again, Captain. Michael tells me you will soon be sailing for Spain." She rushed on with hardly a pause, "I apologize for the delay in our meeting." She looked away to the river. "I was waiting for the elephants to come today. It gave me an excuse to leave the house and be alone with Gem. I—I thought we could talk during a ride to the hatcheries. I've an excuse to go there. I'm looking for Yanna."

"Do you need an excuse to leave the house?" Jace

responded bluntly. "Or merely one to be seen with me?"

She did not reply. He noted the faint darkness beneath her eyes and thought of her ongoing struggle with the fever. He felt uncomfortable. *Just how ill is she?* He knew of some who had died as a result of tropical fever.

"I take no pleasure in causing you unease, Miss Kendall."

Her eyes came back to search his, and the determination he remembered from the past was visible. Despite frail health, she had a strength of purpose many lacked. It was a spirit Jace admired, even if it did lead her toward trouble.

"You will attend the festivities?" came her breathless question.

Obviously, his presence on Kingscote at this particular time disturbed her, although she was trying to pretend that it did not, that the secret they shared about Gem was of no consequence.

His eyes flickered with wry amusement. "You are inviting me?"

"But of course," came her quick reply. She busied herself with Gem.

"Then I would not miss it, Miss Kendall. Unfortunately, neither would the maharaja—if he knew."

Her eyes widened. "Please! Do not speak of that."

He saw her glance about to make certain no one else was within hearing distance.

"I am sorry, but we must discuss it," he said quietly. "When last we met, you intimated only caring for the child. A godparent, was it not? You said you would send him away to school. I agreed that would be safe enough. But now you are making him a Kendall."

Coral smoothed back Gem's dark curls from his

forehead. "Matters have changed." Her voice began to show her irritation that he had shown up to cast a shadow on her plans. "I have my family's blessing for the adoption. And as I once told you, sir, I am not the only one who wishes to keep him. My mother is very attached to Gem. He has in many ways replaced the baby she lost."

"Yes. You told me . . . I sympathize. I, too, am a friend of sentiment, Miss Kendall, but I also respect your father. And I feel he must know—"

She interrupted. "And my father has great pride in Gem. We want him, Captain," she said firmly. "We all want him."

"Not *all*, Miss Kendall."

Jace was speaking of Sir Hugo Roxbury. Evidently she followed his suggestion, for her expression set with further determination.

So, he thought, *she has already guessed Roxbury might one day be the thorn in her rose garden.*

"A formidable fellow, Roxbury," Jace prodded.

"Yes, but he is a good man, however strongly opinionated," she insisted.

He gave a short laugh. "Sir Hugo? Forgive me if my laughter appears rude, but you will permit me to differ. Colonel Warbeck is well acquainted with Sir Hugo. And, I might add, so am I."

She looked at him thoughtfully. "You?"

Jace said casually, "While an officer in Calcutta, I spent evenings at the Roxbury residence, as did others."

Coral was alert now, and she scanned him, saying nothing.

"No matter how we may try to bend the truth for the sake of politeness, neither of us could go so far as to say Sir Hugo Roxbury is a 'good' man. Clever, yes.

Perhaps even ruthless. His ambition drives him. And it is his nature to disapprove of making an Indian child a Kendall silk heir, especially if that position may contest his own."

Jace could see that his words upset her.

She straightened her hat. "It is true that my uncle has tried to change Father's mind, and mine. He has made his case forcefully."

Jace gave a laugh. "I will wager that he has."

"But my life is not my uncle's to control, Captain." She raised her chin. "Nor anyone else's."

"A polite slap, but well taken. Do you think I enjoy this?"

Her face softened. "I appreciate your concerns . . . however, my mind is made up."

"As well as your heart. You have not changed since that night of the monsoon."

She brought her eyes up to meet his, and Jace noticed how her lashes tilted upward at the edges and made a delicate shadow on her ivory skin.

"Yes, my heart is made up. I could not give him up for all India!"

The silence became uncomfortable. Gem stared up at him with luminous brown eyes, and chubby fingers unexpectedly reached over to latch hold of the cord lacing on the front of his tunic. Jace tried to pry his fingers loose without being rough, but Gem was determined to hold on.

Coral hastened to intervene, looking embarrassed. "Gem, do let go of the captain's tunic."

The boy merely giggled and continued clutching the strings.

Jace smiled. "I have a suspicion you do not mind Miss Coral at all," he told Gem.

"Mummy, Mummy."

Jace realized his mistake. She was not "Miss Coral" to Gem.

Jace untangled himself from the boy.

"I cannot believe you would be so horrid as to come all the way to Kingscote to unmask our little secret," Coral whispered.

"I think you know better than that," he gritted. "As you can see—I am loading Kendall silk."

Jace swung into the ghari, seating himself across from her and calling up to the driver: "The hatcheries!" He shut the door, and the vehicle surged forward.

A strained silence passed before Jace spoke. "He's a pleasant child to behold. He looks like his father," he said. "He's going to be handsome."

"Yes," Coral said proudly, glad to have the course of their conversation altered. "Quite handsome. And he shall travel through all Europe and have the best of education."

Remembering his friend with a dagger through his heart, Jace felt his insides tighten. As he stared at the boy, Gem smiled, suddenly shy now, and buried his face in the folds of her silken skirts.

"I can see why he has won over the affections of your father."

"Captain," she said breathlessly. "You are not going to break your promise to me? That night of the monsoon . . . when you were leaving . . . you said you would say nothing . . . that you would leave me to chart my own course."

"And you have. A word of caution: Watch out for Hugo Roxbury," he stated flatly. "He is clever enough to ask questions better left buried in the past."

She settled her skirts uneasily. "What reason would he have for asking questions?"

"Call it instinct on my part, if you will. But the

fact is his coming here now has deeper motivations than merely attending a family ceremony. I've had a month to study him since leaving Calcutta. There is not a sentimental bone in his body."

His tone softened. "Be cautious. Will you?"

"Yes, of course I will, Captain."

"Thinking back . . . have you any idea who may have sent that message to Rajiv? Someone in the mansion, perhaps?"

She shook her head and closed her eyes, as though trying to remember, yet forget, at the same time.

"No, no one. There has been no trouble since the dreadful incident. Rajiv and Jemani are all but forgotten, except by me."

"Someone else remembers. That someone put a dagger through Rajiv. Two or three years means nothing."

Her hand drew Gem closer. "What are you going to do?"

Both Coral and Gem were watching him. The child was sweetly oblivious to his situation, the Kendall daughter all too aware of the predicament, yet unrelenting.

"I shall tell you what I intended when I came here. I told myself I would speak to you first. That I would make you see I am bound by honor to speak to Sir Hampton." Jace looked at Gem. "But it is obvious, Miss Kendall, that I am two years too late. Whatever I do will bring pain, not only to you but to your family. However, the one question remaining is whose heart shall I risk to my silence?"

She said softly: "I shall forever be in your debt."

His eyes caught and held hers. "Bribery, Miss Kendall?"

She blushed. "I only meant—"

"I know what you meant. But I did not come here to collect favors. Nor do I want to bind you with indebtedness. I respect freedom too much to play games."

"You also respect my father, and I appreciate that, truly I do. It may help you to know that I will not be staying much longer on Kingscote. I am going to Roxbury House in London for schooling. In fact, I'll be returning to Calcutta with my uncle and aunt when they leave here. Belinda and I will join my sisters who are already in London. And Gem will come with me. He will be safe in England. I will place him in a good school there."

"A wise decision. Go as soon as possible."

The ghari stopped at the hatcheries. Jace opened the door, prepared to leave without further discourse.

Her voice interrupted. "Do let me tell you something about the production of silk, Captain Buckley."

His alert gaze swerved to meet hers. He had thought she would be anxious to get away from him. He already knew about silk production . . . but he also knew an invitation when he heard one, even though veiled in the disguise of teaching sericulture. He was certain she only hoped to win him over into keeping silence about Gem. Jace found her ulterior motive amusing.

"As you wish. You have my rapt attention. Suppose you explain to me about the silkworm."

"Caterpillar, actually."

He smiled. "How interesting."

The mulberry orchard stood against the backdrop of the jungle. Normally the outspreading branches were thick, the leaves a dark glossy green, but they were in the process of being stripped by the children, and then pruned by the young men in preparation for next season's crop.

The workers' commune appeared a self-sufficient village, with a few shops and hundreds of small huts. Some were made of woven grasses; others were square, low rooms plastered with mud, dried cow dung comprising the floor. Old men, unable to do the heavy work any longer, waited to accomplish their tasks of carrying trays of dried cocoons. Now they squatted in the shade taking turns puffing on a hookah.

The arrival of their ghari was noted, but the adults went on with their work. The children, however, kept looking over their shoulders, giggling among themselves. They were scampering up and down the mulberry trees gathering leaves. Many of them stared and smiled as Jace strolled with Coral and Gem in the direction of the wooden hatcheries.

"All right. What do we see first?" he asked innocently.

"What would you like to know? I am an expert, you know."

"I must confess. The truth is, I know everything there is about caterpillars."

"You?" she paused, and looked up at him, surprised. "How? I thought you adored tea . . . wild, was it not? Somewhere in Darjeeling?"

He picked up Gem and let him ride on his back.

"I do not exactly adore tea either. But it will become a rich market when the East India Company bans shipments from China."

"How do you know that? About the Company, I mean?"

He did not answer how he knew. "As for caterpillars . . . I spent four years feeding the miserable things

115

by hand in China while you were still crawling around on the nursery rug."

"How ancient and wise you sound, Captain. Let me guess . . . you must be about the same age as Michael."

He said nothing. He was a year younger.

Gem seemed only too happy to ride on his back.

"These Chinese silkworms," she taunted, as they walked slowly toward the buildings, "no doubt they belonged to your father?"

"No. The imperial emperor." He glanced down at her and saw her cover a smile. She did not believe him.

"You were a friend of the emperor?" she asked.

He was about to say—*"No, his slave. One of a thousand, until I escaped by wit and charm. Aren't you proud of me, Coral? The other children either died or are still tending cocoons as men, but I escaped."*

But he caught himself. His past would mean little to her. And he did not wish to share it.

"No, not exactly a friend," he said.

They paused to watch a large group of young boys climbing the trees and gathering the mulberry leaves.

"So you know all about sericulture, do you?" came her challenging voice.

"Try me."

"Very well," came the light, musical voice. Coral looked up at Jace with amused eyes and a bright smile. "I shall bypass all the ordinary information such as gathering the tons of mulberry leaves—almost three hundred and fifty pounds for eight thousand worms."

"You are certain it is eight, and not nine?"

"My father has lectured that point, time and time again at breakfast, since I was five years old."

She walked on, and he followed. Gem insisted on

116

removing Jace's hat, then replacing it again every ten seconds.

"I shall also omit boring you with the chopping, the spoon-feeding of the new larvae, and the cultivation in their hatcheries known as a 'nursery'—since you know all about it."

Now she paused and looked at him, satisfied.

"Instead, Captain Buckley, I shall ask you a profound question. One you *must* have been taught by the emperor of China."

Jace smiled, amused. "I wait with breathless anticipation, Miss Kendall."

"What is the process for dealing with a newly hatched worm that will not wake up and eat?"

His mouth curved upward. "Naturally you wish a profound answer."

"Naturally."

"Let me consider . . . ah, yes! I was given a chicken feather and sternly commanded to tickle it awake," came the grave reply.

Coral laughed her surprise. "You are right! Then you truly were involved in sericulture in China?"

"Where else? And no barking dogs, crowing roosters, or eating garlic. It upsets the freshly hatched worms, or should we call them babies? And, you must see to it that they eat, devour their meals, and take naps in harmony."

Coral laughed. "I am shocked, Captain. You are as tedious as my father. He has a hundred rules from China and never deviates. I would not have guessed you knew so much about silk. Did you truly serve the emperor?"

"Yes. But I assure you, he was not the slightest bit grateful. A most dour man. He never walked. I used to wonder if he had feet like the rest of the poor human race. He was carried wherever he went, and he always had a blade in his lap, only too anxious to lop off someone's head."

They passed the large group of older children and women who were busy chopping the leaves. The smaller children carried the trays into the hatchery for young women to feed the worms.

"Shall we visit the nursery?" she said with a smile. "Papa has more 'babies' than he knows what to do with. This is only the west wing of the nursery. There are acres more. But whatever you do, do not talk. You will upset them. Do you hear, Gem?"

Inside the hatchery it was quiet and still, except for what Jace believed was the sound of the silkworms actually munching. He had been told it was his imagination, but he was certain he could hear a "fizzing" sound. They were ravenous eaters.

A hundred or so young women, called silkworm "mothers," were spoon-feeding the chopped mulberry leaves to the larvae. Jace stared at the pastel-hued silkworm cocoons, filling tiny dry cubicles set in wooden frames.

"Most of the cocoons are never allowed to hatch," she explained when they emerged from the nursery. "Although some are kept for egg production. The emerging moth damages the cocoon for unreeling, and in silk production the unbroken thread is desired. But then, you no doubt know this."

Jace followed her out across the yard to one of the outbuildings where the children were busy.

Seated on the mud floor, young girls were busy in the traditional method of spinning silk, known as thigh-spinning. The girls looked up as they entered, and fixing their eyes on him, they took to giggling.

Jace stooped down beside a girl to watch, but she

grew clumsy with embarrassment.

"Ah, I see how you do it," said Jace, pretending to be extremely interested. "You pierce the cocoon at one end, then draw the fiber across your leg."

At the mention of "leg," they giggled even louder. The blushing girl dropped the cocoon and covered her face with both palms while she laughed.

"Do you think I could do that?" he teased her.

One bold girl of ten said soberly: "Leg too big. Too much hair, silk get caught."

The hut became one loud giggle. Jace saw not the girls but himself at that age—lost, an orphan, and soon bent on a sinful path of the worst kind.

"Yanna? You will come back to the house with me," Coral told one of the giggling girls.

Gem was determined to play with the cocoons, so Jace scooped him up and walked outside.

Suddenly Jace wanted to be gone from Kingscote as quickly as he could get the barges loaded. During the ride back to the river, he was silent. If she noticed his withdrawal, she did not let on, and when he made his polite goodbye, she extended a gloved hand, her eyes saying what they both knew she could not say in front of Yanna.

He would say nothing to interrupt the adoption.

8

The church ceremony took place without incident. The day was warm and the sky clear as the family gathered on the lawn beneath a blue-fringed canopy.

Jace stood aloof from the others while the Anglican bishop read the church liturgy, and then from the Bible. Pompous documents were laid out on a long table. Coral, Sir Hampton, and Elizabeth Kendall dipped the gold quill into ink and wrote their signatures, followed by the bishop.

Jace was taken with the joy on Coral's face at the end of the ceremony when she took Gem by the hand, and together they walked up to the bishop and stood before him. Private words were spoken between the three of them; then he lifted Gem into his arms and intoned a long prayer. Coral then placed a tiny gold cross on a chain around the child's neck.

A copy of the signed documents were delivered to Sir Hampton, and a second went to the bishop. "I give you Gem Ranek Kendall," his pious voice announced, and Coral turned toward the family with Gem, smiling. Jace walked away.

There was an abundance of food, conversation, and laughter as the day wore on into afternoon. Jace did his best to avoid Coral, who sat on the spacious green lawn with her silken skirts spread about her. A young Indian girl shielded her from the sun with a white lace parasol. Coral's Bible lay beside her.

Despite her excitement over the adoption ceremony, he noticed that she did not look well. Beside Coral, seated on cushioned stools, Elizabeth Kendall and Margaret Roxbury chatted together, as two sisters do who have not seen each other in a year, balancing their luncheon plates on their laps.

Some feet away, still dressed in black velvet and white lace, Gem Ranek Kendall romped with rabbits, peacocks, and other fowl, under the watchful eye of an expressionless Burmese ayah. A tiny Burmese girl of about Gem's age romped with him. "No, Emerald," he kept saying as the girl won the attention of the peacock. "My turn. My turn. Obey Gem."

Jace smiled to himself. The boy already knew that a Kendall was to be obeyed.

Jace had no wish for company, even though Michael and Alex stood by him, drinking from tall crystal glasses and discussing the upcoming voyage to Spain. Cousin Belinda Roxbury was flirting outrageously with her cousin Alex, who seemed amused by her. Michael did not look happy.

As Jace looked away from Coral, he caught the intense dark stare that momentarily held his own. Sir Hugo Roxbury evidently did not approve of him looking at his niece. Observing that stare, Jace was reminded that Coral's uncle did not appear pleased with the day's events. No doubt he also disapproved of Michael sailing with him to Spain, and of their plans for a partnership in Darjeeling.

122

Jace had no inclination to appease Sir Hugo, for he did not like the man. Yet he had no wish for unpleasantness and was turning to leave, intending to prepare for the trip to Guwahati early the next morning, when a pleasant voice called to him—

"Captain Buckley? Do join us! You must eat something." Mrs. Elizabeth Kendall sat shaded beneath a parasol held by a child. She smiled and beckoned him to their low table.

Mrs. Kendall was a gracious woman. Unwilling to excuse himself and thus appear rude, Jace walked over and heard a rustle of silk as the ladies pulled back their skirts to make room for him on the grass. Mrs. Kendall proceeded to fix him a plate, piling on an assortment of English dishes.

"If you are anything like my two sons, you enjoy a hardy appetite," she said.

Jace accepted the plate, although he was not hungry, answering numerous polite questions from both Elizabeth and Margaret about his upcoming voyage to Spain. Coral was silent. When at last the desserts were served on wheeled carts, there was a lull in the questioning, and the ladies discoursed among themselves.

Coral leaned toward him and said quietly, "You are leaving in the morning, Captain?"

"Yes, aren't you relieved?" Jace smiled. "I shall fade back into the Indian sunset." He set the empty plate down and rose to his feet. "You will excuse me. There is work to do before I leave for Guwahati tomorrow. Thank you for the luncheon." He glanced over at Gem who still romped with the Burmese child in the grass. "And may the shine stay in your eyes."

Jace offered his thanks to Mrs. Kendall, shook hands with Sir Hampton, and with a word to Michael about Guwahati, left the celebration without a backward glance.

Coral watched Jace leave, her emotions a jumble of contradictions. She told herself she was glad he was gone. One slip of the tongue about Gem, and she would have swooned for the first time in her life! She had sensed his unease, just as he must have sensed her own. Not once had they exchanged glances, although aware of each other. She had noticed that he forced himself to eat, to sit quietly, to behave the gentleman, when all the while he had wanted to avoid being there at all. Sitting at her feet, as was expected of an attentive suitor, must have been especially irksome to him, she thought. And quite suddenly, Coral wanted to laugh. She restrained herself, knowing that it would most likely come out as an hysterical giggle, convincing her mother and aunt that the day had been too much for her. She closed her eyes against the sun's glare and tried to cool her emotions.

He was gone now. There would be a long, long voyage to Spain and perhaps to other distant ports. Possibly she would never run into him again. Good. Then she would not need to worry about him saying anything to her family about Gem. But then, somehow she had guessed all along that he would not. Perhaps the captain was not as hardheaded and arrogant as he appeared.

The excitement of the morning was ebbing away. Coral realized how tired she felt, and the heat was beginning to drain her of strength. She excused herself from her mother and her aunt, giving them a customary kiss on the cheek, and calling for Jan-Lee to bring Gem and Emerald.

Today Gem is truly my son. A smile flitted across

her face as Coral made her way back to the house. Soon
the two of them would journey to London to meet
Grandmother Victoria Roxbury . . . and Cousin Ethan
Boswell.

9

It was August of 1795, and already late in the season when the *Madras* sailed from Diamond Point Harbor carrying Kingscote silk. They sailed the Bay of Bengal toward the strait between Ceylon and the Indian coast, then went across the Indian Ocean and came to the island of Zanzibar—isle of cloves, wild coffee, and forests of coconut palms. Here, as planned, they took on spices.

" 'Twas yer father's haven," Seward told him.

Jace remembered the hot white sands and glittering blue waters of Zanzibar, where his father had owned a small bungalow on the beach.

The *Madras* dropped anchor, stopped farther down the coast, then sailed around the African horn, making port at the Cape of Good Hope. From there, the voyage brought them along the Gold Coast of Africa—where the devious slave traders abounded—and eventually they came to the port of Tangiers. Staying a short time, they sailed for Spain and arrived at Cadiz late in December of 1796.

The town of Cadiz, dating back to the times of the ancient Phoenicians, was built on a cliff overlooking

127

the sea. The silk was unloaded in the port, the price was good, and the funds were divided between the three of them. With it they intended to buy heirlooms from Moorish Spain, then sell them to the wealthy collectors in London. Jace expected to return to Calcutta by October of the next year, avoiding the monsoon winds of August and September. Everything, it seemed, was going well. He had almost begun to believe Michael's declaration that heaven's benediction was upon them.

Since the weather for sailing in the Atlantic was questionable, Jace was anxious to leave Cadiz within the next three days. The city was a flourishing port, its bazaars crowded with merchants, soldiers, sailors, slave traders, a few pirates, and many scholars. Although he had friends in the ancient city, Jace preferred to walk the lighted arcade alone. He spent the morning at the famous stall of the Booksellers where he found several copies of old writings to add to his collection. Besides owning a copy of the Hindu holy writings, the Vedas, he had acquired a copy of the Muslim Koran and a King James Bible—but not even Seward knew that he was making a comparison of the three main world religions.

Tired of browsing through manuscripts, Jace left the Booksellers and stood on the corner of the arcade with his purchases. Noise, music, and a babble of voices filled the air. He walked to a tavern-inn on the cliff above the sea to wait for Seward and Michael. They would bring Hakeem, the Arab merchant who specialized in prized antiques.

The low-raftered inn was crowded with seamen when Jace arrived. It was damp and cold outside, and a fire burned in the wall-sized hearth. He found an empty place overlooking the western sea, now shrouded with incoming fog, and ordered portions of roasted lamb.

Michael arrived, tense and excited, seating himself opposite Jace. Leaning across the table, he said in a low voice: "After London, we can return to India and start the plantation!"

Jace cast him a caustic smile. "What did you do, rob a temple? It will be three more years—if all goes well."

Michael grinned, undaunted. "Seward found your merchant friend. And wait until you hear the Arab explain."

They both turned toward the door. Seward strode into the common room, and Jace recognized the wealthy Arab beside him, clothed in a flowing robe and smoke-blue silk turban. His short Muslim beard was well-trimmed, his hawklike black eyes snapping with pleasure when they rested on Jace.

"Greetings, son of the great Captain Buckley! I see you are back to the ways of the sea, and free of the infidel uniform." His crafty old eyes gleamed. "Ah, is it not in your stars to become an auspicious explorer like your father?"

Jace stood and greeted the Arab with a smile. "Hakeem! You old Teller of Tales! How good to see you again! So my father was an explorer, was he?" Jace laughed. "You mean pirate, do you not? Better read your stars again, Father of Hypocrites! What do you have this time for the greedy markets of London?"

"Ah!" Hakeem removed the cloth wrapping from a carved ivory elephant, its emerald eyes glittering like green fire. He set it on the table before Jace.

"The East India director will most appreciate the mate to the one you sold him last time. He has sent an inquiry asking for it."

Rawlings, director of the Company in London, had a compelling interest in collecting antiques from the East, as well as a secret maze of informers who delved into intrigue.

"The elephant is the least of the items he offers," Michael interrupted. "Tell him about the heirloom, Hakeem."

"Ah, yes, the alabaster jewel box."

Michael turned to Jace. "It is from twelfth-century Moorish Spain, dating from the Great Count Roger I."

Jace raised a skeptical brow at Hakeem. "The First Crusade?"

"It is so, my friend. It belonged to the family of the Norman Count. It is worth much on the market."

"Rawlings will be impressed," said Jace, then said deliberately: "But our funds are beleaguered."

Michael leaned toward him and said in a low voice, "If we pool our resources, we can buy it."

Jace knew that, but he was experienced in dealing with Hakeem. Michael was right about one thing. An heirloom belonging to the Norman Count would bring enough money to return to India to buy the Darjeeling land.

Michael's dark eyes snapped with excitement. "Gokul says he can hire tea workers from Nepal. Think of it, Jace! You and I—owners of a tea enterprise. In a few years it is possible to become as successful as Kingscote."

Jace knew what financial success could bring him—complete freedom from the colonel.

"I can marry Belinda," continued Michael.

Jace gave an ironic laugh. "You speak like a vagabond. Are you not a silk heir? You can have Roxbury's daughter if you ask for her. But remember—even after we buy the land, it will take a number of years to grow, harvest, and ship the tea."

Jace turned back to Hakeem. "Where is the heirloom? Do you have it?"

Hakeem spread his palms. "It waits in Cordoba."

Seward groaned. "And why did ye not bring it, I ask ye? Cordoba be days of travelin'."

"I can have it for you in two weeks."

"Two weeks? Are you mad with wine? The weather won't hold."

Hakeem looked out the window with a scowl. "Ah, but a treasure from the glorious past is not easy to come by. Despite the risk, it is worth the wait."

"Let it wait, Cunning One, until we come this way next year," replied Jace, pushing back his chair to stand.

"Ah, but your sea chest will bulge with the rich fatness of Moorish Spain. The alabaster jewelry box is so rich a bounty as to be like a beautiful damsel. If you will not embrace her, she will run to embrace another."

"He has something there," Michael told Jace.

Jace said nothing. He bit into the tender roast lamb, aware that Seward watched him with hungry countenance. He pushed the platter over to him.

"We cannot wait," said Jace.

"Then I cannot hold her until you return from London." The Arab's black eyes glinted, and he whispered, "O Great Ones, the heirloom will bring you at least a treasure chest of English pounds."

"We will wait the two weeks," argued Michael.

Jace silently calculated with one eye on the sea.

"This I will do. I will send a message tonight to Cordoba," said Hakeem. "The owner will hasten his journey. Say, five to seven days?"

Jace had traveled to the great city before and knew

this was possible. "We best travel to Cordoba ourselves."

"We can leave tonight," pressed Michael.

Jace looked at Seward, who rubbed his bearded chin.

"I don't know, lad. Ye know I be as committed to Darjeeling as ye and Michael. But ye be right about the season. Yet, I admit a few thousand pounds be worth a delay. But if ye be in favor of sailin' tomorrow, I be with ye. Maybe we best take us a vote."

"You have it, Seward. We will vote," urged Michael. "What do you say, Jace?"

Jace hesitated. After all, he was the captain, and he knew best when to sail his ship.

"The Deuce! Sometimes one must take a risk if he is to win," pressed Michael.

"Then we'll vote. You first."

"I vote for Cordoba," said Michael, and smiled at him.

Seward frowned in the direction of the harbor, then cast an apologetic glance at Jace. "I be tempted to do the same."

"Well, is it yes or no?"

His brows pulled together. "Aye."

Michael laughed and got to his feet, clapping Jace's shoulder. "Do not look so dour. Are you not a worthy seadog? It runs in your blood like your father before you. Seward will vow to that. Is that not so, Seward? Look Jace, if we weathered the South China Sea, you can get the *Madras* safely to London, then home to India. Sit down, old chap, have some Arabian coffee!"

———

Confidence . . . usually Jace had enough to spare.

As dawn broke on their fifth morning at sea from
Cadiz, uncertainty nagged at his heart, just as the
moist wind tugged at his leather jerkin. He stood on
the quarterdeck while his narrowing gaze swept
across the iron gray expanse of the Atlantic Ocean. The
twelfth-century heirloom was locked inside his sea
chest in the Great Cabin, along with the ivory elephant, waiting for their meeting with Rawlings in
London. The price paid to the Arab merchant had exhausted their pooled funds, but the London market
would be a rich one.

Seward came up beside him, his broad face lacking its good humor. He leaned against the rail, the
wind stirring a thatch of chestnut hair tied at the nape
of his neck. For a moment he did not speak, and along
with Jace watched the murky sunrise color the length
of the horizon an amber haze. The ship creaked and
groaned.

"I do not like it," breathed Jace.

"Aye . . . I be rememberin' long ago . . .'twas but a
lad then. A mere coxswain was I, on one of the meanest
slave ships to sail. We come head on with a storm
havin' the same feel as this."

Jace stared ahead. "I will agree my father was a
blackguard, but he did not trade in slaves. I would
remember."

"No need to get riled, lad. I knew Buckley better'n
ye did. 'Twas not speakin' of yer father, but another
captain, a sure reprobate, that one. A derelict, he was,
by the name of Newton. Been doing a lot of thinkin'
about him lately."

"I never heard of Newton."

"Ye wouldn't. Was before yer time. We was comin'
toward London . . . just like now. Unsuspectin' we
were, and before we get there, we run into wind and

waves. Ain't seen the likes of it since. Ship was near to be battered to sticks . . . them swells rose, I'd say, near fifty feet. Maybe higher. 'Twas enough to scare a sinner into quick repentance. Worst thing ever been through. Aye, 'twas enough to bring the young captain on his face before the Almighty."

Jace was in an ill mood. "Are you hinting I am neglecting the Almighty?"

"Didn't think I needed to hint. I be includin' myself in that."

"Never mind. Where is Michael?"

"Most likely in his cabin. He's a mite sick. Makes a poor sailor. I be thinkin' we best leave him in India when we take to haulin' our tea."

Jace left Seward and went to Michael's small cabin. He was still thinking about Seward's suggestion that he was not devout enough. That Seward considered himself an Anglican was no secret, but Jace had never seen him practice his faith. He tapped on the door. When there was no answer, he opened it. Michael was sprawled on his cot, pale and sick.

"Ah, poor laddie," Jace mocked. "And no lassie to hold your hand."

Michael slowly turned his head toward the door, opening one eye and groaning. "Get out of here."

"Fine way to speak to your captain. I should have you helping the kansamah gut fish. He's making a savory stew."

Michael groaned again and turned his head to the wall. The ship heaved and sank. "How—much—longer?" he whispered.

Jace folded his arms and smiled. "Oh, another ten days. Maybe longer."

"Ten days! My insides will all be heaved overboard by then!"

"Now, now, old chap, all you need is some liquid down you. I can smell the broth simmering. A few fish heads improve the flavor."

Michael moaned and tried to get up as though to slug him. Jace smiled and sank comfortably into the chair, stretching out his boots, his arms behind his head.

"Cheer up. The worst storm of your life is coming. I thought I should warn you."

Michael fell back to the pillow. "Now you tell me. We should have stayed in Cadiz."

"You mean," gritted Jace for emphasis, "we should have left three weeks ago. I think I already mentioned that and was voted down. Next time I will ignore my tea partners and exercise my right as captain of my own vessel!"

"Yes, yes . . . we heard you howling about it a dozen times . . . do not sound so injured. At least we got the heirloom. Ah, Darjeeling! I can feel the firm ground beneath my feet now! I can smell the fresh tea leaves gently moving in the breeze, see the white caps of the Himalayas—"

Just then, the ship pitched, Michael groaned, and a Bible and a stack of books tumbled from the table onto the floor and slid to Jace's boots. When the ship steadied again, Jace picked them up. There was an autobiography of the colonial missionary to the American Indians, David Brainerd.

"Brainerd?"

"Coral gave it to me before I left."

There was also a volume by Whitfield, and another by John Wesley. Jace had heard of both reformers while in London. He leafed through them, pausing to see Coral's signature. No doubt she had plenty of time to read during her bouts with tropical fever. He imagined that she could hold quite a discourse on the Reformers. Jace realized, however, that he knew practically nothing about them. Holding the Bible, he tried to get Michael's mind off his misery.

"After we sell the heirloom, we can decide on the style of our residence. I think we should build us a white Georgian mansion."

Michael looked at him. "You once said you detested mansions."

"I have changed my mind. I want it equal to Kingscote. In fact—I want it to rival anything you Kendalls have."

Michael opened one eye. "What for?"

Jace settled more comfortably. "I have never lived in a sparkling white mansion with a blue roof. I just decided I want one. With furniture from France."

Michael ran a hand over his face. "I care not at all, dear fellow ... I have had my fill of mansions and French furniture. All I want is a humble bunk that does not buck."

Jace leaned his head back against the chair and stared at the ceiling, absently running his thumb over the leather binding of the Bible. "Maybe I will order Persian silk coverlets for my bed."

Michael grunted.

"I will have one of those mattresses that are stuffed with goose feathers, and a hundred servants to wait on me." His eyes glinted with amusement as he looked at Michael. "What do you think?"

"I think you sound like Solomon," came his dull voice.

"I did not say female servants," Jace corrected. "Solomon—the wisest man on earth, yet he took a thousand wives." He laughed softly.

Michael lifted his head and looked at him. "You

know about his wives and concubines?"

"Do you take me to be completely ignorant?"

Michael waved a hand. "No offense, Captain. I simply did not know you had read the Scriptures."

"A most interesting tale how that particular Bible came my way."

"I have always thought you believed in Christ."

Jace scrutinized him. He could not see Michael's expression, for he had one arm across his face, and the other across his stomach.

Actually, Jace had read the entire Bible through, to compare it with the Vedas and the Koran. He had found the person of Christ without fault—more than a mere man. A true Master, but one who demanded all. Jace was not willing to surrender all to anyone.

"About Darjeeling," he said, changing the subject. "Once in Calcutta, we will make an expedition to see the Raja of Sikkim. He will be delighted to see our gold. By the time we get back, Seward and Gokul will have a roof over our heads to protect us from the monsoon." He smiled. "Our Georgian mansion can wait a few years."

"Superb thought . . . land. I cannot say I want to go through this again."

"The upcoming storm will be treacherous. Stay below. Tie yourself to your bunk."

Michael gave a short laugh. "Do not worry, Captain. The only thing that will tempt me from my cot is a sinking ship. May God forbid."

"A sober thought. Where do you want these?" Jace was still holding the books.

"In that drawer. Unless you care to read them."

"Brainerd looks interesting . . . well, maybe I will read them all. I like to discover what goes on in the mind of a man who gives up everything to preach to a bunch of naked savages," he said of Brainerd, "or those who argue church doctrine on the streets of London amid hawkers of fish and posies. The mind of someone who would lie in bed for a month and read them is also curious."

"I do not know the answer to any of their minds. I have yet to reach the spiritual summit of Brainerd, or for that matter, my dear little sister. But one thing is clear . . . Brainerd found the American Indians to be more than naked savages."

Jace handed Michael his Bible. "Ever heard of Newton?"

"No. Why?"

"Never mind. Read Psalms. You need some cheering up. I suggest number 107. Verses 23 to 30."

Michael seemed curious enough to get his mind off his stomach, and began searching through his Bible.

Jace was ready to duck out the cabin door when Michael said, "I suppose Brainerd found in Christ everything he gave up, and more." He paused. "I do not know if I could give up a tea plantation to tell savages of their Creator."

Jace looked at him. "Excuse me, noble Rector, but you do not have one yet to toss to the flames of divine call. Read. I have business with the pilot . . . if you want to see either India or London again."

Michael managed a sick grin, and tried to focus on the words of the psalm. "Ah! It is about a ship! Listen to this—'So he bringeth them unto their desired haven,' " he quoted. "Ah . . . I like that; peace and rest."

Desired haven, thought Jace, as a strong blast of

wind struck him and sea spray wet his face. He walked to the ladder, pausing to squint at the sky. It was an ugly hue, with fierce clouds. The *Madras* rolled and pitched, and a hissing spatter was carried along the deck.

Desired haven. . . . Jace was not ignorant of the claims of Christ. Yielding to His Lordship would mean giving up control of his own plans. The last thing Jace wanted was to be vulnerable. He knew enough of what was in the Book to understand that Christ would not settle for anything less than his surrender. Jace did not like the word surrender . . . the times that he had laid bare his emotions to others only brought memories of rejection. He knew that Christ was not a hard taskmaster, and yet—what would He demand of him? To give up his ambitions? His ship? Perhaps to become an Anglican minister walking about in a robe—

"Captain!" shouted Jin-Soo. "Ginseng tea answer to all things!"

Jace turned. The beloved old man was determined to serve Jace personally. He stood in a baggy knee-length black kimono holding a bronze urn and cup, a smile on his crinkled face. The wind whipped at his white pigtail as he bowed low at the waist.

"Jin-Soo! You know better than to be on deck when it's pitching like this. Go below, now!"

"I go, Captain, but you drink tea first. Need much strength. Dragon-devils stir up sea, spew waves instead of fire. You up all night, yes?"

The Chinese miracle brew was the last thing Jace wanted now. "Where is my coffee? I want it black and scalding. And do not bring it up to me. I'll send the coxswain."

"Captain is very stubborn." He added in labored English: "Arabic coffee is no good. It is very bad. Chinese tea is very good. Captain needs a woman to look after him. Jin-Soo fail. Yes, I go, I go!" he shouted above the rising wind as Jace glowered. Turning, the old one struggled back down the steps.

The deck, deserted now by all but the best of his experienced seamen, heaved up and sank again beneath Jace's boots. The *Madras* shuddered its complaint and groaned, while the wind doubled its velocity.

"Cap'n!"

"What is it, lad?"

The coxswain was pasty white as he clung tenaciously to one of the shrouds. "Pilot say 'e dinnae 'no what 'e to do. Cannae pilot 'elm. Say 'e done lied aboot sailin' Indian Ocean in monsoon—"

"Lied? Of course he lied. Did he think I believed him? But I will have his head if he leaves the helm now!"

"Aye, Cap'n, I tell 'im."

"Where's Seward!"

"Methinks 'e be below, Cap'n!"

No doubt checking on Michael, Jace thought.

Below at the bottom companionway steps, Jace took a moment to shrug into his oilskins, shouting at the same time, "Seward!"

Jin-Soo thrust his head out a cabin door. "Seward is not here, Captain. He went to Great Cabin looking for you. You want coffee now?"

"Later, Jin-Soo, and keep an eye on Michael. He is sick."

"But—"

Jace turned heel without another word. He imagined his ship a piece of driftwood tossed on the waves, being sucked toward the open jaws of a hungry behemoth. It took an experienced seaman to maneuver down the passage; he leaned into one wall, then the other, as the ship pitched and rolled. As skilled as he was, it took longer than usual to climb the narrow wood steps leading topside. Jace threw open the companionway door and ducked out into the roaring squall, intending to go to the helm.

The thrashing wind took his breath away, and he held to the door, his boots planted squarely apart to avoid stumbling crazily across the heaving deck. Black swells of seawater washed over the rail onto the main deck, lashing up about his calf-length boots like snarling dogs. Torrents of rain struck against his face. The daylight had darkened to twilight. For a second he stared ahead of him, disbelieving what he saw.

Impossible! Michael had vowed he would not come up on deck!

Yet there he was!—grasping the rail and staring into the mountainous swells as though in a trance. Had he gone mad?

Jace moved toward him, then saw the danger coming—a dark swell rising above the side of the ship like a breaking black avalanche.

"Michael! Hold on!"

But the wind sucked his words into a cavern of noise and silenced them. The monstrous wave swooped over the railing onto the deck, instantly burying everything in its flood. The icy force slammed Jace back, knocking him off his feet. Half-blinded by stinging salt, his mind shouted: *Michael!*

Jace caught sight of him in the seawater that rushed down the ship's tilting deck. He heard Michael yell, caught a glimpse of his attempt to grab a shroud line, and saw his hand touch nothing but air.

Jace hurled himself after him, lunging to grasp the back of Michael's collar before he was washed overboard. Jace grabbed his drenched hair instead, and held relentlessly to the line with his other hand while the sucking wash tried to rip them apart. The sea engaged Jace and Michael in a tug-of-war, demanding to fish them both overboard into its watery net. There was little between them and the mountainous dark swells. *God! Not Michael—*

The ship heaved portside, throwing Jace against the railing. Pain stabbed through his body like red-hot daggers as he felt his ribs crack. Weakness assailed him, and only after the water rushed back to sea did the ugly realization rip through his mind. He no longer had hold of Michael! He had lost him!

Still grasping the rail, Jace leaned over the side of the ship and searched the swelling dark caverns. "Michael!" he shouted, but his voice mocked his feeble effort. "Michael!"

Despair flooded his soul, then rage.

"Filthy curse!" he screamed at the sea.

The *Madras* vaulted. Jace slid across the deck like a slippery fish on its belly. He slammed into the ladder that led to the quarterdeck and the Great Cabin. Unable to move, pain from his cracked ribs made it difficult to breathe. His numb fingers touched a rung, fumbled, then wrapped about the wood. Struggling to his knees, Jace gritted his teeth against the pain. A second surge of water flooded after him, wrapping about his legs like a viper trying to snatch him back. Jace crawled up the ladder and clung there between the two decks trying to gain his breath.

"Captain!" shouted his first-mate.

Jace yelled his orders, though he knew it was too late. "Man overboard! Sound an alarm! See if you can spot him!"

Like a drunken man, the first-mate staggered

across the afterdeck, shouting as he went.

The ship rolled, and Jace stumbled onto the deck, leaning against the rail for support while edging his way toward the captain's cabin.

The open door slammed back and forth on its hinges, and Jace stumbled inside, grasping hold of his desk. The storm made the cabin as dark as evening.

God, why? Why! "Why did you not take me instead!" Jace gritted into the silence. *You know he was worth two of me!*

The emotional loss stabbed at him with a retching pain far worse than his cracked ribs.

Jace fumbled to remove the oilskins, and then his jerkin, but could not. His body sprawled over the desk.

"Jace!"

Seward ducked his head under the doorway, knocking off his tricorn, taking in the scene with a glance. "Ye be hurt!"

"Michael's overboard. I lost him."

Seward's voice sucked in, then snapped with emotion. "Aye!" He stood there in shock.

"I gave orders to search for him, but . . ."

The ship rolled, and too weak to balance himself Jace fell against the chest of drawers. Pain brought a moment of blackness, but he fought against it.

Seward grabbed him and lowered him onto the floor. Quickly he lit the swaying oil lantern above the desk.

"Bind my ribs and get me to the helm."

Seward glowered over him, wild with fury. "Nay, lad! Will I lose ye also? I vowed to Captain Jarred Buckley I'd be yer surety! Ye'll not leave the cabin!"

"Pull yourself together! Do as I say, Seward!"

Jace tried to raise himself to an elbow, but Seward's big hands slammed him back to the floor, and pain lashed through his ribs. He glimpsed Seward's wild expression, the lank hair hanging in his eyes.

"Ye be goin' nowheres, laddie."

"Don't be a fool! I'm captain of this ship! Now get me to the helm, that's an order!"

As though struck with an icy blast, Seward blinked, and slowly his hold loosened.

"Aye," he growled darkly. "I be hearin' ye. Captain, eh? Better ye stayed in uniform! And would to God I'd never let Hampton's son come!" He turned away, smashing his fist against the wall. "Now the only son of Jarred Buckley be followin' his drownin'. 'Tis the devil's storm out there!"

"Snap out of it! You speak to me of God! Where is He? Is it the Devil or your Christ who commands the wind and sea?"

Seward sobered. His ice-blue eyes narrowed as he knelt beside Jace. He removed Jace's oilskins, and used his knife to slit open the leather jerkin, exposing his chest.

"Well said. It be the Almighty's storm all right, and there be a message in it for us all. Ye be as stubborn as yer father was, nay—worse, ye are!"

"Stop your grumbling and do something!"

Seward glared down at him. With strips of cloth he bound Jace tightly.

"Ow!—easy, you grizzly! You want to crack the rest?"

Seward grunted and stood unsteadily. "Nay a bad idea if it keep ye safe." He pulled Jace onto his boots. For a moment Jace's brain spun and nausea gripped him.

"Ye be standin'. Walk alone, Captain, or ye'll not be goin' to the helm!"

"Then I will get there alone. If the *Madras* sinks,

this captain's going with her!"

Jace swayed toward the door, but was so dizzy that he slammed into the wall. He tried again.

Seward winced, mumbling under his breath; then throwing a hefty arm about his shoulders, he turned him toward the cabin door.

"Like yer pirate father ye be. Damnation awaits ye!"

"Silence your cursed tongue!"

"Nay! Damnation awaits us both! Do ye think 'twas a mistake that the Almighty took a goodly lad, and left the stubborn, rebellious son of a pirate?"

Jace swung his fist, but he was too exhausted, and it missed as Seward ducked. Blackness swirled in Jace's brain, and he stumbled, crashing upon his desk and into unconsciousness.

Seward grabbed him. "Ah, lad! I didn't mean it! God forgive me, I didn't mean it!"

The coxswain appeared, sopping wet and shaking, bracing himself with both hands in the doorway. Seeing his captain unconscious, and Seward weeping, he too broke into a bawl.

"God 'ave mercy on us, Cap'n! Christ 'ave mercy! Dinnae find no Master Kendall! And 'elmsman 'e ran, and 'e too done gone overboard! Cap'n—"

"Silence, boy!" Seward thundered. "Get yerself in here! Take care of the captain. He be unconscious, do ye hear?"

"Aye, sir!"

Seward grasped the boy by the scruff of his tunic, lifting him up off his heels, his eyes blazing. "And if ye show yerself above, I'll throw ye to the sea myself!"

He dropped the coxswain, who fell to the cabin floor. "Aye, Mister Seward, I 'ear ye!"

Seward stumbled toward the door. "May the mercies of the God of Jonah be upon the filthy lot of us!"

145

10

Kingscote
July 1796

Coral laughed as she leaned over the small bed in the upstairs nursery, Gem's arms holding tightly to her neck. The large brown eyes ringed with dark lashes stared up at her and he giggled, refusing to let go.

"Kiss me again, Mummy."

"There—on the forehead."

"Nuther one."

"Time for bed. You must be rested if you are going to ride with me on the elephant tomorrow."

"Not sleepy."

"Not sleepy, indeed," Coral teased, giving him a squeeze. "You can hardly keep your eyes open—why, you are even making me sleepy. . . ." and Coral pretended to yawn.

Gem smiled, and a tiny dimple formed at the corner of his mouth. "Sleep here, Mummy."

"Mummy must sleep in her own big bed, but I will sit with you until you are asleep. Are you ready to give

147

thanks to God for the day we have had together? You got to see your great-uncle Hugo today, and Great-aunt Margaret."

Gem nodded and shut his eyes so tightly that his nose wrinkled. "Thank you, Lord Jesus. Amen."

Coral smiled and covered him lightly with a blue cotton sheet. "Good night, Gem."

"Night, Mummy . . . Mummy? Ride baby elephant tomorrow?"

"Yes, I think so. Go to sleep now."

She dimmed the light on the table beside the bed until only a golden glow shone in the nursery. Dolls, blocks, and other toys were neatly stacked in their blue-painted bin. She drew the mosquito net about his bed, then walked to the open verandah.

Before going to her room down the hall, she stepped out into the darkness, breathing the scents coming from the garden. From the silk workers' huts near the distant hatcheries came the smell of woodsmoke.

Alone, and without the sharp eyes of Jan-Lee scrutinizing her for signs that she had overextended herself, Coral took advantage of the solitude to lean wearily against the verandah rail and draw a long breath. She did not dare tell them how exhausted she felt! Would she ever be strong again? There were so many activities she wanted to experience with Gem, but could not because her strength failed her. Fever and weakness, the result of tropical illness—her second relapse since the birth of Gem—had left her thin and tired. Even simple tasks, like bathing and dressing Gem, she had been forced to leave for Jan-Lee.

Her delicate brows came together. She had promised to ride with Gem on the elephant, but would she even have the strength? *I must go to bed,* she thought. *I must get some sleep.*

Later that night, the air was full of jungle sounds seeping in through the net gathered around her bed. Coral tossed restlessly, slowly coming awake.

She strained to hear what had awakened her, but heard little except the thump of her heart. Then, the thud of horses' hooves and shouting voices stabbed the night. One of the voices belonged to her father!

Coral flung the covers aside and pushed her way through the mosquito net. Scurrying across the floor to the verandah, she peered below. Male servants ran in all directions while Sir Hampton shouted orders.

"Father, what is it?"

Coral could not see his face as he looked up at her, rifle in hand. "Stay inside, Coral. Marauders! They appear to be sepoys. The swine set the mulberry grove on fire."

Fire! Horrified, Coral looked off in the direction of the jungle. Faintly, through the thick darkness of the trees, she could see the orange-red piercing through the blackness of branches. On the breeze came the foul odor of smoke. *Marauders!* Her father had said they looked like armed sepoys—the Indian infantry. Were these renegades who had mutinied against their commander?

A scream came from below, and she caught a glimpse of Mera and Rosa running from the house.

"Fire!" Hampton shouted in Hindi. "The silkworm hatcheries are in danger!"

The children! thought Coral with trepidation. *Who will get the untouchables out of the huts?*

Natine ran from the stables bringing two horses. Hampton swung himself onto the saddle.

"Hampton, wait for Hugo! Do not go alone!" Elizabeth Kendall shouted from the front doorway.

"Father!" Coral shouted over the rail. "The children!"

"Hugo is coming now!"

Other workers on horseback galloped toward Hampton. The war cry of trumpeting elephants shrieked through the blackness and Coral covered her ears. The trained mahouts arrived, prepared to lead them into battle. Her father galloped toward the hatcheries with Sir Hugo Roxbury, and the yard was left in silence except for the anxious dialogue of her mother and Natine. Coral watched flames leaping up from distant branches.

A fire, she thought, dazed. *Why would there be a fire here? Did the enemies come from Burma?*

Still stricken, Coral glanced below. Her mother now stood with Margaret and the female servants, staring after the galloping horses. But Natine was looking up toward the mansion, past Coral, in the direction of the nursery.

The nursery was safe from the fire, of course— Coral froze with sudden horror. Fear gripped her like iron bands. She whirled, and like a mad woman, she screamed, running and stumbling from her room. "Gem! Gem! Come to me! Quick, Gem!"

Coral stumbled down the hall, her shift clinging about her ankles. Grabbing the silk and pulling it to her knees, Coral ran down the hall, whispering, "Lord, protect my son!"

She reached the nursery door, flung it open and burst inside. "Gem!"

She stopped, a scream dying in her throat. Jan-Lee lay on the floor, unconscious. Coral's eyes darted to the small bed. *Empty.* She went weak. Her gaze sought the verandah and met the glittering black eyes of a sepoy in a soiled brown puggari. He clutched Gem under his arm, one leg already swung over the verandah.

"Stop! Stop!"

"Mummy, Mummy, Mummy—!"

Gem's hysterical screams thrust Coral in his direction. Reaching the verandah, she clawed the sepoy's face as he grabbed for a rope to make his escape.

"Let go of my baby!" she screamed as the man slapped her backward. Coral stumbled to her feet, grabbed the heavy pot from the floor and hurled it at his back. Whirling, his fist smashed into Coral's face, sending her crashing to the floor.

———

Coral had no recollection of how many weeks had lapsed since the abduction of Gem. Now and then, she would awaken from a fever-induced delirium to see her mother beside her bed, haggard from lack of sleep. Sometimes it was Aunt Margaret who answered her tormented cries. Other times it was Jan-Lee murmuring sighs as she wiped Coral down with cool cloths, her dark eyes saddened.

When Coral's eyes did open to a greater awareness of her surroundings, she realized that she was in bed and so weak she could hardly turn her head. The room was in shadows, with the sunblinds drawn, and one small golden lamp burned on a table. Silence surrounded her, and the chair beside her bed was empty. Somewhere in the distance she could hear the wheels of a horse-drawn wagon nearing the front yard. From below, came voices.

151

Coral tried to speak—"Mother. . . ?"

The feebleness of her voice alarmed her. It was not Elizabeth who responded, but Jan-Lee who came swiftly from the shadows and bent over her with serious eyes searching her face.

"Hush, hush. You must sleep. Miss Elizabeth will be back soon."

"W-what . . . is all that . . . that noise? Tiger—"

"There is no tiger. You dream."

"Noise . . . I hear . . . voices—"

Jan-Lee wrung the water from a cloth and wiped Coral's face. "Do not worry yourself. Your mother will come soon."

"Gem . . . any news—"

As Coral tried to focus her gaze, she saw that Jan-Lee's face twisted with grief.

"Miss Coral . . . there is something I—" she paused, then turned toward the door. She left Coral's side and spoke in a low voice to someone, but Coral could not make out her words. She struggled to raise herself to her elbow; never had she felt this weak. *Maybe I am dying* . . . she thought, and strangely she felt no alarm.

Coral heard a rustle of skirts, and her mother came toward her, pale and drawn in black satin. "Coral, dear." Elizabeth reached a cool palm to the side of Coral's face.

Coral's eyes absorbed her mother's stiff black funeral dress and ankle-length veil. She saw the black prayer book with the embossed gold cross and the white handkerchief. Her gaze darted back to her mother's face. All at once the truth stabbed. She choked back a wrenching sob, her cold fingers flying to her mouth.

"Gem!" A horrid cry escaped Coral's lips.

Elizabeth fell beside her, her eyes swimming with tears, her face contorted with grief, and Coral felt her mother's sobs even as she gathered her into her arms.

"I am so sorry, darling, so sorry. They found him by the river—"

"No!" Coral clutched her mother, her fingers digging into her flesh with uncontrollable rage. "No! It is not fair!"

Elizabeth Kendall held Coral against her breast, her trembling hand stroking the tangled hair as she rocked her tormented daughter.

"Lord," whispered her mother. "Give us your grace. You have promised—comfort my daughter."

Coral stiffened and cried: "They killed him! Jace was right! Oh, my poor baby! What did they do to you, what did they do—"

She sobbed deeply until her lungs could no longer inhale. Her heart thundered in her ears, sending the blood pounding in her head until she felt it would explode.

Her mother continued to hold her, rocking her as though she were an infant. Coral could feel her mother's tears mingling with her own. Horrid images of the abductor plunging a dagger into Gem's heart burned within her mind. She could hear his last words begging her—the hysterical screams, *Mummy, Mummy, Mummy!* brought convulsions of pain. Coral wept until her throat ached and burned, and she was numb with pain.

"Why, Mama?" she choked into Elizabeth's breast.

"Only God has the answer," came her mother's whisper.

"But why did God take him from *me*—I . . . I was

teaching him Bible stories, I was helping him to memorize Scripture verses—I taught him to love Jesus—why, Mama? Why did God take him from *me?*"

Elizabeth shook her head, her eyes welling with tears. "I do not know—" and her voice broke—"I asked Him that when He took Ranek—"

They held to each other in silent grief. "His steps cannot always be traced, my darling. He wants us to trust Him in the dark, and in the howling storm."

Elizabeth continued to rock Coral, speaking softly through her tears. "We may never understand in this life why bitter things happen to us, why God permits pain and loss. But He is perfectly wise, and His tender mercies endure forever."

She tilted Coral's face toward hers, brushing away the tears with her handkerchief, scented with lavender. "If we cannot understand the wisdom of His actions, then let us draw near to the rich bounty of His consolation.

"Go ahead, dear, cry all you wish, and I shall cry with you, it is necessary. But we sorrow not as those who have no hope." She smiled through her own tears. "Christ is our hope. Today we buried Gem with the words of Christ: 'I am the resurrection and the life; he that believeth in me, though he were dead, yet shall he live: and whosoever liveth and believeth in me shall never die.'

"Today, the Almighty has given us a cup of gall to drink. But even in this, let us find thanks. For He would not give it to us to drink if there were not some good within. We can find the sweet taste of peace in that. Gem is safe now, my darling. Nothing can ever hurt him again."

Nothing can ever hurt him again. . . . Slowly Coral's sobbing ceased, and a deep weariness settled over her. Her eyes were swollen and her mind heavy with sleep. Elizabeth brought a cool glass of water to her lips. Coral drank and could feel nothing but her mother's heart thumping beneath her ear.

In the weeks following, Coral's emotions were dazed, while her health had taken a swift turn for the worse. She recalled only snatches of what had taken place during those days. They had found Gem, Coral was told, dead in the river. The details were not given, and Coral did not want to hear them, yet. She knew of the crocodiles. Her mother explained that the silk hatcheries had been saved. The untouchables were not hurt. The fire turned out to be smaller than first suspected, and when Hampton and Sir Hugo had arrived on the scene with armed workers, the marauders had already withdrawn and disappeared into the thick jungle.

It was clear to Coral that the attack on Kingscote had been only a ruse to lure them from the house, with the abduction of Gem being the primary motivation. Jace Buckley had been right. *Jace!* If only she could see him now and talk to him. If only he were still in the military and stationed at Jorhat! But he was on the other side of the world. Gone. Like Gem. Everything was gone.

When six weeks had passed and Coral showed no sign of improving, a hastened family gathering was called for in the library, and a decision was made. Coral would make the voyage to London.

"Your cousin Ethan is an expert on tropical diseases," her mother explained. "According to your uncle, Ethan studied the illness while spending time with the Company in Rangoon. We have expectations for your recovery. It is worth a try, dear. We cannot go on like this—" Unexpectedly her voice broke, and Coral felt her mother's damp cheek against her own. "Will I lose you, also?"

"I will be all right, Mother," but Coral wondered if she spoke only to cheer her. "But . . . I don't wish to go . . . I'm so tired . . ."

"It is a risk to send you on the voyage now, but your father and I agree it's a far greater one to keep you here."

"But—"

"Hush, darling. I will journey with you as far as Calcutta. And Uncle Hugo and Aunt Margaret will care for you aboard the ship. Your father and I agree this is the best decision we can make. We could ask Cousin Ethan to come here, but it would take a year. This way, you will be in London in half the time."

Caught amid illness and the need for her grief to heal, Coral's feeble efforts to thwart the family decision met with failure. Her sisters were already enrolled at school and writing for her to join them. And Grandmother Victoria was anxious for Coral to come and stay at the family estate. If the treatment was successful, she would have private tutors, and perhaps in the future, a year at Lady Anne's Finishing School.

But Gem! She would never have her baby to embrace again.

The Madras, *off the coast of London*
February 1797

*The storm raged on for several days. When the
wind exhausted itself into periodic gusts, and the rain
dwindled to scattered squalls, the coast of England
emerged from the gray wisps of fog to beckon with open
arms the storm-battered ship. The seasoned crew of English and Indians, interspersed with a few haggard but
expectant Malaysians, responded with a shout as the
dawn broke on the London estuary. The East India port
waited, a safe haven.*

*A roar of voices sprang up in a familiar English
lymeric:*

"Ohhh—the King 'e loves 'is bottle, me lads,
The King 'e loves 'is ale!
An betwix 'is bottle and 'is lass,
'e'll drink us all to 'ell!"

Captain Jace Buckley watched the gray swells
ease before the ship, his bronzed features fatigued
from lack of sleep. He supposed his ribs were healing
well enough, but his soul was not. He tried to mask
his moodiness. No one must guess how badly he hurt.
Jace would not easily recover from what had happened to Michael.

Nagging thoughts plagued him: *If we had sailed
two weeks sooner . . . if we had not gone to Cordoba . . .
we would have missed the storm, and Michael would be
alive. If . . .*

Jace did not wish to discuss his feelings. He only
knew that he was in a black mood, and his relationship
with Seward was none the better for it.

He blames me for his death, Jace thought grimly.

157

And maybe he is right. I was the captain. I should not have listened and stayed at Cadiz. I knew better. But I gave in to Michael. Michael was a novice . . . he did not know, he could not have guessed the seasons. But I knew. Yet I stayed. And I let him down. I failed them both.

The sense of infinite loss that he had experienced when first realizing that Michael had slipped from his grasp haunted him. How would he be able to explain to the Kendalls?

His hands tightened on the rail, his eyes narrowing. It made no difference that Michael had disobeyed orders and gone topside. The result was the same. He was dead.

Jace tried to shed the nagging feeling that the alabaster heirloom was tainted with the blood of the eldest Kendall son. He could not.

What of the Darjeeling tea plantation? Should he set it aside, or pursue it? At the moment, it did not seem to matter. There were few people he had truly cared about. Seward was one, Michael another. The loss only gave Jace excuse to further harden his heart. If he learned to care about some thing or someone, it was ripped away. *No more,* he thought. *Never again.*

Seagulls screamed and wheeled above the churning wake, and shifting his gaze from the coastline, he observed the two boatswain mates who swung like monkeys above him, inching their way along the wooden yards to unfurl the main sail. Overhead, the canvas flexed and snapped to the salt-laden wind, while foam splashed over the bow.

The crew became alert as the sound of his boots on the oak ladder preceded the captain's arrival onto the deck.

His leather jerkin, breeches, and calf-length boots

differed little from those of his crew. His coloring from the sun was as golden as his Indian kansamah's, causing the blue-black of his eyes to become piercing. His long hair and scraggly beard made him hardly recognizable from the once polished and ceremonious Major Jace Buckley of the 21st Light Bengal Cavalry.

Greeted by a grinning crew happy to be coming into port, Jace knew that the loss of Michael meant little to them. He had been only a stranger, just another English civilian. The loss of the helmsman had been forgotten in a day. The crew had weathered the bleak storm without damage to the ship, the cargo was safe—and they would be paid. The crew was satisfied. Now the brawling alehouses on the wharves awaited their celebration.

Jace passed by his jubilant crew members and entered the Great Cabin with its dark overhead beams, throwing back the shutters on the stern windows. A shaft of sunlight fell across the scarred oak desk, where Goldfish jumped up and down and performed cartwheels for his dreary master. Jace scooted the monkey aside.

"Go ahead. Keep it up. And as soon as we dock, I'll exchange you for a parrot."

Apparently undisturbed by his master's idle threat, Goldfish grabbed the oil lantern swaying over the center desk and sailed happily across the compartment, landing on a chest of drawers as though home in the Indian jungle.

"Useless creature," Jace murmured, sinking into the chair behind his desk. Every bone in his body complained at the harsh treatment of the last ten days. His eyes ached from lack of sleep, and his brain buzzed. He squinted at his sea chest. Within it were a number of precious items, and safely stashed away at the bottom was the heirloom from the Norman kingdom of Sicily.

Jace yielded to frustration and smashed his boot against the sea chest, sending it across the wooden floor.

Opening the desk drawer, his eyes fell on the small black Bible that had belonged to Michael. Jace hesitated, then opened the cover, once again reading the delicate inscription:

May 1795, Kingscote
To my dearest brother, Michael
May His words grant wisdom, peace, and life everlasting. A special thanks for your support in the matter of Gem's adoption.

Your sister, Coral

His jaw tense, Jace leafed through the delicate pages. He had gone back to Michael's cabin to pack his belongings and found the Bible. He opened it to Psalm 107 and discovered Michael had taken time to underline the verses that Jace had mentioned to him before going on deck. Jace read them:

They that go down to the sea in ships, that do business in great waters;
These see the works of the LORD, and his wonders in the deep.
For he commandeth, and raiseth the stormy wind, which lifteth up the waves thereof.
They mount up to the heavens, they go down again to the depths: their soul is melted because of trouble.
They reel to and fro, and stagger like a drunken man, and are at their wit's end.

Then they cry unto the LORD in their trouble, and
    he bringeth them out of their distresses.
He maketh the storm a calm, so that the waves
    thereof are still.
Then are they glad because they be quiet; so he
    bringeth them unto their desired haven.

How long he stared at the words he did not know.
That nagging phrase stuck in his brain again—*desired
haven.*

At last Jace closed the Bible and placed it with
the three volumes of Brainerd, Whitfield, and Wesley.
Out of memory and affection for Michael, he would
read them. Then he would return the books to the Kendall family with the rest of his belongings. When that
would be, he did not know. He would be in London
until June. Seward was writing a letter to Sir Hampton Kendall now, explaining his son's death. Jace too,
as captain of the ship, would write his explanation and
condolences. But the news of Michael's death would
not reach Kingscote for months. Again, he looked at
the inscription in the Bible. Someday, he would also
return the Book to Coral.

The next day they anchored in the London port.
Early morning discord echoed on the wharves of the
East India docks where the *Madras* was moored in its
narrow berth. The London estuary swarmed with men
of various nationalities and dress, a fisherman's pie of
alien tongues mingled with rough English.

Jace was standing with Seward when he heard
Jin-Soo and turned to see the old Chinese man hurrying toward him.

"Captain receive message. Expected to eat dinner
tonight with Sir Rawlings at company headquarters.

Dinner at seven. I will ready the bath, Captain. I will lay out your garment."

A fleet schooner eased itself beside the *Madras*. Dock workers began to unload the treasures stashed in its massive hold. On the docks below, horses strained to pull the overloaded drays, while men sweated to stack barrels and crates.

Later, as Jace soaked in the wooden tub, he watched Seward pace. Now and then he would stop, pull a timepiece from a deep pocket in his waistcoat, scowl, then begin his pacing again.

"You prowl like a caged cheetah," said Jace. "And the sound of your boots is grating to my nerves."

Seward glanced awry in his direction. "The hour be awastin', lad. Cannot ye soak another day?"

Jin-Soo poured another bucket of water over Jace's head. "Hand me the shears, Jin-Soo. The disgruntled Mister Seward is about to starve. The side of mutton he devoured this morning was not enough. He awaits roast goose at Rawlings' table."

Unintimidated by the irritated twist to Seward's lips, Jin-Soo laughed with merriment in memory of Seward's noted appetite.

Jace tossed the shears to Seward, and Jin-Soo held a mirror for Jace's approval.

"I be doing me some hard thinkin'," said Seward. "The death of Michael be a lastin' grief to me. Won't be easy goin' back to Kingscote, facin' Sir Hampton and Miss Elizabeth. And I be doin' some thinkin' about Captain Jarred Buckley's son, too. While we be waitin' to sail, I've decided to stay in Olney."

Olney! Seward's news took him by surprise, and Jace fixed the mirror on him, looking at Seward over his shoulder. The grave expression was a familiar one in recent days. Neither of them was in a pleasant mood. The tea plantation in Darjeeling had not been mentioned once in their conversation, nor had the Moorish heirloom. And even though Michael had not been Seward's charge, and Sir Hampton had approved of the voyage, Seward felt responsible.

"I did not know you had family in Olney," said Jace.

Seward scrutinized Jace's thick dark hair and chopped the curling tendrils to the nape of his neck. Jin-Soo swept them up. "Aye, ye be right, I don't. They be in Aberdeen—what be left of them. 'Tis a man in Olney I wish to season with." His sharp eyes met Jace's in the looking glass. "Truth is, I be wantin' us both to call on the captain."

Jace became alert. "A sea captain?"

Seward's expression darkened as though memories of his own past bore him trouble. "A shipmaster of a slave ship. Long ago. I hear he be in Olney. Time I looked him up."

"The one you told me about, the one in the storm?" Jace felt uncomfortable. Evidently a horrendous storm at sea had wrought some manner of spiritual change in the culprit's life.

"Aye, 'tis the man. Captain John Newton be his name. 'Twas a vile bloke back in me youth. Be a man ye ought to meet while here in London."

Jace said nothing and ran his fingers through his hair, satisfied. Unlike the present style of long hair, he preferred it short. "I gather this Captain Newton is a minister?"

"Aye, so it be said. He was the rector at Olney for some time. Still might be. Be interestin' to hear what happened to him."

Jace was noncommittal. "You go stay with this captain friend of yours, Seward. It will do you good, and like you say, we won't be sailing until spring."

He felt Seward's gaze.

"Be hopin' ye might come. Good to escape the *Madras* awhile."

Jace was unreadable. "I have work to do."

Seward's silence pricked at his insides, but he did not like to be cornered.

"Like I said, if I get a chance, I may come and meet Newton. But do not count on it. I will be busy while in London. You know how Rawlings is. He will have work for me to do at the Company. There is also repair to be done aboard ship."

Seward grunted. "Ye be makin' an excuse."

Were they excuses? Why should he be uneasy about meeting this man Newton? And yet he was. . . .

Jace changed the subject. "Jin-Soo, hand me the razor." He touched his short beard. Except for a mustache he had worn in the military, he preferred to be clean-shaven. When Seward took out his watchpiece for the second time, however, he relented, sighed, and reached for the towel in Jin-Soo's hand. "What is this?" he asked him, squinting at a floral tin that Jin-Soo offered.

Jin-Soo smiled widely. "Sweet powder, Captain. Heavenly Lotus Blossom. You like, yes?"

"I like, no. One would think I was calling on a damsel instead of the cheroot-smoking, burly-headed Rawlings."

"Consider makin' time for Olney, lad. If for no reason except I be askin' ye."

Jace turned and scanned him, then went to his bunk where Jin-Soo had laid out the garments that had been packed away. Systematically, Jace eliminated what he did not like, using deft fingers to toss aside a silk shirt with ruffles about the cuffs, the lacy jabot, and the smoke-blue silk waistcoat that matched the narrow breeches that were much too tight. Instead, ignoring Jin-Soo's protestations, he unlocked his sea chest, then removed a cream Holland shirt with full gathered sleeves that tightened about the cuffs and a V neck that laced below the throat. Next came a pair of black light woolen trousers, the calf-length boots coming up over them. He belted on his scabbard and grabbed his dark cloak, then paused—

Jin-Soo stood extending the Moorish heirloom wrapped in a cloth. "Prize to buy us tea plantation, Captain. Jin-Soo will work very hard there, with Gokul and Mister Seward."

Jace was aware of Seward's penetrating stare. He did not need to be reminded of its cost in blood. Without a word, he took it from Jin-Soo, placed it back within the chest, turned the key, snatched up the carved ivory elephant, and wrapped it in a handkerchief. He stopped when he saw Jin-Soo's expression of bewilderment.

"Another time, old friend." Jace walked out.

Seward gave an affectionate tug at Jin-Soo's pigtail as he strode toward the cabin door. "Keep the captain out of mischief till I return. Feed him much Ginseng tea."

Jin-Soo grinned and bowed low at the waist. He attempted to quip Mister Seward's jargon: "Sooo long, Mister Seward. You take it easy."

Jace expected a comment on leaving the heirloom

in his trunk, but he was grateful when Seward seemed to understand and said nothing. There needed to be a time of healing before either of them could face it.

With the setting sun, the London night had turned damp and chilly, with tendrils of fog wrapping about the district's warehouses and buildings.

Jace turned up the collar of his cloak as he strode with Seward down the creaking quays. Beyond, tiny clapboard rooms and houses built atop the buildings leaned precariously toward the littered street. Barefoot waifs were out begging, and sharp of eye, caught sight of Jace and Seward, receiving a coin. The old and sick slept in the dark alleyways. Acrid smoke curled from chimneys as home fires were stoked against the seaborne chill. Soot mixed with the driblets of misty fog covered every surface. An echo of horse hooves announced the coming of a cabby, and Jace whistled for the driver.

A plump man with scraggy white hair drooping from beneath his hat pulled up and leaned down from the driver's seat to unhitch the door. "Aye, gov'na, where to?"

"Leadenhall. East India Company."

Jace climbed in, Seward after him, dragging the door shut behind him. The coach lurched ahead and rounded a narrow corner.

"What about Olney?" Seward pressed.

Jace leaned his head back against the seat, lowering his hat as if to snooze. "You never give up, do you?"

"I promised yer father before he died I'd take good care of ye. Done a poor job."

"Thanks. But I believe I am doing well enough. Salve your conscience. I am no one's problem but my own. You have been a friend. That is all I've ever wanted."

"Then humor an ol' friend with gray in his hair. Come to Olney before we sail."

Jace raised his hat to squint at him. "Perhaps. But I'll not vow to it. Understood?"

"Aye, lad, 'tis enough." Seward settled back in the leather seat, suddenly relaxed and pleased. After a moment, he asked: "Did ye say ol' Rawlings was servin' roast goose?"

11

Known affectionately by many as the "old converted sea captain," John Newton was no longer the curate at the church in Olney in 1797. He had retired, and Walter Scott was minister, but Seward had located the house Newton shared with his wife of many years and the hymn writer William Cowper.

"Master Cowper be best known for his hymn, 'There Be a Fountain Filled with Blood, Drawn from Emmanuel's Veins,' " Seward told him, and started to bellow forth a stanza.

Seeing the glitter of black in Jace's otherwise blue eyes, Seward stopped, shrugging his heavy shoulders. "Admit a frog sounds a wee better, lad. But remember 'tis the words that count."

"I am not altogether dense, Seward. You need not explain."

It had been with uncertainty that Jace gave in to Seward and accompanied him to Newton's house one rainy night in March. Jace told himself that he could endure the old captain's tale of heaven's intervention. After all, it was not as though he himself were a heathen. If he chose to, he could debate theology with the best of them.

But hours later, when John Newton left the cottage room to get a book from his study for the "young Buckley," Jace used the opportunity to turn on Seward. "You vowed—'no sermon.' He has discussed everything from Calvin to the pope!"

"God forbid I should seek to silence the man. 'Tis no fault of me own if he wishes to share his fair words shown him by the grace of God."

"Not your fault!" Jace scoffed. "He has been preaching for three hours!"

"Easy, man, 'tis not preachin', but 'talk.' "

His eyes narrowed. "Call it as you wish. I call it sermonizing."

Seward's sharp eyes riveted on him. "One would think ye faced the bars of Newgate Gaol, instead of fair company with a saint of God."

"Never mind," Jace gritted. "Just keep your tongue silent, will you? If you would stop asking a hundred questions, I could make an excuse to leave."

Seward obstinately folded his arms across his broad chest and leaned back in the chair, his gaze narrowing. "I be apologizin' for no such thing. A bit of goodly news be balm for yer conscience and mine." He suddenly smiled broadly beneath his reddish mustache. "Just sit awhile, lad. 'Twill do ye good. Ye be as fidgety as Goldfish."

"Now look here—"

Jace stopped and cast a glance toward the door leading into the kitchen. Seward followed his look, then rose awkwardly to his feet, clearing his throat.

The silver-haired and plump Mrs. Mary Newton entered with tea and sweet biscuits. Jace too stood and with little effort displayed his most charming manners, helping her with the tray.

"Your kindness is appreciated, Mrs. Newton," he said smoothly. "I cannot recall the last time Seward and I have enjoyed freshly baked sweetbreads. I am afraid my kansamah aboard the *Madras* has settled for cooking with mold and seawater."

He looked at Seward, waiting for a perfunctory reply to the offered tea and cookies. When Seward only shifted his stance, Jace quipped, "Is that not right, Seward? You like tea and biscuits."

"Oh, aye, aye, 'tis so, Madame . . . er . . . we thank ye much," and he leaned over the tray, taking several of the tiny biscuits into his big hand.

"Use a plate, Seward," said Jace dryly.

"I beg yer pardon, Madame."

Jace managed a charming smile as he accepted the detestable cup of tea, watching in mute horror as she added a heaping spoonful of honey.

Newton had returned with not one book for Jace to take back with him on the *Madras*, but two. Jace gravely accepted them, saying something about how he had read Brainerd and Whitfield, and was well into John Wesley.

He immediately saw his mistake. Newton admitted that he had been greatly influenced by George Whitfield and the Wesley brothers, then launched into a discussion of Whitfield's belief in predestination, versus Wesley's belief in free will.

Jace bit into a biscuit. What would have been instantly devoured aboard ship felt dry and tasteless in his mouth. He glanced at Seward, who was clinging like a drowning man to every word, prolonging the discourse by asking questions that even Jace was able to answer.

The rain continued to pelt against the window,

and the fire leaped and danced in the hearth as if pleased that Jace had to sit and listen. He wanted to take off his coat and loosen his cravat, although logic told him that the room was not too warm. In fact, the expansive cottage room was pleasant and nicely decorated. But somehow Jace was sure he would feel more comfortable in his own tiny cabin on the *Madras*.

There was a moment of silence. Jace did not like the quiet. He quickly opened the *Olney Hymns*, published in 1779. The hymns were written by Newton and William Cowper, a member of his congregation. According to Seward, Cowper had been invited to take up residence with the Newtons due to periods of deep depression. It seemed that William Cowper had once tried to commit suicide.

"Yes, it is true," began Newton. "One day Brother Cowper ordered the coachman to bring him to the London Bridge where he intended to jump off and end it all. The trip took longer than necessary, and when it seemed to him that they should have arrived, Cowper impatiently halted the coach and got off—only to find himself at his front door! They had gone in circles for an hour."

"Blest be God!" said Seward, deeply moved.

"The coachman blamed the mistake on the fog, but Cowper knew the hand of God had spared his life that night. He has since written hymns that lift the depressed soul heavenward."

Jace said nothing. The thought that the Almighty might be so personally involved in the affairs of men could be intimidating to one who wished to escape.

Together William Cowper and John Newton had published the *Olney Hymns*, now used by many Christian groups meeting in homes or in small free churches throughout London.

Jace casually leafed through the hymnal, his tanned, rugged expression refusing to show anything. If he were honest with himself, he would admit that the incorrigible slave trader turned parish curate had baited his curiosity. It was amazing indeed that a man of Newton's background could write such tender words about Christ.

In spite of himself, Jace listened, moved by Newton's description of his youth, for there was much in his tale with which he could associate.

Newton's father, like Jace's, had been a sea captain. But unlike himself, Newton had known his mother during early childhood, and she had proved herself to be a devoted Christian who prayed, as mothers often do, that her son would grow up to become a preacher.

Jace, on the contrary, had never seen his mother. He did not even know who she was. She might have been a tart from some exotic port, or as Seward said, a lady; although the latter seemed quite improbable. And he was certain that no woman had ever prayed for him.

"My mother died when I was a young boy, and I followed my sea captain father to a sailor's life," said Newton. "I soon joined the Royal Navy, but loathed the discipline."

Jace thought of his own dislike of the military. He set his tea cup down, then picked it back up again, drinking the stuff for lack of something to do. Again he leafed through the hymnal.

Newton told of deserting the ship, of being caught and flogged, and eventually discharged.

Jace thought of his brevet of courage earned in Rangoon. There was a difference.

"I then headed for regions where I could sin freely,

and ended up on the west coast of Africa, working for a slave trader," said Newton.

There, Newton had been treated roughly by the trader and was soon engulfed in a life of wretchedness.

"I was a horrid-looking man, toiling in a plantation of lemon trees on the Island of Plantains . . . my clothes became rags, I had no shelter, and was begging for unhealthy roots to allay my hunger."

He had managed to escape the island, he told Jace and Seward, "And in the following year my ship was battered by a treacherous storm . . . I had been reading *The Imitation of Christ*—aye, I fell upon my knees crying out to God for mercy. I was a wretch who found amazing grace."

Jace paused. *Amazing Grace*. The words caught his attention. *That song . . . those words*—he had heard them before. Where? He turned to that hymn in the book he held, and now the words stared up at Jace as Newton's voice went on glorying in the grace of God.

> *Amazing grace, how sweet the sound,*
> *That saved a wretch like me!*
> *I once was lost, but now am found,*
> *Was blind but now I see.*
> *'Twas grace that taught my heart to fear,*
> *And grace my fears relieved;*
> *How precious did that grace appear,*
> *The hour I first believed.*
> *When we've been there ten thousand years,*
> *Bright shining as the sun,*
> *We've no less days to sing God's praise,*
> *Than when we'd first begun.*

Jace felt the rain in his memory, could feel it on his face, could hear the sweet voice of a woman singing.

He closed his eyes as it came back to him. The monsoon on Kingscote. The little whitewashed hut where the Kendall daughter and her mother had delivered the Indian girl's baby ... it was the funeral. Mrs. Kendall had sung that song.

"Aye, I remember that storm aboard ship," Seward was saying darkly. "I didn't believe the change in ye would last. Thought it was born of the hellish night. Now I've seen and heard ye, and I be knowin' for a surety." He shook his head. "I believe in this Christ, and yet—there be no assurance, naught but the fear of damnation. I be sure of nothin'."

Jace closed the hymnbook with a soft thud, scanning one man and then the other. This was getting out of control. He started to speak, but Newton looked concerned and leaned toward Seward, resting a firm hand on his broad shoulder.

"Wesley, too, feared damnation. He found no peace in the liturgy of the church. Scriptural faith is a very different thing from a rational assent to the gospel."

"Michael had that faith," said Seward, and unexpectedly his eyes filled with tears.

Jace sat in stunned silence, watching the tears run down Seward's creased face. A big man, a strong man, weeping like a child! It frightened him, for it meant that a man could lose control, could become vulnerable—

Newton was speaking to Seward now in a gentle tone, almost a whisper, "Faith in your Savior, Seward. That's the assurance."

Jace felt his heart wrench. *I must get out of here!*

Suddenly, he found his own voice interrupting, sounding cynical, challenging: "You speak of faith! What *is* faith? It is merely what a man wants to believe it is, and nothing more. I have seen a Hindu carve his flesh into bloody ribbons to appease Kali. I have seen a Muslim with his forehead flattened from bowing on stone toward Mecca. I have seen those devoted to Rome weeping, their knees bloody as they crawl to beg mercies of the Madonna. And I have seen Protestants baptize by the edge of the sword and destroy one another for differences in interpretation. They *all* claim they are motivated by faith."

He had thought he might anger Newton, but the man was not disturbed at all—and that disturbed Jace.

"What others may describe as faith is not so at all, my friend. It is human activity engaged to please the god of their religion, usually a god of terror.

"This is Christian faith: a renouncing of everything we are apt to call our own, and relying wholly upon the blood, righteousness, and intercession of Jesus. You see, there is a wide chasm between a religion of works and the Christian's faith in a finished work accomplished by God himself in Christ."

Jace was silenced. Whatever frustration had motivated his outburst was gone. But an internal struggle ensued, one he had been desperate to avoid. God wooing, convicting. It was gentle, yet painful, and Jace felt his will striving to retain its lordship.

As though being burned upon his soul, the words rang through his mind—*"You must yield every area of your life to the Captain of your soul."*

Abruptly, Jace stood to his feet with books in hand, surprised at his reaction. "I have found our discussion interesting, sir, but I must be going. Books are hard to come by, and expensive. Perhaps it is best if I did not take them."

Newton looked at him. Jace felt transparent. *He*

knows . . . he understands what I am feeling. For the first time in his life, his self-confidence was cracking. *Danger.*

"No need for that. You can return them to me the next time you are in London."

It sounded like a challenge, one that Jace could not bring himself to back away from. As their eyes locked, Jace heard himself saying calmly, "Very well. I shall be back one day."

"Good." Newton smiled and stood to his feet. "You are welcome here, any time. Next time you must tell me about yourself, Captain Buckley. Seward has shared a little of your upbringing in India, and I am most interested. I would like to hear more."

Somehow Jace managed to retain his outward indifference. He shook Newton's hand, thanked him, made the correct compliment about Mrs. Newton's tea and biscuits, then turned toward Seward with a challenging gaze, though his voice was casual. "Coming?"

Seward cleared his throat and stood. "Aye. One thing more—" he turned to Newton.

Jace sighed within.

"They say ye retired for ill health and be failin' in memory, but there be no evidence of it tonight."

"My memory is nearly gone, but I remember two things: that I am a great sinner and that Christ is a great Savior!"

Jace opened the cottage door and escaped into the rainy darkness, unnerved to discover that the tenderness and strength of Christ was like a sword, able to slash through his bulwark. He felt exposed. Vulnerable. He was not sufficient in and of himself. He had known that, of course; but tonight, quite by accident, he had tasted it.

A stiff wind sent the droplets of rain against his

face, cooling him. He would not go back. He would send the books to Newton.

Jace had prided himself in his ability to avoid emotional entanglements of any sort. Was he vulnerable after all? The thought was disturbing. Where would it lead? What strange, winding paths were these that he had no control over? Like William Cowper and his eerie ride in the fog, would divine providence lead him back to where he must grapple with the infinite—and yield?

To believe, to trust, meant removing his armor and laying bare his heart for scrutiny. No hands other than his own must touch the bruises that were there.

Irritated by this new feeling of weakness, he fumbled with the two books belonging to Newton, trying to protect them from getting wet by placing them beneath his coat, yet feeling as though they were pricks in his side. Now he had the responsibility of seeing them safely returned.

Jace doubted if he would ever find the time, or the desire, to read through *The Imitation of Christ,* even though he was a little curious about the book that had made such an impression on a man like Newton. And as for the *Olney Hymns*—it might be pleasant to read, but he hoped Seward did not find the book a necessary cause to start bellowing out hymns aboard the ship!

Jace knew his irritation with Seward was greater than the situation warranted, but at the moment he did not care. It was Seward who had entangled him in this dilemma.

Jace started down the cobbled street toward town without Seward, lowering his hat against the rain. Despite his nettled mood, the words of Newton echoed through his brain, and he could not silence them, though he tried.

"This is faith: a renouncing of everything we are apt to call our own, and relying wholly upon the blood, righteousness, and intercession of Jesus."

The water on the darkened cobbles glistened under the street lamps, and his boots echoed in the otherwise silent night.

A few minutes later he heard Seward hurrying to catch up with him, but he did not speak as they walked along beside each other, and Seward, as though he understood his mood, wisely remained silent, increasing his stride to catch up.

After twenty minutes, Seward began to whistle "Amazing Grace," stuffing his big hands into his coat pockets, his boots making crunching sounds on the cobbles.

He is quite pleased with himself, Jace thought irritably.

12

Roxbury House, London
June 1797

The shiny black coach boasting the Roxbury coat of arms brought Coral, Margaret, and Sir Hugo through the wrought-iron gate and up the cobbled carriageway. Coral's gaze was fixed ahead upon a green rise with a backdrop of elms, where Roxbury House dominated the English countryside.

So this was her mother's home: the imposing estate where she had been born and raised until her marriage to a maverick Kendall cousin named Hampton.

The three-story gray stone baronial mansion reminded Coral of a castle. The building was heavily turreted, and flaunted some forty rooms of state with elaborate artisan friezework and marble.

In 1660, Aunt Margaret explained, Charles II had awarded the estate to Great-grandfather William, the first Earl of Roxbury, along with the estate's lands and a summer house built on the fashionable London Strand.

"This was during the Reconstruction after the

181

rule of Oliver Cromwell."

Coral found herself greeted at the heavy wooden mansion doors by Simms, a gaunt-faced butler in spotless black, who escorted the three of them through the massive, chandeliered hallway into the parlor.

Coral decided that Grandmother Lady Victoria, the grand matriarch of the family, was as imposing as the mansion. Her skin had not seen a day of sun in her seventy years, leaving it porcelain clear, and her sharp blue eyes did not apologize for an appraisal that made Coral imagine herself a slave on the auction block. Family jewels glittered on Lady Victoria's earlobes, her throat, her fingers; and the handle of her walking stick flashed with emeralds.

Behind Grandmother stood Simms, who now held the leash of three small, shaggy white dogs with diamond collars. Simms wore a frozen expression that looked dour upon everyone except the matriarch.

However, Coral had underestimated the depth of her grandmother. Lady Victoria's imperious facade melted when she unexpectedly embraced Coral. "My dear grandchild, how precious to have you here. A pity your sisters couldn't be here to greet you, but of course they are away at Lady Anne's. However, Ethan will be pleased."

Ethan will be pleased. . . . Coral felt the pressure of family unity wrap about her like a python. They had already assumed she would marry him. At twenty, she was considered too old to delay marriage much longer.

Sir Hugo's voice interrupted her thoughts: "Coral, this is your cousin, Doctor Ethan Boswell. Ethan, Coral Kendall."

Coral turned toward her cousin and paused,

swallowing back a start of surprise. A tall, handsome man with ash-blond hair and drowsy gray eyes walked up. Evidently he had just been out riding, for he wore a fashionable tweed jacket and brown breeches. He smiled down at her, and tossing his horsewhip to a groom, bent to brush his lips against her forehead.

"Cousin Coral, welcome to Roxbury House."

"Yes, thank you . . . Cousin Ethan."

He continued to smile. "In a few months I will have you well enough for Grandmother to introduce you to London society."

"Yes, yes," Lady Victoria responded, "but first, my dear Coral, I believe a tour of Roxbury House would be in order."

Grandmother Victoria took pride in showing Coral the house, especially what she called the *Royal Hall*. Here, Coral found an elaborate collection of silk tapestries depicting the kings and queens of England. But Coral's favorite room was the all-yellow Morning Room, warmed by the rising sun over the Thames. From here she could step outdoors onto a flagstone court and wander the gardens, which surrounded a large diamond-shaped courtyard.

It was several days later, when Coral was alone in her suite of rooms, that she found the courage to unlock the small cloisonne box that her mother had given to her before she sailed. Inside were the mementos she had asked for, which had belonged to Gem.

"The Lord gave, and the Lord hath taken away. Blessed be the name of the Lord," Coral quoted. She found needed solace in knowing that her little lamb had passed through the gate into the presence of the Great Shepherd.

Inside the box, Coral saw the adoption papers signed by the Anglican bishop, and smiled in memory of that long-awaited day.

She picked up the carved elephant that Michael had made for Gem. It was a miniature of her pet, Rani. Fingering it gently, she remembered how Gem had carried it with him everywhere.

There was something else she was looking for now, the object that had caused her to open the treasure box. She leafed through the mementos, but it was not there. Where was the tiny gold cross that she had placed around Gem's neck on the day of his adoption? She emptied the box on her bed and sorted quickly through the other objects. It was gone! Or had her mother forgotten to place it there?

Coral frowned . . . and then she saw a small red silk pocket embroidered with a Burmese dragon. She smiled.

Jan-Lee had wanted to give her something . . . the cross? No doubt. Had she not been the one to ready Gem for burial?

Quickly she reached her fingers inside, expecting to feel the cold metal, but felt only a small piece of paper. She drew it out and smoothed it open, reading:

September 1796

I do not want to burden your soul, Miss Coral. I do not want to light false candles of hope when it is best to put yesterday far from us. But I find no rest and must write these words. I feared to tell you what I thought when you were so ill. I also fear for the lives of everyone on Kingscote if I rekindle coals of trouble. I fear the fire will destroy the hatcheries, maybe take your life too. I could not bear that.

By now you are safe in London. I will tell you what is on my heart. It was I, Jan-Lee, who readied the child for Christian burial. I wondered why there was no cross on Gem. It was on him when the sepoy stole him from me. It is important that you know the child I readied for burial was badly injured beyond description. But I keep thinking why no cross? One thing is very important. The child had a scar on his heel. I do not remember that Gem had a scar. Maybe you will remember.

Jan-Lee

Coral sank to the bed, so weak that she could not move. She stared at Jan-Lee's letter, unable to even think. *Scar . . . did Gem have a scar?* No! No! She would have remembered! Or had such a thing escaped her? No, that could not be, she would remember if Gem had injured his foot! "Oh, dearest God," she whispered. "What does this mean? What could this possibly mean?"

She ran a trembling hand across her forehead when a rap sounded on her bedroom door. Coral jumped to her feet. "Yes?" she called shakily.

"It is your uncle. May I come in?"

Coral stuffed the letter into her bodice. Before she could answer, the door opened and he stood there, an imperial figure in black broadcloth and a white frilled shirt. His lively dark eyes studied her, then fixed upon the treasure box with its spilled contents.

In three brief strides he was beside her, a hand on her shoulder. Drawing a white handkerchief from his pocket, he commanded, "Blow your nose like a brave girl and wipe your eyes. You are much too ill to torment yourself like this."

Before she could find the strength to react, he

gathered the mementos scattered on the bed, along with the adoption certificate, and placed them back into the box, snapping the lid shut.

"Ethan has suggested the need to wait awhile. Your emotions are highstrung."

Coral made a sudden move to retrieve the box, but Sir Hugo caught her, his brows furrowing with annoyance.

"As I feared. You're becoming obsessed with this loss. You must go back to bed at once. I will call Ethan."

"Uncle!" Coral's voice was indignant. "I am quite all right! Give me the box!"

Footsteps interrupted from the hallway. Margaret Roxbury came into the room, her eyes taking in first Coral, then her husband holding the small box. Her expression tensed.

"Hugo, what are you doing?"

Coral did not miss the sharp glance exchanged between them. But Hugo offered a somewhat mocking smile. "Never mind, darling. I wouldn't want to interrupt your letter writing. The colonel will be expecting *your* response."

Coral was shocked at Hugo's inflicted barb. Her aunt Margaret's cheeks turned pink, and her brown eyes grew distant. She tilted her head to the side with recovered dignity.

"On the contrary, *darling*, I was writing Elizabeth. I have no reason to answer Colonel Warbeck's letter. It was addressed to you, was it not?"

"So it was, my pet." He lifted the box. "She has been looking at the child's toys. It has upset her. Who is responsible for giving her this box now?"

"It must have been Mother. Oh, Coral—it is too soon. You should have waited."

"I will send for Ethan. A sleeping powder will make her rest until morning."

"Do not call Ethan!" Coral protested, her voice becoming shrill with exasperation. "I am fine, and the box belongs to *me*."

Without a backward glance, Sir Hugo left Coral's room, holding the box beneath his arm.

"Whatever are you doing to that child?" snapped Grandmother Victoria from the corridor. Hugo said something quietly, then walked on, and a moment later she came into the bedroom.

"Margaret, good heavens!"

"Mother, she is crying over Gem again, and—"

"Well of course she is going to cry. It is only natural." Her sharp blue eyes snapped with impatience as she rustled across the room and took hold of Coral's arm, easing her to the side of the bed. "When Henry died I wept incessantly for months! I cannot tell you how weary I became of those forbidding it. It did me a world of good. And when the tears stopped, my sorrow was over. Margaret, if you do not wish to see the child cry, then remove your presence from her room. I will sit with her."

"Mother! I was not scolding her for crying over Gem. It—"

"Uncle has taken my treasure box with Gem's mementos," cried Coral. "The adoption certificate—"

"Tsk! Well! I shall get it back at once," Lady Victoria said crisply. "Margaret may find him intimidating, but I do not."

Margaret placed hands on hips and looked toward the ceiling with exasperation. "Mother, I do not find my husband 'intimidating.' "

"Where is he?"

Margaret sighed and threw up her hands. "Downstairs. He is sending for Ethan."

"Good. Coral needs to sleep. In the meantime, I will get your treasure box back," she assured Coral.

Grandmother swept toward the door, and Margaret followed her. "Mother, please do not create a scene."

"Why should I? Hugo is reasonable, is he not?"

Coral sat weakly and watched them disappear from her room, hearing their voices rise and fall as they went down the hall. *Thank God for Granny V!* Coral realized that she had one tower of strength in the house, and if she was to share her hope about Gem being alive to anyone, it would be her grandmother.

True to her word, the cloisonne box was returned. Ethan arrived and handed it to her with a sympathetic smile.

Coral emptied the contents on the bed. Everything was there. Including the adoption certificate.

"Everything in order?" he asked soothingly.

Coral nodded. "Yes—I am sorry about the ruckus."

He smiled, stirring the powder that he had mixed in a glass of water. "No need to apologize." His eyes held hers, and Coral glanced away, busying herself with the box.

"You will feel stronger in the morning. Here, I know you do not approve of this, but do drink it. In time, you will notice marked improvement in your fever."

Ethan handed the glass to her, then sat in one of the tapestry-covered mahogany armchairs. "Uncle is overbearing, but he means no harm. He is concerned, as we all are. If ever you are to get well, Coral, you must give your mind and body time to rest and heal."

Coral knew that and was irritated at being treated like a child.

Ethan stayed until she drank the medication, then excused himself. When he had gone, Coral fought against the drugged sleep for as long as her mind allowed.

No cross on Gem. What does it mean? Anything at all? Could Gem's abductor have removed it and tossed it away? Perhaps her mother had taken it and simply forgotten to include it with the other items. But the scar . . . Gem had no scar—or did he? She would have noticed! And Jan-Lee bathed him—

Coral struggled between dashed hopes and rising excitement. Could the child they had buried on Kingscote be an untouchable? Made to look as though he were Gem?

Coral removed Jan-Lee's letter from her bodice and tried to read it again, but her eyes could not focus clearly as sleep weighed heavily. Her hand too felt heavy, and before the powder made her completely inept, she struggled out of bed and placed both the letter and the adoption certificate—not in the cloisonne box—but in the drawer with her undergarments. She stumbled back into bed, exhausted.

"Thank you, Lord," Coral murmured drowsily. A small candle now flickered with the light of hope in a sea of darkness. But she reminded herself that she was in London, and if Gem were alive and being held by his abductors, he was trapped somewhere in India. What could she possibly do?

"I will write home tomorrow," she thought sleepily. "And also to Jan-Lee. I will tell Grandmother too."

And Jace Buckley—should she risk trying to contact him?

Coral fell asleep with the name of Director Rawlings on her mind. Rawlings, of the East India Company. Her father knew and trusted him. She could trust him too.

———

The weather was warm for a London June, and Coral had been at Roxbury House for a week. She walked with her grandmother across the green toward the small lake created for the estate. Tame ducks and white swans paddled, but a black swan held Coral's attention. The sweet smell of cherry blossoms from the nearby orchard infused the breeze that ruffled the gold curls beneath her sun hat. Still frail from months of illness in India, she remained under the medical supervision of her cousin.

Grandmother sat down on the bench, holding the jeweled handle of her cane, while Coral wandered to the edge of the lake to feed the ducks bread crumbs from the basket on her arm.

There will be no more journeys into the valley of depression, she told herself. The question of why the Lord had permitted the loss of Gem remained obscure. Perhaps she would never understand. She reminded herself of what Job had confessed when losing all that was dear to him. *The Lord gave . . . the Lord took away . . . blessed be His name . . .*

Ahead was the cherry orchard, where the extensive stables awaited her growing desire to ride the well-bred line of horses. Ethan had suggested they go riding together soon in order to show her the rest of the estate grounds.

"What do you think of Ethan?" Grandmother asked bluntly.

Coral laughed. "Really, Granny V, do you expect

me to fall in love so easily?"

Grandmother did not blanch. "Tsk, tsk, dear, I did not ask you if you were in love, did I?"

"No," Coral admitted, "but—"

Grandmother Victoria wore a triumphant expression. "However, since you have brought the matter up, I shall offer my opinion."

Coral tried to lure the black swan to come near. "I am sure you would offer your advice regardless," she said with a little smile.

Grandmother did not appear the least bit disturbed. "You are quite right. I shall. Ethan is possibly the best match the family could make for you, considering your health, and the noteworthy fact that he is Sir Hugo's only nephew."

"Uncle Hugo does agree that his nephew is noteworthy," said Coral in a humorous tone. "Nevertheless, I shall not be rushed into anything as important as marriage. I hope the family does not intend to pressure either of us. Cousin Ethan seems quite engrossed in his medical research." She glanced sideways at her grandmother. "And I too want to begin my studies as soon as possible." Coral was thinking of a linguist who taught Hindi, but she doubted that anyone in all of London could be found. There was also her interest in the music of Charles Wesley, and the new hymns of the Dissenter Movement, which were placing a new emphasis on congregational singing, something that was frowned upon as strange by the state church.

"No one is going to demand that you marry Ethan, child. Unlike Hugo, I happen to agree with your mother and Margaret on the matter. A woman ought to love a man before she is expected to vow her fidelity to his name. Nonetheless, I cannot stress strongly enough the importance of marriage within the family.

We cannot trust the fate of the Roxbury/Kendall dynasty to the greedy appetites of strangers. Heavens! With four granddaughters to arrange for, and a hundred penniless scamps running about with titles who are only too anxious to please an heiress, the family must be careful indeed. You do see the difficulty facing us, do you not? Coral! Do pay attention when I speak to you."

Grandmother Victoria's voice cut through the dark memories that had momentarily held Coral in their grip, making her shiver with coldness and reminding her that she was now in London to begin a new life. The words of her grandmother pressed along the same theme that she had heard from Sir Hugo on the voyage from Calcutta, and now, as then, they made little impression.

"Yes, Granny V, I am sorry. My mind wandered."

"Whatever were you thinking of, child? Are you still grieving over the Indian boy?"

Coral turned, her feelings evident on her face. "Oh, Granny V! You should have seen Gem! He was such a winsome boy, so bright, so beautiful, you would have loved him. I should have had his portrait painted—" She paused for a moment, unable to go on. She walked over to her grandmother and sat down beside her. "If I had his portrait, I would at least have something to look at."

The black swan wandered onto the grass nearby and Coral tossed more crumbs. "Gem adored Bible stories. He could repeat them in perfect English. Everything was going so well until the night of the fire—" Her voice faltered.

Grandmother leaned over and placed her thin veined hand on Coral's. There was a moment of silence while Coral brought her emotions under control. She squeezed her grandmother's hand.

"Poor child. Sir Hugo is right. You have traversed a wretched path. I did not mean to upset you like this. Well, you say you taught the boy well," she concluded lamely. "There is that consolation to enhearten you."

"Yes, and if Gem is dead—I have every confidence he is in the state of the blessed."

Coral felt her grandmother's piercing gaze.

"Life is plagued by 'ifs' my child, but I cannot understand why you would question the fact of the boy's death?"

Coral met her gaze. "Grandmother, there is a possibility Gem is alive . . . that the child found was not my son, but one of the untouchables working in the hatcheries."

Coral wanted to squirm under her grandmother's scrutiny.

"Good heavens! Hugo told me you might—" She stopped, and for the first time appeared unable to cope with the situation.

Afraid she would lose her support, Coral rushed to explain about Jan-Lee's letter.

Grandmother's eyes brightened a little. "You have the letter?"

"Yes. I will show it to you before I write Director Rawlings. You might as well know that I have decided to hire mercenaries to try to locate Gem."

"Mercenaries! Forbid! I could never allow such a thing. Whatever will Elizabeth say if I permit you to make contact with the seamy side of London?"

"Sir Rawlings is a gentleman and quite respectable."

"The director of the East India Company? Posh! He is a knave if there ever was one."

"He is a friend of my father," Coral soothed.

193

"Oh, and indeed! Hampton was a knave himself, in the old days, until Elizabeth settled him down. I will have no scandal surrounding your stay in London."

"There will be no scandal, Grandmother, I promise. I will do it in secret. No one will even know."

"Tsk, tsk, no scandal you say. It was scandal enough that you were permitted to adopt an Indian child. Have you any notion the gossip Lady Vivian has sown about London?"

Coral glanced at her uneasily. "No, but I do not particularly care."

"The precise reaction I would expect from a granddaughter being raised in a raw and heathen environment like India! If I had my way you would never be permitted to return to that land. And that goes for your sisters as well. I shall tell you what the gossip is saying."

"Granny V—"

"It is said the child belonged to Michael or Alex."

"You do not mean—"

"I most certainly do. And the Indian woman is believed to be a concubine on the plantation. Why else, they say, would Sir Hampton Kendall allow his adoption?"

Coral jumped to her feet. "Jemani was my friend, and I made a vow to her that I would look after Gem." Coral's cheeks were flushed with indignation. "The English can be positively—pigheaded!"

If she expected Grandmother to become upset at that, she showed no alarm.

"You are quite right," she said. "But since such goings-on do take place in London royalty, as well as among those working for the East India Company, well, you can see the natural path to which the feet of men do run."

"I will not listen to their gossip, and I am certainly not going to let it upset me further. If they want to believe he is the offspring of a Kendall son—then let them. They will believe it regardless of my denials."

"That is true. However, I must say that I, for one, do not believe it. Knowing how Elizabeth and you feel about Christian matters, I do not find it all that surprising that you took the boy in. But child, you must be reasonable about your feelings. Regardless of his parentage, hiring mercenaries will do nothing to bring him back."

Grandmother snatched bread crumbs from the basket and tossed them to a fat white goose that had waddled from the cherry orchard. "This is most upsetting."

Coral felt a new tide of weariness and sat down, her outburst leaving her more subdued. The last thing she wanted was to lose her grandmother's support.

"I am sorry, Granny V. I did not mean to alarm you."

"I want nothing more than to see you happy, Coral, but—" and she sighed. "While I dislike admitting this, I suspect that Hugo may be right after all."

Coral felt a rise of uneasiness. "About what?"

Grandmother glanced at her, her pale eyes troubled. "About your inability to adjust to the boy's death. Grief is one thing, and I think I have made it clear you need not go into a closet to have a good cry. But this matter of Gem being alive, of this letter . . . your thinking is not quite . . ." she halted, "what shall we say—stable? I am not blaming you," she hastened. "It was not a pretty thing to come upon that wretched savage in the process of stealing Gem from the nursery. Ethan

195

is convinced that such an experience can leave a mother scarred indefinitely. He is quite sympathetic toward your position."

Coral stared at her, confused. Is that what the family thought? That she was beside herself?

Coral steadied the frustration rising within her, then began calmly, "I admit the fever does cause nightmares, even hallucinations, but I am over that now. There is nothing wrong with my thinking. Did Uncle Hugo tell you there was?"

Grandmother looked pained. "It was a mistake to have allowed you to adopt the baby. You were too young and impressionable. Naturally you grew attached, and his loss has done this to you. I do not blame you at all. I blame Hampton. He should have known the trouble it would cause you, and Kingscote, not to mention Elizabeth. I suppose he did it because of baby Ranek, but I fear Hugo is right."

Hugo . . . Hugo. It appeared the entire family believed him.

"Uncle Hugo means well; however, he is wrong about Gem, and about me. I know he thinks I am unstable, but it is not true, Grandmother. I have the letter from my ayah. My conviction that Gem is alive has nothing to do with grief. And if he is, he is in the hands of his abductors. I intend to continue the search in India."

Coral stood, looking down at her grandmother, her eyes pleading. "Granny V, please understand how I feel. I cannot rest until I know what happened to him." She felt hurt by the alarm in her grandmother's eyes. She bent and planted a kiss on her forehead. "I love you, Granny V. Do change your mind about Director Rawlings. Do you not see? I must write him. I need your support. You will help me?"

Lady Victoria said nothing. Coral waited for a moment, but when her grandmother remained silent, Coral gathered up her skirts, turned, and left.

13

Grandmother Victoria watched Coral walk across the green toward the mansion, removing her hat as she went. She was a determined young woman, so much like Elizabeth. She had lost Elizabeth by refusing to understand her love for Hampton Kendall, and her determination to go to India. She must not make the same mistake with Coral's devotion to the Indian boy.

I have already lost my daughters. I will not give up my granddaughters too. One of them should belong to me, to London, and to Roxbury Silk House. If I cannot have Coral—then I will have Kathleen, Marianna, or Belinda. Why should India take them all?

Using her cane, Lady Victoria stood to her feet, staring thoughtfully after Coral. It might be wiser to sanction Coral's mission to write Director Rawlings, even though Hugo would resist. Giving her granddaughter moral support would win her devotion. How splendid if she could manage to keep Coral and Ethan in London!

Coral believed the boy was alive. But that was impossible. Margaret had explained to her that the child's body had been found a few days after his abduction, but if it would make her granddaughter happy, then why not allow Director Rawlings to look into the matter?

She emptied the remaining bread crumbs from the basket onto the lawn. She had no reason to doubt Margaret's assessment of what had happened that night on Kingscote. After all, she and Hugo had been there in full control of their senses, while her granddaughter's health had taken a dire turn for the worse.

She sighed. It was painful to see Elizabeth's daughter this distraught.

There must be something Ethan can do to make her well again, she thought. *And I will tell her this afternoon to go ahead and write Director Rawlings.*

Satisfied, Grandmother Victoria looked up, surprised to see Sir Hugo standing a few feet away in a dark riding cloak. He stood under an elm tree staring after Coral.

"Good heavens, Hugo, you startled me," she snapped.

"Oh, did I? My apology."

She cast him a tiresome look. "How long have you been there?"

"Not long. I was out riding with Ethan. I decided to come back early."

He walked the short distance from the path to where she stood, his dark eyes empty of expression. "You must not tire yourself, Victoria," he said solicitously. "You know what Ethan told you about your heart. Let me help you back to the house."

"I am quite all right. Stop fussing over me. By the by—Margaret wishes to see you. She is waiting in her room. You have been neglecting her something beastly."

"This dreadful business at Parliament has kept me busy. I'll make it up to her."

"Men, such insensitive creatures. They forever deceive themselves into thinking yesterday can be 'made up for.' It is you, she wants—though heaven knows I don't know why," she said.

Hugo laughed as they strolled across the velvety grass. "Dearest Victoria, how your honesty bears the sting of briars. But what your daughter may want might surprise you."

She cast him a guarded glance. But he said, "You are wrong. One day I will make up lost time with Margaret. But for now, perhaps a month or two at the house on the Strand will help. I was also thinking that it might be good for Coral to come with us."

Lady Victoria looked at him, askance. "This is rather unexpected, is it not? And if it is Margaret you're thinking of, whyever do you wish to bring Coral?"

"Coral's illness and the loss of the boy has been quite hard on her," he said smoothly. "I worry about her. Margaret can help."

"Are you insinuating that her grandmother cannot?"

"Now, now, Victoria, I would be the last to question the diligence you invest in your granddaughters. Belinda can attest to that."

Victoria looked at her son-in-law, feeling somewhat guilty. Belinda had come to her room in tears the night before. It seemed she was in love with her cousin Alex Kendall, but Hugo insisted she marry Sir Arlen George in Calcutta, a distant relative of the governor-general.

"Belinda wishes to marry young Alex. Do not be so hard-nosed about it, Hugo. Sir George is old enough to be her father. Is it not your own ambitions you are thinking of? Margaret tells me you spend too much time with the governor-general."

"Nonsense. My position demands time with the governor."

"Perhaps, but that does not help Belinda."

"Belinda has a head for every handsome young rascal that comes along. Arlen George will be good for her frivolous nature. He is not the jealous sort. A few flings, and he will look the other way."

"You are odious."

"Belinda and Sir George will announce their engagement when we return to Calcutta."

"And Alex? He has nothing to say about this?"

"My dear Victoria," he said wearily. "Alex Kendall is passionately in love with his music. Belinda does not exist in his world. She would never be happy."

"Posh. Alex is interested in more than music, I dare say. Elizabeth mentioned some girl in Vienna. The daughter of his music instructor."

"Which is my second point. Alex, too, is wild, and perhaps too much like Belinda. Tensely emotional. Any marriage between them would provoke temper tantrums. Now, about Coral—it was Ethan who suggested that she come with Margaret and me to the summer house."

The fact that it was Ethan's idea mollified her. He was like a son, and she trusted Ethan when she wondered about Hugo. But when had Hugo and Ethan discussed a two-month stay for Coral at the summer house? Grandmother Victoria felt nettled. Would the family forever persist in making plans without consulting her?

Hugo looked toward the mansion, his face grim. "Coral was distraught at breakfast."

"I did not notice," Victoria said crisply. "Coral insists she feels well enough. Perhaps she would improve if we simply left her alone to adjust on her own. She is quite religious, and finds strength in that."

"Ethan is concerned that she imagines things. He spoke to me a short time ago."

Victoria glanced at the side of his face, noting the square cut to his jaw, the ruggedly handsome features, the spartan look to his lips. Yet he lacked the masculine sensitivity Margaret needed.

She should have married John Warbeck. Another of my sins, Lady Victoria thought unhappily. Aloud, she said: "Did he? He said nothing to me. When did you see Ethan?"

"This morning at the stables. He mentioned the possibility of placing her back on the powders."

Lady Victoria paused, remembering that Coral had mentioned a letter about the boy from her ayah in India. Had she imagined it?

"Coral does not approve of those Eastern powders Ethan is prescribing—or are they your drugs?"

"Mine! Since when would I meddle with drugs?"

"Oh, come, come. Anyway, she claims they keep her mind confused."

"Rubbish. It is her mind that is confusing her, not Ethan's medicine. Stop fussing, Victoria. He's a physician! He knows what he is doing."

"So you wish to take her to the summer house?"

"Ethan believes it may help her. He will keep her entertained with carriage rides, picnics, and boat trips on the Thames. It is a healthy idea. She is becoming morbid."

Victoria studied his sympathetic expression. "She insists there is a letter from her ayah questioning the boy's death. Coral believes Gem is alive."

"Sorrow often creates delusion," came his quick reply.

"Coral does not seem the dramatic sort."

"On the contrary, her strong will makes her quite dramatic. Hampton and Elizabeth sent Coral here specifically to be turned over to Ethan's medical care. We can trust his decisions."

"About this letter. She insists it was in the small cloisonne box you took from her."

"Ah. That again? If I recall, you stormed after me, snatching it away. There was no letter. I would have noticed it at once. There were only mementos. Sentimental objects to send her into fits of tears. Why anyone wishes to keep such things I do not know. Death ends this existence. Why prolong the memory by suffering?"

"You sound positively heathen! I suppose you sympathize with those gurus who spout reincarnation? Posh! Coming back a hundred times as this creature or that, or some ancient tyrant! No wonder Margaret has lost the sparkle in her eyes. I should never have allowed it. I should have agreed to that young buck Warbeck."

"Lady Victoria, your tongue knows the venom of a viper, however well-bred."

"Indeed. I shall report your heretical beliefs to Bishop Canterbury," she said tartly.

Sir Hugo gave a laugh.

"Curse the day my daughters sailed East on Company ships. . . . By the by . . . I nearly forgot—there is a letter waiting for you from a Captain Buckley. It was delivered this morning. You look surprised. Do you know him?"

"Quite well, as a matter of fact. Colonel Warbeck is his father."

Lady Victoria walked on. "Then he did eventually marry. I did not think he would after—"

"No," came the smooth interruption. "He adopted Buckley. The young man is insolent. But I admit he is an excellent swordsman, and knows his way about India. He could be a valuable man to the Company if he were not so independent."

"What could he want with you?"

"I am sure I do not know. But Michael is aboard his ship, which is docked here in London. They intend to open a tea enterprise in Darjeeling."

"Not another plantation in India! You say Michael is aboard his ship? Why am I not told these matters? My grandson is in London, and he has not yet come to Roxbury House?"

"Give him time. Perhaps they have only just arrived."

"Strange that he would leave it to Captain Buckley to get in touch with us. Well, no matter. Coral will be cheered to see her brother."

"Say nothing yet, Victoria. Let me handle this matter, and see what Buckley wants. It may have nothing to do with Michael."

"Very well. I left the letter on the library table. My memory is getting terrible these days. Tell Simms that Michael must bring Captain Buckley with him for dinner. I want to meet this adopted son of John Warbeck."

14

After leaving her grandmother at the pond, Coral walked across the lawn, entered the house, and stood thoughtfully midway up the staircase.

Contacting Director Rawlings and writing home to Kingscote would raise the ugly issue of deceit, and cause untold upheaval for her parents. If Gem was alive, then some other poor child had died, and someone in the village had done this dastardly thing to make them believe it was Gem. Unearthing the scheme and digging into the motives could mean further risk for everyone. Yet she had an obligation to Gem, and to the truth. She would find him. Whatever the cost.

Jan-Lee had understood the risk involved. That was the reason she had been cautious in making known her suspicions to the family. But had she done so immediately, the problems now facing Coral might have been solved with less heartbreak. As it was, she could not ignore Jan-Lee's letter.

Coral thought of Sir Hugo and the cloisonne box. The letter . . . thankfully she had been wise enough to place it inside her bodice before he entered her room. Had she not done so, he would have found it. *But what am I thinking about my uncle!*

"Perhaps I *am* a trifle overwrought," she mumbled to herself.

The house was silent, the servants busy elsewhere, and she slipped into the library with its towering walls of books, crossing the rose carpet to the door that led into a small office. It was a rigid sort of room, crowded with dark furniture, and the drapes were pulled shut. The smell of sweet tobacco clung to the air.

Coral sat down at the desk and proceeded to write two letters: the first to her father, and the second to Director Rawlings at the East India Company on Leadenhall Street.

A short time later, she heard a soft tread in the outer library, followed by a rustle of paper. She stood, again placing the letters inside her bodice, and walked to the door.

Uncle Hugo stood before the window with his broad back toward her. She best let him know of her presence, but before she could, he seemed to sense that someone stood there, for he turned toward her.

His dark beard always made it difficult for her to judge the expression on his face. There was astute silence, growing more tense by the moment. Then his voice came quietly:

"Were you looking for this, my dear?"

Confused, her eyes dropped to his hand. He held up a torn envelope and a sheet of paper.

"I found it on the library table," he said. "It is from Captain Buckley."

Coral's heart began to pound. The captain! But why would he write a letter to Sir Hugo?

Confused, she said, "*Jace* Buckley?"

Sir Hugo stared at her, as though deep in thought, and when he spoke his voice was surprisingly kind.

"Sit down. Alas, we have another tragedy to be borne."

Another . . .

Her mind jumped to the possibilities of disaster. Jace was dead. His ship had sunk. No! Not if he wrote the letter—"What is it?"

"I fear the adventurous Buckley has been derelict in his duty as captain of the *Madras*. It is something I might have told Michael had I thought him willing to listen."

Derelict in his duty? She envisioned him as he was when they had first met—the precise and disciplined major—and her mind struggled with the conflict her uncle's words brought. She could not conceive of Jace Buckley ever being derelict. What was her uncle saying? What had happened?

"His license should be revoked," Hugo insisted. And as she watched him, bewildered, he ripped up the letter in apparent rage and flung it into the small hearth. "The Devil to pay!"

"Uncle!" She hurried toward him, taking his arm. Dark eyes stared down at her.

"I can only believe the worst."

"The worst?" cried Coral. "About the captain? But why would you need to? Tell me what's wrong!"

"A clear mind is needed to captain a ship," he was saying. "The young scoundrel ought to be hung!"

Coral's icy hand fell from his arm, his rage frightening her.

"Michael is dead," he announced. "He was washed overboard in a storm. The captain was not at his post, but drunk in his cabin."

Coral stared up at her uncle as though she'd not heard a word he had spoken. *Impossible.* Her brother was not dead. No, not Michael too! And Captain Buckley would not have been drunk . . . would he? But what

209

did she know about him, really? The Lord would not take Michael so soon after taking Gem. No. It was not true. Dead? Michael? No.

Coral shook her head. Dark waves rolled over her mind, each sending Sir Hugo farther and farther away. His sharp words seemed to repeat themselves in her mind: *Michael is dead . . . Michael is dead—*

"—he ought to be hung!"

15

The gilded clock in the Long Gallery chimed five times. In the library, Doctor Ethan Boswell watched from the rectangular window as the big man named Seward left Roxbury House, shouldering his way into the waiting coach, which rumbled out of sight into the London fog. He had delivered a detailed report of Michael Kendall's death to Sir Hugo, but at the moment, it was not his cousin's death that disturbed Ethan. It was the letter from Captain Buckley addressed to Coral.

Ethan let the red velvet drape fall into place, and with his jaw set, looked across the library at his uncle.

Sir Hugo sat with his head resting against the winged-back leather chair, staring up at the high ceiling. He drew deeply on the tube connected to the side of a long-necked clay pot. With veiled distaste, Ethan watched him exhale a cloud of dark smoke. Hugo's heavily lidded black eyes came to rest on him. The water pipe used in India, known as a hookah, gurgled as he drew on it again.

Hugo exhaled, then spoke between his teeth: "Never mind Buckley. I shall take care of the matter.

211

Do you have Coral's letter to Rawlings?"

Ethan hesitated. He had no reason to question his uncle's account of the boy's death, but the fact remained that his patient believed otherwise. Accepting the letter Coral had written to the Director of the East India Company on the pretext of delivering it left him feeling uncomfortable.

"I have it," he admitted. "Victoria gave it to me. She wants me to deliver it to Director Rawlings. She supports Coral's decision in this."

Ethan felt his uncle's heavy gaze boring through him.

"Come, come, Ethan. The letter." He held out his hand, a ruby winking in the firelight. "The last thing the family needs is a pack of mercenary jackals prowling about Kingscote sniffing out trouble. Victoria means well but is wrong. The boy is dead."

Ethan went to warm himself at the hearth, where a fire crackled.

His uncle continued. "Did you make that fact clear to Coral before you put her to sleep?"

"She understands the facts. She refuses to believe them."

"She's hallucinating again. As her physician, it is your responsibility to see that she recovers from her delusion."

Ethan's expression hardened. "You can be certain I will do everything in my power to see Coral well." He added, looking at his uncle evenly: "Something else. She insists there was a letter from her ayah, and now it's missing."

"There was no letter in the box. Am I accused of thievery?" he asked sarcastically.

"Assuredly not. She may believe that the child is alive, but she will come out of this unreality soon. Her grief over Michael has worsened matters. Two deaths in so short a time would leave anyone in her frail health somewhat erratic. We must be patient."

Sir Hugo tapped his fingers on the arm of the leather chair and watched him evenly. "Remember one thing, Ethan. The silk dynasty is not in business to adopt Indian orphans. A letter to Rawlings will do little except increase the problems on Kingscote. As her guardian in London, I cannot permit it. The boy is gone. So is Michael. You are right, however. This unfortunate loss can only reinforce her instability. Perhaps if you explain the powders are necessary until her mind accepts reality, she will be more inclined to accept the truth."

Ethan looked away from his uncle to the fire. "I was thinking a letter from Sir Hampton might also help. He saw the child for himself, did he not?"

"A letter? To eliminate *her* doubts, or yours?"

"Of course I do not doubt you. Why should I?"

"Just remember, Ethan. You have as much reason to see Kingscote flourish as I. If you want that research lab on the plantation, you will need a silk heiress for a wife."

Ethan flushed angrily, and he shoved his balled fists into his trouser pockets. "I have more interest in Coral than the finances to start a lab."

"I do not doubt that at all," Hugo soothed. He drew on the hookah, closed his eyes, and leaned his head back.

Ethan watched him coldly, but there was little he could do to thwart his uncle.

"I know Rawlings," Hugo went on. "He has two avid interests: collecting antiques, and meddling in Eastern intrigue. He will try to make something of her overwrought suspicions, and I can't allow that. I must do what is best—not only for Coral but for the silk. The boy was slain by angry Hindus over the Christian adoption. I warned Hampton, but he wouldn't listen. Matters are quiet again now . . . rekindling the ugly incident will stir up flames. Hampton and Elizabeth will insist whoever's to blame be brought to justice."

"Entirely just! Let them hang!" snapped Ethan. "If it was a conspiracy, Sir Hampton does well to seek them out. Killing a child! A despicable act!"

"Must you think as a sentimental fool? Will you have Kingscote a smoking rubble?"

"But surely—"

"Stay out of the cobra's den, Ethan, lest you also be bitten and die!"

Ethan stood rigid, understanding the veiled threat. He stared at his uncle. *Uncle.* . . . There was always some question of his being Sir Hugo's nephew. When a child, Ethan had once overheard the filthy talk of two servants saying he was Hugo's illegitimate offspring. The idea that Hugo may actually be his father did little to soothe him.

"With Burma invading Assam, the last thing we need is a Hindu mutiny on the plantation," Hugo continued. "If there is another fire, this time the hatcheries will go up!"

"But if the boy *was* murdered—" Ethan insisted.

"Rubbish. What to us is murder is to them mere religious ritual."

"Them? Who is 'them?' "

"My dear fellow, you know India!" yelled Hugo. "Ghazis, of course! The English may tamper with many things, but India's culture must be left alone. If not, we will have a mutiny on our hands, and the Company will lose all rights to trade. We cannot handle further uprisings instigated by discontented maharajas and holy men. The Company has already crossed swords with Burma. There is trouble with Nepal—Bhutan in Sikkim. The last thing we need is Bengal!"

That his uncle could be ruthless, Ethan knew. He had been a boy when Sir Hugo had first become his guardian. He knew little about his mother. He had a vague recollection of a woman's death, a woman with golden tresses and soft gray eyes.

Soon after that, Hugo had arrived in a carriage and took him away from another young woman who had cursed and spit at him. Hugo had calmly shoved her away from him, and Ethan remembered crying when she landed in the mud.

Hugo had been named his legal guardian by a family barrister. Presently they had come to Roxbury House where his attractiveness, and early interest in medicine, had made him his grandmother's darling, and his uncle's heir.

Sir Hugo was a man driven by his ambitions, but Ethan respected his mind. He told himself that however callous his decisions may appear, it was for the good of the family, and therefore, to contest him was unnecessary. And, Hugo was right about one thing: If Ethan married into the Kendall side of the family, the resources he needed for his research would be available with the stroke of a pen. No longer would he need to please Grandmother Victoria, or Uncle Hugo. He would be in control of his own destiny.

The thought of possessing the freedom to open a lab on Kingscote made his heart pound. After all . . . his passion was unselfish. The long years he had dedicated to medicine, years of utter self-denial, were beneficial to humanity. Think of the thousands suffering from tropical diseases across India and Burma that he could help. Was he not helping Coral now? She would get well and strong. He would see to that! Why should he not cooperate with his uncle? Besides, cousin Coral was a lovely girl and would make a perfect wife.

Ethan's fingers thoughtlessly ran along his gold-colored silk doublet and frilled shirt. The chocolate-brown cravat about his throat was meticulously pressed, as were the fawn-colored jacket and matching trousers.

"Well?"

Ethan came back to the moment. He walked up to where Sir Hugo sat calmly in the chair. The hookah gurgled its disgusting sound again. He reached inside his jacket and removed the letter addressed to Director Rawlings.

"As her physician," stated Hugo, "I am certain you will agree a long stay at the summer house will do medical wonders. Say—two months?"

Ethan's jaw tightened. "Only if I accompany her. She will need close supervision under the powders."

"Of course. My next suggestion."

Ethan handed him the letter.

There came a quick tap on the door, and it opened wide. Grandmother Victoria stood there, her silver hair immaculate, her blue eyes going immediately to Ethan.

"It's Coral. Meg says the poor child is having a most dreadful time. She is crying out in her sleep. I do so detest seeing her this way!"

"Yes, Grandmother. I am on my way to her room now." He glanced at Sir Hugo, who had gone to the hearth and was facing the flames. Ethan's gaze dropped to see the letter curling into white ash.

"I certainly hope so, Ethan," Grandmother said in a half-scolding voice, as though he had been neglecting his duty. "Are you certain this trip into London will not be too much for her after the news of Michael? This relapse is unexpected."

"She's on the medication, Grandmother. She will be getting better soon."

Lady Victoria hesitated. "I was thinking I should accompany her."

Ethan was about to agree when Sir Hugo's steady voice interrupted. "Do not forget your promise to the Duchess of Sandhurst."

"Oh posh! My memory again. Then it appears as if I shall be visiting Sandhurst for a few weeks. She will be offended if I do not."

Her satin skirts rustled stiffly as she turned and left with only a glance toward Sir Hugo's back.

Meg, the upstairs maid, waited nervously on the upper landing, one hand holding the banister, the other tugging at her crisp white dustcap.

She curtsied quickly. "Begging your pardon, Doctor. I know it's near your dinner and all, but I can't seem to waken her from the nightmare."

"The nightmare again?"

"A very bad one, sir!"

The woman hurried to lead the way down the hallway to Coral's room. "She's thrashing about something awful, sir, and her nightclothes are sopping wet. She keeps calling the Indian child, and I didn't know what to say or do, and—"

"Yes, Meg, no need to apologize. I was on my way up anyway. You can go down to the kitchen and have a cup of tea, dear. I will send for you later this evening."

Meg curtsied, her face flushed gratefully. "Yessir, thank you, sir."

Downstairs in the library, Sir Hugo removed a second letter, this one from his jacket. He tore it open and read:

June 20, 1797
Miss Kendall:
I received your letter of inquiry into Michael's death today. I will try to excuse your rude questioning about my loathsome and damnable drinking habits. I understand Michael's death is a grave loss to you. I have some books and the Bible that belonged to him. I could have sent them with Seward, but prefer to give them to you in person, as well as my explanation of what happened that day at sea. I will be sailing to Calcutta on June 22, and wish to speak with you before I sail. If you are willing to see me, and to listen without hurling false accusations, send a message to the Madras *at the East India Docks.*

Respectfully,
Captain J. Buckley

Sir Hugo stared at the letter. So Coral had sent an inquiry.

Hugo intended to leave for the summer house tomorrow. It was best that any relationship with Colonel Warbeck's son be put to a stop before it began.

He dropped the letter onto the glowing coals.

The House on the Strand
July

Was she hallucinating? Coral drifted in and out of sleep in her bedchamber, which faced the London estuary. In the shadows of her room she saw Sir Hugo hovering near her bedstand, arranging her medications.

Coral's head felt swollen and painful, and thinking was too hard . . . she must sleep.

Gem—she tossed restlessly, soaked with sweat. No, she must not think of him now. It would hurt too much in the dark. Everything hurt worse at night. She must get strong! She was a prisoner of her own frailty!

Disjointed thoughts came tumbling through her mind. The family insisted her baby was dead. *He* was alive. It was Michael who was dead—buried at sea.

Coral let out a cry, visualizing fish with jagged teeth eating his flesh. No godly burial for her beloved brother! He was cast upon the angry sea, his cries for help smothered by dark brine, his clutching hands grasping at seaweed. Jace Buckley did it! He let her brother die. His screams for help went unattended while Jace drank himself into oblivion in his cabin!

Sobbing, Coral drifted in and out of nightmarish sleep. She could sleep for hours, or was it days? She must be alert to think, to plan her return to India, to pray, to fight; yet inevitably she grew weaker and more helpless. Sleep would come, though she fought against the effect of the medicine, and with sleep came the blackest vision of all—

As if akin to the storm blowing in from the London estuary, the nightmare that had plagued Coral during the worst month of her illness in India came sweeping through her soul.

Loss smothered her heart in the humid Indian night. Once more she slipped out from under the mosquito net encircling her bed. The tender soles of her feet brushed against the mat rugs. She floated to the open verandah. Humid darkness no longer surrounded her. It was dawn.

She leaned over the rail where the emerald lawn ran down to the Brahmaputra River. The clear lemon light touched the quiet water where the wooden barges were being loaded with raw silk. She turned her attention away from the river to the thick jungle, hearing the happy voices of the children working in the hatcheries.

The whimsical voice of a particular child reached out and gripped her heart. Her pulse quickened—Gem! He was in danger! She tried to scream. Her voice became a mocking whisper, "Gem, come back!"

Again she was running as she had in a hundred dreams, searching for the child that remained just ahead but out of sight.

The soft innocent laughter echoed in her soul. Where had he gone to? Why was he hiding from her? Gem never ran away. He always came running to meet her, his soft brown eyes shining under long dark lashes, his shy smile greeting her with the trust between mother and child.

"Gem, my baby, come back!"

She raced down the well-worn path in the direction of the thatch huts belonging to the silk workers.

The workers seemed to scowl at her; then they reached out to stop her. She fought her way through the mob and ran on.

Instinctively she knew that sorrow awaited her behind the thick trees, yet she felt compelled to take the path that she had trod a hundred times in her memory.

At that moment she came to a clearing in the jungle. The stark scene enveloped her in despair. Gone! The huts were all in flames. She whirled to look off in the direction of the Kendall house for help, but it too was burning!

Her hair clung to the sweat on her neck. She stumbled forward, her skirts snagging on thorny bushes. Vines wrapped their tentacles about her ankles to thwart her progress. Foolishly she looked for Gem under a shrub and then behind the charred rubble of a hut. In dismay she dropped to her knees and *gazed up into the heated sky of whitish haze.*

Gem's voice played in the branches of mulberry trees like wind whispering through the leaves, singing the rhyme she had taught him,

"Shepherd, Shepherd, where be your little lambs?
Don't you know the tiger roams the land?"
"Softly, little lamb, softly. I AM always here.
My rod is your protection, My arm will hold you
    near."

Coral bolted awake with a gasp. A dim lamp burned on the table beside her bed, and Ethan leaned over her. "It's all right now, dear, it's all right. It was only a nightmare."

She sank against the damp pillow, struggling for composure. "Oh, Ethan, it is always the same . . . as though Gem is trying to call me—" her voice broke off, her fingers gripping his hand. "Maybe he *is* calling me! I cannot stand thinking about it. Ethan—suppose he thinks I deliberately abandoned him, that I do not love him anymore? Who knows the tormenting thoughts of a child ripped from the safety of his nursery? Suppose they mistreat him, suppose—"

"Coral." His voice was firm, sounding a warning.

She took in a deep breath, exhaling slowly, as he had taught her to do.

After a moment, she relaxed a little. She thought of the letter she had given to Simms to deliver to the *Madras*. Had Captain Buckley received it?

"H-has any letter come for me?"

Ethan smiled. "You know it takes five months for mail to arrive from India. Maybe by Christmas."

"N-nothing else?"

His smile vanished. "Were you expecting a letter

from someone in London?"

"Yes, I wrote Captain Buckley before I left Roxbury House. I wanted to ask him about Michael."

Was it her imagination, or did he grow cool?

"The *Madras* sailed for India in June. This is July. It is no wonder he did not answer you. If he has any conscience at all, he knows guilt over Michael's death."

Coral turned her head away. *July.* Had she been in bed, drugged with medication, for six weeks? She tried to reject her disappointment that Jace Buckley had refused to answer her letter. She would not have thought the cool and restrained major would become a derelict sea captain, but it was known that he was an adventurer who sailed the wicked ports of the East. And did not her mother once tell her that his father had been a pirate?

I will not think of him, she decided, her fingers tightening on Ethan's comforting hand.

"Ethan? The letter to Director Rawlings ... Grandmother said she gave it to you before we left the estate. Did you deliver it?"

She felt the pressure of his fingers tighten about hers.

"Let's wait and discuss the matter when you are feeling stronger," he said softly.

Coral's eyes pleaded. "No, Ethan, now."

His gaze held tenderness, and she warmed to it. She had felt so alone. Scripture reading had proven impossible, and prayers died on her lips unspoken as sleep took control of her mind.

"I am trying to help you. I want you to trust me, Coral."

She moistened her lips. "I want to trust you. I believe I can."

He smiled. "Then listen to me now with your mind and not your heart."

"I will try."

"If you persist in tormenting yourself about Gem, you may never get well enough to go home to India. Michael's death is wrenching! I understand that, but we must leave them both to God. The matter of the boy is settled."

"It cannot be settled until I get him back. Gem was abducted by the maharaja. Who else could it have been?"

"What raja do you speak of?"

"I—I do not know."

He looked dubious.

"But I am certain!"

"But you do not know who this raja is?"

"No. The major kno—" she stopped. She would not think of him. "Director Rawlings may be able to help me."

He sighed. "The letter was useless. It could only stir up trouble for your father and Kingscote."

"Useless!" She tried to sit up. "But Ethan, I just told you that the director may be able to help."

He studied her with sober gaze, and Coral felt uneasy.

"Gem's body was found two days after his abduction. Sir Hugo told me everything."

"But I told you, Ethan! Jan-Lee doubts that it was his body. The body they found had a scar."

"But there is no letter from this ayah of which you speak."

"I tell you there was a letter! It is missing! It was with the adoption certificate. I put them away before the news about Michael. Uncle Hugo took it, he—"

Coral stopped when Ethan simply patted her

223

hand. She wanted to wince. He was humoring her. She stiffened. "It should have been there. But I have been too drugged to keep watch—"

His hands held hers tightly, and his eyes were troubled. "Coral. Good heavens! Do you think we are your enemies? You must calm yourself. Listen to me. Even if there was a letter, and your ayah mentioned a scar, it proves nothing."

"It proves the child was not Gem."

"You were ill much of the time during his first years. He could have hurt himself, and you might know nothing about it."

"But Jan-Lee bathed him! She would know. It was she who asked me about the scar. I must write her—"

"Listen. Your mother also cared for him. It could have happened during that time."

Coral paused. She frowned. Her heart sank. She felt the knifelike pain of crushed hopes. "Yes . . . yes."

"Dearest . . . then there were times when the ayah did not have Gem in her care. And more importantly, Hugo was there when they found him."

Sickened, she could only stare at him, clutching the bed covers with trembling fingers. "I remember everything that happened that night—the fire, the sepoy in the nursery, Jan-Lee on the floor—Gem calling for me—" she stopped, aware of his gaze, and it caused her unease.

"Do you remember what happened in the days immediately following his abduction?"

She swallowed, plucking at the cover. "I do not remember them as clearly. I was not well before his abduction, and afterward I had taken to bed." She stopped, her eyes coming to his. "My mother said only that he was found by the river, and I never asked for more details." She thought of the crocodiles. "I was not ready to hear them. I expected the worst."

"Coral, we cannot ignore the fact Hugo was there that night. Do you remember that?"

"Y-yes, he and Margaret were there for the adoption ceremony. And there was something about his meeting with the ruling family at Sibsagar about trouble with Burma."

He looked hopeful. "You are right. He is here in London for the same reason. Uncle is a witness of Gem's death. According to him, your father did tell you the details that night, but even then you refused to listen. It was only then that you became so ill and for weeks were delirious with fever. That could account for your lapse of memory."

Coral felt the cold tentacles of fear. *Had she forgotten? Was there something wrong with her mind?*

Ethan squeezed her hand gently. "Perhaps you have permitted yourself to forget reality because it is too painful."

It cannot be!—Or was it? Was it possible that they had told her, but like Ethan suggested, her memory had rejected reality? Perhaps she had only been too feverish to remember. But the letter from Jan-Lee. She could not have imagined that.

"Ethan, I feel so confused. It is the powders. I do not want to take them again. I—I want to talk to Uncle Hugo. I want to hear what happened to Gem from him."

"Coral, not now. You must rest. You can speak to him in the morning. I will stay beside your bed tonight. Then there will be no nightmares."

"No, *now*, Ethan. I want to talk to him now. I want to hear it from him."

He studied her face, and she knew she must look agitated, even a little wild. He drew in a breath. After a moment, he nodded gravely. "Then you shall. I will ask him to come."

16

Coral sat up, trying to compose her features as the two men entered her chamber a short time later. Suddenly she wished that she had asked Aunt Margaret to come too. Strange . . . she had not seen her aunt in weeks. Was she even at the summer house?

Sir Hugo stood there for a moment in silence, as though analyzing her emotional state. He came to the side of the bed, and she rejected the feeling of being intimidated. His bearded face was masked in shadows. Coral found herself feeling like a child ready to be scolded by a stern father. She must be cautious.

"Good evening, Uncle. I have not seen you in several weeks. Not since we arrived on the Strand."

"I feared to impose upon you, child. I asked Ethan to keep you sedated. Your emotional state is so delicate at present."

She looked at Ethan. Uncle Hugo had asked him to keep her sedated?

Coral showed no alarm under Hugo's steady gaze and made room for him to sit on the bed beside her. She was grateful for one thing: She had known many strong-willed men. Her father, Seward, Michael, and now her uncle. She refused to cower.

"I have not seen Aunt Margaret."

"It was necessary for her to return to the estate soon after we arrived. Your cousin Belinda came home from school and has taken to bed for a week."

"Nothing serious I hope?"

He smiled. "You are the one we are concerned about. Margaret will be here by week's end. She will bring your cousin. You will enjoy that?"

"Yes. I am beginning to feel a prisoner."

"Ah, as soon as you are well, Ethan will have you out at the seasonal balls."

The very thought of waltzing sent her mind spinning and her stomach churning. She must get off the medicine.

"Ethan tells me you wish to discuss the death of Gem. Do you think it wise at the present?" His sober look made her uneasy. Did he expect her to snap like an autumn twig?

"I want to discuss it, Uncle. You must not worry about me. I am no longer grieving over Michael. I know his Christian experience was genuine."

"If your faith enables you to be at peace, so much the better."

She knew that her uncle was not a religious man, but it was disturbing to hear him dismiss the Christian hope as a comforting fancy.

"You feel certain you wish to discuss the death of Gem?" he asked.

The death of Gem. How certain he made it sound. "You—do not recall a letter from Jan-Lee? I kept it inside a red silk pocket. Just before the news arrived about Michael, I put it in a drawer in my room at Roxbury House with the adoption certificate."

He patted her hand. "No, my dear. I have seen no

such letter. I am not in the habit of sneaking about searching through bureau drawers." He smiled, obviously trying to lighten the moment.

"It is missing."

"You are certain it existed?"

Ethan sat down on the other side of the bed and took her hand. The gentle squeeze he gave her was reassuring.

"I am certain."

"Then perhaps it will yet turn up at Roxbury House."

"Uncle—I think Gem may be alive and in danger."

He said nothing but looked knowingly at Ethan.

Coral tensed, looking from one to the other. "I want to hire mercenaries to try to locate him. You will help me? I want to visit Director Rawlings."

Sir Hugo sighed. "Coral, I wish I could help you. I do not want to sound cruel, but I am forced to be blunt in the matter. I know you loved the child, and his loss is a grief to you. Margaret and I understand. So does your grandmother and Ethan. But the boy is gone. He has been dead for over a year. I and your father were both there the night he was found. Try to remember!"

Her heart thudded . . ."You—found him?"

She felt his probing gaze.

"No. It was not I."

Would she have less reason to doubt Gem's death if it had been someone other than Hugo who found him? She wondered if he realized the turmoil of her thoughts.

"Then, who?"

"We were all out looking that night. Your father went in one direction, taking workers with him, and I in another. We arranged to sound an alarm if we found anything. Those in my company had the misfortune of coming upon him by the river."

Coral restrained her emotions. She said, surprised by her calm voice: "You are certain it was Gem?"

"I had no reason to doubt it."

"If *you* did not find his . . . body, then who did?"

"There was confusion among the workers and much carrying on, as one would expect. I believe it was the man named Natine."

Natine. Coral tried to remember what it was about Natine that had upset her the night of the fire.

"Then how—how did you know it was Gem?"

"I saw him. But I did not know for certain; I only knew it was a child of the same age."

"Then there is the possibility—"

"It was Natine who first identified him. But I wanted to be positive. So I sounded the alarm for Hampton."

Her hopes crashed. *Father!*

"Then we all returned to the house to wait for him. Neither I nor Margaret said anything to your mother. Margaret thought it best to let Hampton tell her."

Coral had heard nothing yet to discount Jan-Lee's suspicions.

"But it could have been another child," she insisted. "Whoever abducted Gem did not want us to search for him. What better way than to make us all think he was dead?"

"I would be inclined to agree if Hampton had not identified him."

"My father looked at him?" she asked weakly.

"I, of course, would not take so serious a responsibility upon myself. You do not remember Elizabeth coming to your room and telling you?"

Coral searched her memory. "No," she whispered,

and despite her efforts, successful until now, her voice cracked. "I do not remember, Uncle. I remember nothing but awaking the day of the funeral when she came to my room."

Sir Hugo showed none of his normal constraint or dislike of tears, and his arm went about her shoulders. "There, there, my dear."

How could she forget anything so painful and vivid as this?

"Perhaps there is a solution to this whole matter. Ethan has suggested I write to Hampton. If you have difficulty believing your uncle, surely you will believe your own father."

She did doubt him, but how could she possibly say so?

"It is not that I do not wish to believe you, Uncle, but why do I not remember? And the letter—"

"Ethan suggests it is due to the shock of discovering the sepoy in the process of abducting the boy. He believes it will all come to you in time. Through the dream itself perhaps." He stood. "I will write Hampton tonight. But you must promise to let the matter of Gem rest in silence until you hear from your father."

"Uncle is right," urged Ethan. "You must put all your thoughts into getting well again. If you do, I will try taking you off the powders."

No more medication! She looked at him gratefully. "Yes, I will wait to hear from my father."

"Good," said Sir Hugo, standing. "That should be time enough to see you on your feet and pursuing your education."

When Hugo and Ethan left, Coral lay in her bed, disturbed. Her uncertainty about her uncle was growing, despite her reluctance to mistrust him. *I too shall*

231

write Father again . . . just to make sure the first letter
was mailed.

The next few weeks remained difficult ones. True
to his promise, Ethan had taken her off the powders,
and within a couple of weeks she was strong enough
to get out of bed for short periods. Everyone seemed
pleased with her progress, and quite unexpectedly Sir
Hugo decided they should return to Roxbury House.
Coral wisely spoke no more of the missing letter from
Jan-Lee or of Gem for fear that her family would think
her ill again. Whatever she did in the future, she would
need to do on her own. And that meant getting well.

Restricted as she was to the boundaries of the
Roxbury estate, Coral was eagerly anticipating the beginning of her studies and getting Gem off her mind.

Now that midsummer was upon them, and her
sisters and cousin were home, life picked up its tempo
to include a whirlwind of gala balls, dinners, and out-
ings. Marianna was considered too young for the balls
but was allowed to attend the picnics. Coral was not
strong enough to begin her social debut.

As they sat in the garden having luncheon with
Grandmother and Margaret, Coral's sisters and cousin
were discussing the upcoming ball to be given by the
Duchess of Sandhurst, and Kathleen's amber eyes
sparkled. "I am going to design my own ball dress. I
showed my idea to Aunt Margaret, and she approves."

"It is quite nice, Kathleen. I think you have tal-
ent," Margaret agreed.

Kathleen reached up and gave an unconscious
touch to her chestnut-colored hair and exchanged a
glance with Grandmother. "And, I am going to stay in
London when I graduate Lady Anne's. I shall become
a couturiere at the Silk House."

Coral noticed the arched brow of Aunt Margaret as she turned toward her mother. "Will Elizabeth permit Kathleen to stay?"

Grandmother Victoria looked undisturbed. She said in a defensive tone: "With you and Elizabeth in India, the Silk House needs the blood of a Roxbury woman. Kathleen is the eldest. And with her interest in design, it is appropriate that she should stay. I am going to write Elizabeth and Hampton."

"Unlike Coral, I have no desire to go back to India," said Kathleen quickly.

"Oh, but you must, Sissy," breathed Marianna, wide-eyed. "Papa wants the three of us to marry and live on Kingscote."

Marianna, the youngest of the Kendall daughters, had recently turned fifteen. She was the only one to have blue eyes and strawberry hair, taking after Grandmother's side of the family, and her tiny frame and heart-shaped face suggested fragility. Coral knew that her younger sister had not yet been able to get over separation from their mother and that Marianna was anxious to return to Kingscote.

"Papa said you must marry Captain McKay."

Kathleen gave her baby sister a wearied look. "For your information, Father's mind can be changed. Grandmother will see to that."

Cousin Belinda Roxbury frowned, and looked up from her soup to her mother. "I, too, wish to stay in London with Grandmother." She looked at her mother hopefully. "Have you spoken to Father? The idea of marrying Sir George is ghastly! Why, he is all of thirty-five! He shall die before I ever have a gray hair in my locks."

Margaret pushed her plate away, as though her appetite were gone, and took in a small breath. "I said

233

we would not discuss your engagement to Sir George at the luncheon table."

Belinda's dark eyes fell, and she dipped her silver spoon into the mushroom broth without tasting it. "Yes, Mother."

For the first time, Coral noticed how much her cousin looked like her father, Hugo. She had the same striking black hair, the flashing dark eyes, and a certain look that attracted men, despite Margaret's vigil.

Coral knew that her cousin wanted to marry Alex, but engagement to Sir Arlen George was all but certain and would be publicly announced in Calcutta when Sir Hugo and his family returned to the East India Company.

Coral became aware of a pause in conversation and cleared her voice. She had been waiting for this moment.

"Granny V, now that I am well enough to have private tutors in September, I have decided on a music instructor. Anne Peddington's brother, Charles."

"Peddington?" asked Grandmother Victoria as if tasting the name. "Never heard of the man. How did you learn of him?"

"Um . . . at church, Grandmother."

The mention of church did not go over well. The family was strict Anglican, and Coral had been attending a small nonconformist group connected with John Wesley's Methodist movement.

"Anne Peddington's father is a minister. Charles is very gifted with music and has a waiting list for students. But Anne assured me he would make room for me in September."

Grandmother lifted her diamond-studded lorgnette to look at her suspiciously. "I do hope you are

not becoming too seriously involved with the Dissenters."

Coral felt the eyes of all those seated at the luncheon table. There was a puzzled look from Cousin Belinda, who vigorously avoided attending any religious
services.

"The group is quite respectable, and . . . Ethan has
been accompanying me."

Coral felt the prick of her conscience for using
Ethan to try to persuade her grandmother. He could
do no wrong in Lady Victoria's eyes. Yet this time, even
the mention of Ethan did not satisfy her.

"Lady Villary has recommended Mr. Latimer. He
teaches her daughter Frances."

"Charles Peddington is an excellent teacher,"
Coral pressed. "And he knows William Cowper. They
sometimes work together on music."

"Cooper?"

"Cowper."

"Am I supposed to know the man?" asked Grandmother. "Goodness knows I have been forgetting
things."

"No, you have not met him, but he has a growing
reputation as one of London's leading new poets."

"Heavens! Poetry. Not another Charles Wesley?"

"He has met both Wesley brothers, Charles and
John. Mr. Cowper works with a minister named John
Newton. Mr. Newton wrote 'Amazing Grace' and—"

"Tsk, tsk, dear Coral, these names mean nothing
to me. Let us not get carried away with the noncon-
formists, it only makes for conflict."

"Mr. Newton is an Anglican," said Coral quickly.
"He was the rector in Olney."

Cousin Belinda exchanged glances with Kathleen.
Coral ignored them. They found her interest in spiri-

tual matters dull and could not understand why she did not put up a terrible fuss about not being allowed to attend the balls. *"You are so pretty, Coral, but you never flirt,"* Cousin Belinda had told her. *"You are no fun at all!"*

With relief, Coral heard Margaret coming to her defense. "Now, Mother, if Mr. Peddington is a good music instructor, what does it matter? As ill as she was, we should be grateful she can even begin her studies. And Elizabeth did make it clear to me when Hugo and I left Kingscote that Coral could choose her own instructors."

Grandmother looked guilty. "Elizabeth told you that? Well, you are right about one thing. We should all be grateful Coral is up and about again. Ethan's done so well by you, Coral. There is new color in your cheeks, and you are gaining your weight back."

"I know you will like Mr. Peddington," said Coral.

"I do doubt that, child, but very well, if you truly want this Dissenter, I shall see to it this afternoon."

Coral breathed a sigh of relief.

17

Roxbury Silk House, London

"Legend tells us that silk was introduced into India by a Chinese princess who smuggled caterpillar eggs into Hotan," Margaret told Coral as they wandered through the salon. Margaret stopped before an intricately embroidered map showing the routes of the silk caravans traveling from the Orient into Persia and Spain, called The Old Silk Road.

"Father insists the caterpillar is native to northern India," said Coral.

Margaret smiled. "He may be right. I suppose we will never know."

Already acquainted with the family history in sericulture, Coral was nevertheless surprised by the elegance of the Silk House with its white-veined marble floors, French chandeliers, and floor-to-ceiling mirrors. The walls of the grand showroom were draped with silk tapestry panels, brocaded with gold on a background of red.

Coral was visiting the Silk House in order to choose the colors and textures for the new garments

Grandmother had promised. While they waited for the head couturier to arrive, she found herself intrigued with the five hundred doll miniatures that were on display in the showroom.

Margaret's eyes flashed with excitement, and a warm blush tinted her flawless skin. "Many of the dolls date back to the rule of King James I. They all wear an original costume designed by Roxbury women."

Margaret took her arm and swept Coral away in the opposite direction. "Wait till you see the silk room."

With rustling skirts, Coral quickened her steps to keep up with her aunt, surprised over the sparkle in her eyes and the joy in her step.

This is her passion, thought Coral. *She loves this facet of silk the way Papa is devoted to the hatcheries.*

As Coral followed after her, stepping through the draperies into the silk room, she paused. The September breeze that came through the open court gently touched the mannequins on display. Cascades of silk quivered and sent a whisper through the atelier belonging to the couturier.

"Soft as a baby's sigh," said Margaret. "Look at these colors. They represent the success of the combined efforts of the family in London and India."

Since Kingscote silk was harvested from muga caterpillars that thrived in the humidity of the Assam valley, it produced a unique, shimmering golden variety, lovely in its natural form. And the silk from the muga bleached and dyed more easily than did the silk from the tussa caterpillar of China.

"Look at this one—coral pink. I think you can guess who Granny V named this after?"

Coral smiled with pleasure and ran her palm

across the slippery variety called satin-silk.

"And these . . ." Margaret swirled the material of a half-dozen new shades. "Sumatra orange, blue-green jade, amber gold, and ivory snow."

"They sound splendid enough to eat for dessert," Coral said with a laugh.

Margaret's eyes shone. "The Duchess of Sandhurst has ordered a new ball dress in each of the new shades for her daughter. Imagine!" She laughed. "Please, do not tell Belinda! She has the notion that being a silk heiress entitles her to keep up with royalty."

Margaret then introduced Coral to the new textures of crisp brocades woven with threads of gold, silk-velvets, paisleys, and taffetas. Coral wandered through the aisles, dazed. "How will I ever decide on the colors for my wardrobe? Why, look—the material looks alive," whispered Coral.

"It is the triangular shape of the silk fibers—see how it reflects the light like prisms?"

Margaret chose a bolt of a golden hue, and draped the silken yards over a mannequin. "Protein gives it a pearly sheen. It moves . . . I know exactly how the material will react to the cut and needle." She ran her fingers beneath it, then let it fall softly.

"Look how perfectly it would match your flaxen tresses and golden coloring!" Margaret sighed with pleasure. "Just being here makes me want to do something with it."

Aunt Margaret held it toward Coral, and then toward the windows, letting the light show its luster. She swirled the yards of shimmering fabric onto the mannequin. "Look how it suggests its own design." She gave the material a few twists and folds, then let it fall. "What do you think?"

Coral was watching Aunt Margaret—she, too, appeared surprisingly beautiful. Was this a reflection of Margaret Roxbury at twenty?

"I think it reminds me of a summer gown in a garden of lilacs," breathed Coral. "Oh, Aunt Margaret! You are so experienced in this. Uncle Hugo should insist you work here for at least part of the year."

The September breeze picked up its intensity, and Margaret closed the French doors. On the way back, she paused to gather up some velvet, touching it to her cheek. Her mood altered like a mist moving across a sunlit sky, and Coral suddenly wished that she had not mentioned Hugo.

"I thought he might stay and run for Parliament. It appears as if we will return to Calcutta sooner than expected. The governor-general has elevated him to a new position in the Company."

Coral masked her surprise. "He must be pleased. I know how much the East India Company means to him. What will his position be?"

Margaret touched the velvet absently. "Hugo is not certain. He will meet with the governor-general when we get back. I confess, Coral, I am frightened."

"Afraid?" Coral said, startled. "Of what, Aunt Margaret? Certainly not of—" She stopped.

Margaret's eyes softened as they came back from her thoughts, and aware once again of Coral, she smiled. "Afraid of Hugo? Is that what you wanted to ask?" she laughed. "No, darling, not in the way you may think. Oh, I know what Grandmother says about being fearful of standing up for my ideas, but it is not so. He has always been gentle with me. Does that surprise you?"

"Well, I . . ." Coral stammered, and did not know what to say. It was obvious from Margaret's smile that she understood her embarrassment.

"Your uncle can be hard. We both know that. He is a complex man and has his dark moods, but I knew that when I married him. Perhaps it is the energy that can drive him to the edge that makes me worry. And then there is Belinda." She turned back to straighten a bolt of silk. "Now that she has graduated Lady Anne's, she will return with us. As you know, her engagement to Sir George will be announced next year. Her disappointment is no secret to anyone, including Sir George."

Coral thought of Belinda's vow to not marry him and wondered how she could possibly thwart Sir Hugo's will. Belinda's hope for a relationship with Alex rested in Margaret's willingness to talk to Hugo. Perhaps this is what worried her—the inevitable conflict that would arise.

Margaret brightened and changed the subject. "Grandmother has not told Kathleen yet, but for her birthday next month she has arranged for your sister to train here with Jacques Robillaird!"

"The head couturier?"

"An exceptional man. He will do your wardrobe."

Coral wondered what her parents would say of Kathleen's interest in design. That Granny V was scheming to keep Kathleen in London came as no surprise, and like her cousin Belinda, Kathleen's engagement to Captain McKay was all but announced. Captain Gavin McKay was from her father's side of the family and was serving in the British military at the Calcutta garrison. Their father took pride in his Scottish ancestry, although he had not been in Scotland since a boy, and he took pleasure in Gavin, the son of his cousin.

Coral understood that it was to Kathleen's benefit that the young Captain McKay was not anxious to marry. Had he wished to do so, he could have pressed the issue of marriage to Hampton, and Kathleen would be forced to marry, since she was a year older than Coral. But Gavin McKay was somewhat of a maverick and seemed more amused with Kathleen's maneuverings to avoid him than he was determined that they marry.

Sometimes Coral thought that Captain McKay was in love with Kathleen but was waiting for her to admit her feelings for him. But Kathleen was adamant. She wanted a career at the Silk House in London. Granny V was just as determined to see that she had her opportunity.

"We will sail for Bengal in May," Aunt Margaret was saying.

Coral felt a tingle of excitement as she realized that she would be free from Uncle Hugo's watchful eye. Her thoughts of Director Rawlings were interrupted by a deep French accent:

"Ah, Madame Roxbury!"

They turned. Coral expected to see a slight man with gray hair. Instead, a robust man in his thirties stood holding a silk ball dress.

"You have come to see, to feel, to smell the silk, that is so?"

"Jacques, how well you know me," Margaret said with a smile. "And to decide on a wardrobe for my niece." She turned to Coral. "This is the man I boasted about in the carriage. May I present Paris couturier Jacques Robillaird, Roxbury's most talented designer. Grandmother 'stole' him from the French Huguenots in Spitafields," she said, speaking of the silk district in London.

Jacques smiled down at Coral. "We Protestants who escaped the fiery stake came to London and brought our knowledge of silk weaving with us."

"For which we are thankful," said Margaret. "Jacques will work with you on your wardrobe, Coral. Jacques—my niece, Lady Coral Kendall."

"Mademoiselle, a pleasure. I have met your sister, Mademoiselle Kathleen."

"Monsieur," Coral greeted with a small curtsy. "I am sure my sister will be pleased to be working with you in the months ahead."

"And now, we have much work to do," he said. "Madame Roxbury has previously told me of your hair and skin coloring. And there must be something grandiose to wear to the Octoberfest Ball given by the Earl and Duchess of Sandhurst."

He drew aside a curtain, and Coral gave a cry of delight.

Fed by her enthusiasm, his hawkish eyes became tender. "I am pleased you approve."

The ball dress was made of billowing watered-jade silk with numerous flounces and gathered up at the left with clusters of amber silk fringe. The shoulders were bare except for tiny puffed sleeves of sheer silk over amber glacé. There were matching gloves that came just below the elbow, a headdress of lace and September mums sprinkled with jade stones, and matching jeweled slippers.

"It is stunning," said Coral, imagining herself at the earl's ball. "It is almost too lovely to wear."

"*You* shall be its life," Jacques replied. "And the rest of your trousseau shall be equally inspiring."

———

Fall came, was lost to winter winds, and Coral joined in the family festivity of strewing Christmas evergreens and red plaid ribbon along the fireplace mantels, archways, and banisters at Roxbury House.

Outside the rectangular window in the music room, snow flittered onto the holly bushes where red and green peeped through the bed of white.

Today was her last music lesson until after the holiday festival, and she left the window, humming Charles Wesley's Christmas hymn. Charles Peddington was already forty-five minutes late, and she sat down at the piano waiting to hear his carriage. Usually prompt, she attributed his delay to the snow.

Her fingers practiced on the ivory piano keys as she sang the first verse of the hymn:

"Hark! the herald angels sing,
'Glory to the newborn King;
Peace on earth, and mercy mild;
God and sinners reconciled!'
Joyful, all ye nations rise,
Join the triumph of the skies;
With the angelic hosts proclaim,
'Christ is born in Bethlehem.'
Hark! the herald angels sing,
'Glory to the newborn King!' "

Coral's hands fell silent. She sat, her eyes fixed upon the keys . . . remembering Gem. Where was he now? Was he alive?

By now her father had received her inquiry into Uncle Hugo's account of Gem's death, and of Jan-Lee's suspicions, and she expected to hear from Kingscote sometime in late spring. There had been several letters from home since she had sailed from Calcutta in 1796, and a package from Elizabeth. By now the news of Michael's death at sea had arrived on Kingscote. She bowed her head, praying for comfort and strength for her parents, and for Alex.

How would her brother accept this loss? Despite the difference in their personalities, he had been close to Michael.

The rattle of carriage wheels and horse hooves sent Coral to the window. Charles Peddington alighted from the coach, paid the cabby, and came bounding up the steps to the door.

A minute later she heard Simms let him into the hallway, taking his worn cloak and cap, with Charles apologizing for tracking in snow.

Coral smiled to herself as she turned from the window to greet him. Charles seemed anything but a learned music instructor. He was, in fact, but a year her senior, and his youth was couched in boyish exuberance for the music of Wesley, Cowper, and Newton. The singing of hymns was far from being endorsed by the clergy, and still banished by many churches, but Charles insisted the birth of the golden age of hymns would eventually change the worship service.

He came rushing into the music room, out of breath, his brown eyes alert to the fact that he was an hour late. His round face was tinged pink from the biting cold. He brushed back a shock of unruly brown hair from his forehead and shifted his stance, heaving a parcel that he carried under his arm.

"Sorry I am late, Coral . . . it was Anne. You know how she loves books of all sorts. Well," and he heaved a sigh, "my sister came across an old copy of the Olney hymnbook by Newton and Cowper at the book shop, and she wanted me to bring it to you for a Christmas present." Almost shyly he held it out to her. "We wish it were new and leather-bound."

"An Olney hymnbook! Oh, Charles!"

"I fear it is a trifle scarred up."

"As if that makes any difference. I could not have a better gift."

He looked pleased as she took the package from him and brought the book to the piano. "Let's sing!"

She sat down and played several hymns, while Charles joined in. Inevitably she was drawn to "Amazing Grace." When at last they lapsed into reflective quiet, Simms brought hot mulled tea and Christmas cakes. She smiled at Charles and walked to a table where several Christmas packages were wrapped and stacked neatly in a basket. There was a new greatcoat, a hat, and a dashing cape for Charles; a Paris hat, a muff, and a fur-lined cape for Anne; and a number of presents for their rector father: butter cakes, plum and raisin puddings, tins of French chocolates, English toffees, and cookies from the Roxbury kitchen.

"You and Anne are coming to the Christmas Ball next week? Grandmother hopes to meet your father."

Charles blushed. "I am sorry to say he is unable . . . that is, well, our father is somewhat puritanical. He disapproves of balls . . . but," he hastened, "he has no set rule for Anne and me. He has left it up to us, as he has with the meetings at Clapham."

Coral had been attending the meetings at Clapham for several months. The fashionable suburb was three miles outside London where a number of wealthy Dissenters had their homes.

The group of Christian laymen under the godly leadership of their rector, John Venn, was meeting in the great oval library of the banker Henry Thornton.

It was here, amid great books of learning, that Coral's love for the greatest of all books was awakened into something fresh and personal. Coral listened to such great men as the chairman of the East India Company, Charles Grant, speak zealously for the support of missions in the American colonies. And William Wilberforce proved to be not only a fighter for emancipation, but a profound scholar on biblical teaching.

"Are you coming tonight with Doctor Boswell?"

"Ethan is on medical call."

Charles hesitated as though concerned. "I should warn you that Mr. Wilberforce will be there again tonight."

Coral was aware that Wilberforce's debates in Parliament over the abolition of slavery in England had earned Uncle Hugo's disfavor. *"His self-righteous meddling is not to be borne,"* he had stated at the dinner table. While courts had made the ownership of slaves illegal, Wilberforce, and men like John Newton, were striving to try to get Parliament to pass a law that also banned Englishmen from participating in the slave trade.

"Sir Hugo has a meeting at the East India Company."

That night, she went to Clapham in a Roxbury carriage with Charles, and they laughed and sang as the snow flittered down.

The Clapham meetings stressed a practical expression of Christianity, gained not through church liturgy, but fanned to flame through personal involvement in Scripture study and what were now labeled "seasons of intercession."

Although raised an Anglican, and steeped in tradition and ritual, Coral had learned to pray and study the Bible on her own through the many years of illness that had kept her confined to bed. But the meetings in Henry Thornton's library had become a pivotal turning point in her relationship with Christ, and had engendered in her a new awareness of the need for evangelizing the heathen.

It was of interest to Coral that the chairman of

the Company, Charles Grant, attended the meetings, and that the head of the colonial office gave a large amount of aid to the missionaries working in the American colonies. *What would Uncle Hugo think of that?* she wondered with a faint smile.

The meetings stressed the interest of God in the nations. The heathen were people of His desire, not objects of human sympathy; souls whose value to Him was far more costly than silk and rubies, whose liberty from satanic bondage had already been bought by the extreme value of His suffering and death. They were precious trophies to be won and given to the Glorious King.

She thought of Jemani's conversion and wondered how many others on Kingscote might learn of Christ if her father had a small chapel built on the plantation. But then she remembered Rajiv and shuddered. Who would dare come? And at what cost?

Coral decided that the idea of a chapel, like a momentary flame, was best left to flicker and fade.

———

"I cannot understand it," Charles commented to Coral a month later. "Even though God knows I am grateful to teach music, I feel there is something more I want to do." He shrugged. "And yet . . . I see no possibilities."

"Maybe you should enter the ministry, like your father," Coral suggested.

"I have already prayed about that. I feel the need of some work outside England." He smiled ruefully. "I am easily swayed, I fear. I have been reading Brainerd and now have little on my mind but the savages."

"Perhaps you should speak about your concerns with Mr. Wilberforce, or Mr. Thornton."

"I have, and they arranged a meeting with Andrew Fuller of the Baptist Missionary Society. Who knows? Perhaps each of those steps will bring me to a new door."

For Coral, a new door opened a week later, when she learned of a growing Christian movement for children on the London streets called the Sunday School Movement, established in 1780 in some of the free churches.

The Sunday School Movement, made popular by Robert Raikes, not only emphasized the teaching of Scripture to children, but also instruction in reading, writing, and simple arithmetic. The concept had seized her interest at once, and upon mentioning it to Ethan, he offered to take her to observe the meetings.

"Anything, if it brings a smile to your face," he said, and took her gloved hands into his. "Coral, you are looking so well. My hopes for your complete recovery soar like an eagle!"

She smiled up at him. "I have so much to be grateful for, Ethan. The Lord is truly good. And I believe he has blessed you with wise medical knowledge. How good of you to look at Billy Morley today. He is an orphan, you know."

"I did it for you. I like to see you smile."

"There are so many like him on the streets who need a doctor. If only something could be done."

"For me, Coral, it is enough to see you well and strong again. The color is back in your cheeks, and your eyes dance."

She laughed and looped her arm through his as they walked from the small church built in the slums of London. "It is because it is spring."

"So it is." Ethan paused, and stooping to the ground, unexpectedly came up holding a bluebell in his hand.

249

"For you. The first bluebell of spring. Even the seamy side of London celebrates the good fortune of having Miss Coral Kendall walk her cobbles."

Coral smiled and took the small flower. Her eyes faltered under his intense gaze.

"I am indebted to you, Ethan."

His hand tightened about hers. "You are not well yet. But I will confess my selfishness. I like to hear you say I am the cause behind your smile."

"You are far from being selfish. No one could convince me otherwise."

"I want you to be indebted to me," he said lightly as they walked along toward the carriage.

Coral cast him a glance, laughing, but he was not smiling.

He stopped and turned to gaze down at her, his gray eyes bright and warm in the sunshine.

"I want you in my favor so you will not be able to refuse my marriage proposal. No—do not look alarmed. I am not proposing . . . yet." Ethan smiled. "I am willing to wait as long as necessary. But I will be sorely disappointed if you will not become my betrothed before you return to India."

Coral looked down at the bluebell, feeling the breeze touch her bonnet, and his fingers tighten on her wrist. Betrothed to Ethan . . .

"You know the entire family expects us to marry."

"Yes."

"I will be pleased enough to have you as my wife, Coral. Yet, I want it to be your wish also."

Her voice came with poise: "I will be truthful. Until now I was more concerned with discovering the extent of your Christian faith than anything else."

"And now?"

Coral had to admit Cousin Ethan's behavior was

above reproach. She had only to mention a meeting, and if he were not on medical call, he would show up with his carriage. The mention of London waifs being taught in the Sunday school, and the sickness of some of the children, had prompted him to come today to treat them as best he could. *"I have always considered John Wesley's free dispensary in London a godsend,"* he had said. *"There ought to be more."*

Coral had no justification to doubt his Christian faith. And he was stable. Reckless adventure was the furthest thing from his mind. She respected all of this.

"I . . . I am growing fond of you, Ethan."

His hand squeezed hers. "I am more than delighted. I will be wise and say no more now." His voice became cautious. "Then there is no one else?"

"Oh no," Coral rushed to reply.

He smiled. "As long as you say that, I will try to be patient."

"Oh!" A sudden gust sent her blonde curls and bonnet flapping in the wind, and the bluebell in her palm scattered its petals across the dirty London street.

"Come, I will buy you an armful of roses," he said with a laugh and swept her across to the waiting carriage.

Coral, laughing too, glanced back to where the bluebell now lay strewn on the cobbles, and somehow her laughter died.

———

Spring of 1798 came to London with the nodding heads of many bluebells and the delicate scent of lilacs; and Uncle Hugo, Margaret, and Belinda departed on an East Indiaman, bound for Calcutta. Coral stood with Ethan, Grandmother Victoria, and her sisters on the East India dock, watching the ship leaving the harbor. She felt the crisp sea breeze on her face and lifted a gloved hand to wave goodbye.

The outward-bound East India Fleet paraded down the English Channel. The nautical sight took her breath away. She counted at least twenty great three-masters in double line, escorted by proud Royal Navy frigates. The East Indiamen crested through the choppy sea with flags billowing triumphantly from their mastheads, the white canvas swelling out like clouds against the gray-blue sky.

A diverse collection of passengers lined the rail on every ship for a final glimpse of England. Coral could make out soldiers on their way to join the Company's army in Calcutta or Bombay, women seeking husbands, Company officials—like Sir Hugo—and their families taking up a new post, and undoubtedly, adventurers out to seek their fortunes in the East.

"It is the first convoy of the season to be sailing to the Orient," Ethan told her.

Thinking of ships sailing in the Atlantic brought Coral's mind to Michael and inevitably to the derelict young adventurer who was responsible for his death.

"We will see them again in Calcutta," Ethan said in her ear.

Coral looked at him. He was smiling, his gaze sympathetic, and she understood that he had mistaken her gravity for sadness over her family's departure. She smiled at him, then looked back toward the departing ship.

Now I am free to seek Director Rawlings.

18

The letter from Sir Hampton arrived in June. Wishing to be alone with its contents, Coral slipped away from the others and went upstairs to her room in Roxbury House.

After shutting the door behind her, Coral tore the envelope open, and with shaking fingers, read her father's scrawling hand:

Kingscote, November 1797
Dearest daughter Coral,

Your mother and I have received a double sorrow. A letter from Captain Buckley arrived last week. By now you also know that Michael was lost at sea. Your mother has taken his death well, yet Alex is most grieved, and we do not know what to do. He has turned uncontrollable, angry with God and man. Remember to pray for him, for this is a sore tribulation for your mother and me.

As for little Gem . . . God rest his soul. It grieves me to the core that Sir Hugo told you the circumstances surrounding his death. He has written ex-

plaining the reasons why he was forced to do so. Your mother and I were worried about your health. It seemed best to us at the time to spare you these details.

Yes, your uncle was with me that dreadful night when many from Kingscote were out searching for Gem. As Hugo said, it was Natine who found him washed up from the river. But it was I who identified the little one—what was left of him. He'd been attacked by the crocodiles and was beyond recognition. However, it was Gem, despite your convictions to the contrary. He wore the nightclothes he had on when he was stolen from the nursery, with his name embroidered on the bedshirt, and the tiny gold cross was yet about his neck where you placed it at the time of his adoption. I have enclosed it within this envelope for you to have. Proof, dear daughter, that our heart's wishes cannot change what is the will of the Almighty.

I am sorry to write you these dark words, but you wished to know, and I could not keep them back any longer. I was concerned with shielding you from the ugliness of his death. While there is no evidence as to who is responsible for this wicked deed, I am sure it is the work of someone on Kingscote—or in the village—someone resentful of his Christian adoption.

May God's peace keep your heart. If you love your father, you will not let this loss shroud your future with continued unhappiness and ill health. You must choose to get on with your life, and look forward to marriage with your cousin Ethan, your own children, and a future on Kingscote."

Always with love, your father,
Sir Hampton Kendall

With blurred vision, Coral stared at the tiny gold

cross resting in her palm. Her heart swelled with re-newed grief. It seemed only yesterday that she had placed it around Gem's neck.

She walked to the velvet settee and sat down. At-tacked by crocodiles . . . beyond recognition. . . . Her mind wrestled with a dim possibility. Was Jan-Lee correct? Was she being unrealistic, groping at illusive bubbles? It dawned on Coral that her father had not mentioned her ayah, or the scar that Coral had in-quired about on the heel of the child. Perhaps Jan-Lee would write.

Coral struggled to keep a firm hand on her racing emotions. Suppose the abductors had done this hide-ous thing to convince Hampton to stop the search? It would be simple enough for them to have exchanged garments.

Her decision came calmly enough and brought new resolve. *I will not be able to get on with the future until the questions about the past are settled in my heart. I owe it not only to Gem, and to myself, but to Ethan.*

At the East India Company, the odor of ink, paper, and lamp oil beset her nostrils as Coral was an-nounced and ushered through the heavy oak door of the director's suite. The first thing that greeted her was a large desk on which lay an open leather case holding a menagerie of exotic safari miniatures: Bengal tigers, cheetahs, monkeys, birds, and even crocodiles. Coral was immediately intrigued.

Sir Edward Rawlings, director of the company, had an oil lamp pulled close to his silver head while looking through a magnifying eyepiece. He was so en-grossed that Coral wondered if he knew she was there. She saw that he was evaluating a carved ivory ele-phant, and what appeared to be its mate sat before him. Were the green eyes made of jade or emerald? Her father had spoken of his old acquaintance as a shrewd man, and the affable English gentleman before her was not what she had expected of Sir Rawlings. In reality, he was a key figure in a network of varied individuals who dappled in the dark and dangerous world of Eastern intrigue. The network was one of several working against each other for various causes. "A delightful surprise to meet a daughter of Hampton."

His voice broke the silence, and startled her. He did not look up but went on with his examination of the elephant. "Do have a chair, Miss Kendall, and tell me what brings you here. I suppose your uncle has sailed for Calcutta by now?"

She did not know why she was surprised that he would mention the departure of Sir Hugo. Naturally, as director of the Company, Rawlings would know what Hugo Roxbury was doing.

"My uncle and his family sailed last week. The governor-general has given him a new position, although I know little of what it is. I believe it has something to do with Burma."

Rawlings looked up for the first time, his sharp gray eyes analyzing her. "You are aware that the king in Assam has signed a treaty with the Company? Thankfully, war has nearly ceased. You say there was an attack on Kingscote a couple of years ago?"

"Yes, that is why I am here. My child was abducted. However, the attackers were not Burmese, but Indian. They were sepoys."

Rawlings looked horrified. "What! Sir Hugo said nothing of the abduction of a European child!"

Coral hastened, "Gem is of Indian blood." Seeing his disinterested expression she added firmly, "He is adopted, possessing the same rights and privileges as any child born into the Kendall family."

A shaggy white brow arched with understanding, but surprise. "I see . . . sepoys abducted him you say?"

"Yes, I entered the nursery as Gem was being carried out onto the verandah . . . I tried to stop the sepoy, but to no avail. I caught a good look at him. He was definitely of East Indian blood. I am here, Mr. Rawlings, because I believe Gem is alive, even though I was informed of his death."

"And what exactly is it you wish of me?"

"My father has spoken of you. I . . . understand you are acquainted with many adventurers in India and Burma. I wish to hire a mercenary to try to discover my son's whereabouts. I want to know for certain if he is alive or . . . dead. And if he is alive I want to get him back. I will pay handsomely for any information."

Rawlings ceased to examine the carved elephant and turned instead to study her, as if pondering whether the determination of such an unworldly young woman should be taken seriously. He looked down, inspected the elephant again for another long moment, then spoke.

"The governor-general in Calcutta has already been in touch with Hampton about the attack on Kingscote. Officially, the Company can do little more, except send word to the raja asking his cooperation in turning up any new information on the boy's abduction. All that, I am sure, has already been taken care of by Hampton."

"And unofficially? Are there not other doors to knock at?"

Rawlings set the elephant aside and scrutinized her again. "Quite . . . but as a friend of Hampton, my dear, I hesitate to involve his young daughter without his prior knowledge. Hampton is not likely to approve of your dabbling in intrigue, and if he wished to use those doors himself, he could."

"He has not done so because he is convinced Gem is dead. My father can be a stubborn man, Mr. Rawlings. He loved my son, and feels his loss. If I can get some glimmer of hope proving Gem is alive . . . I am sure he will listen to me and pursue the matter on his own. But my uncle has convinced him that my determination to find Gem is born of ill health."

"Sir Hugo?"

"Yes."

The older man drummed his fingers, watching her, and Coral was sure she would fail in her endeavor when suddenly he reached for a pen and ink.

"I can give you the name of a man in India who may be able to help you. He knows the area well and has contact with Indian and Burmese spies." He looked up, his sharp eyes meeting hers evenly. "Without apology, I warn you now that this will cost you."

Coral's heart thudded with excitement. "I shall do all I can to meet the price."

"A mercenary risks his life. They do not work cheaply. His contacts also expect to be paid for their risks."

Coral had no money except her allowance while in London, but she pushed that from her mind for the present. "I understand." She must also wait until she arrived back in Calcutta . . . but to have even the name of a mercenary was a start. Suddenly she felt elated. Was the Lord going to answer her prayers after all?

Rawlings folded the paper and placed it in the envelope. "I take it you are not returning to India for a time."

"I am afraid not. There is some schooling to attend, and I am under a physician's care for tropical fever."

"Nasty business, the fever . . . had it myself in younger years." Rawlings paused a moment, studying the young lady before him. "Miss Kendall, I need not tell you to guard this name carefully. Do not banter it about. When you arrive in Calcutta, contact him at the address given in this envelope. I have given you his pseudo name. As I said, it is a risky business."

"Yes, I understand." Coral placed the envelope in her bag with trembling fingers. "Thank you. You have been very helpful, Mr. Rawlings, very kind." She smiled. "My father was right about you. You are a friend, indeed."

Rawlings stood, smiling, and held out his hand. "Let us hope Hampton still thinks so when he discovers just how I have helped his daughter."

───────

Besides the Clapham meetings in the library of Henry Thornton, Charles Peddington was also attending what was known as the Exeter Hall group.

Here in the hall in London, where most of the missionary societies held their annual gatherings, the debates were having so strong an influence on the nonconformist community that the government was being swayed to act favorably on missionary matters.

"Especially the notion of white settlers and traders exploiting the natives in the colonies for gain," Charles told Coral.

Charles had just come from one of the meetings, and Coral noticed that he appeared more excited than usual. "I met Andrew Fuller tonight, from the Baptist Missionary Society. He told me about William Carey, and I knew at once that you would be interested."

"William Carey?"

"He sailed to Bengal in 1793. Mr. Fuller has said that Carey intends to translate the Scriptures into every language of India!"

"India!" Coral cried with delight.

"It was Master Carey who first founded the Baptist Missionary Society. Doctor John Thomas came from Calcutta in 1792 and spoke to the group at Kettering, and Master Carey was there. Thomas spoke of the poverty and superstition, and of three brahmins who sent him a letter pleading for help. The Society accepted Doctor John Thomas as their representative. But that is not all. As Thomas spoke to the missionary gathering in Kettering in 1793, he pleaded for others to aid him in the colossal undertaking. It was Master William Carey who stood to his feet and volunteered to go to India with him. Look—I have brought you Master Carey's treatise on world missions. They say it is a literary masterpiece, a charter for the church."

Coral took the pamphlet and read the long and laborious title:

"An Enquiry into the Obligations of Christians to Use Means for the Conversion of Heathen in which the Religious State of the Indifferent Nations of the World, the Success of Former Undertakings, and the Practical Ability of Further Undertakings Are Considered."

"Andrew Fuller was there the night Doctor Thomas spoke at Kettering," Charles went on. "He knows William Carey well. He said that when Carey got up to speak, he vowed right then and there to go with Thomas. Thomas then jumped to his feet, and falling on Master Carey's neck, wept with joy.

"Andrew Fuller said, 'There's a gold mine in India,

but it's as deep as the center of the earth.' He asked, 'Who will venture to explore it?' and Master Carey said, 'I will venture to go down, but you must hold the rope.' "

Coral was moved and sat staring at the pamphlet.

Charles laid a hand on hers. "And Coral—I vowed to the Lord tonight at Exeter Hall."

Her eyes rushed to meet his. "You?" she whispered.

"I do not know what the Lord may have for me, but . . . hearing about India from Andrew Fuller was all I needed to convince me to join my brother Franklin. He is at Calcutta working for the East India Company. I hope to find William Carey and Doctor Thomas."

"Oh, Charles . . . when will you go?"

"Soon. In fact, I am going to tell my father and sister tonight. Franklin has been after me for years to join him. But it was not until talking to Andrew Fuller about Doctor Thomas and Master Carey that I knew what I wanted to do." He took her hand. "Now I know why the Lord brought you into my life, Coral. You have showed me the heart of a nation called India. Through your eyes I have seen her need, her pain, and her beauty. It is where I belong."

Coral's eyes welled with tears.

"And, our friendship can continue after you go home," he said. "I will be able to visit you and your sisters at Kingscote."

In her bedroom, Coral prepared for the night, situating herself beneath the satin covers, pillows fluffed behind her back. With the lantern lit on the stand beside her, she began reading the eighty-seven pages of William Carey's pamphlet—the work of eight years.

Carey's knowledge of world geography, of the racial and religious conditions of the heathen, and of the profound difficulties in bringing the gospel to the world was remarkable. Coral was awed.

Having come from India, she could easily relate to Carey's zeal and compassion for the lost. Her heart knew a sudden excitement as she read how God had filled his mind and soul with the command to go into all the world and proclaim the gospel.

And now he is there, she thought. *He is in* my *India!*

Coral read in the pamphlet that the command to go, and the promise of His companionship, was not simply to the apostolic church, but to all Christians of every generation.

When she finished reading, she laid the pamphlet aside, picked up her King James Bible, and turned to Isaiah 54:2–3, the scripture reference that Charles had written down from William Carey's sermon to the Baptist Missionary Society.

Enlarge the place of thy tent, and let them stretch forth the curtains of thine habitations: spare not, lengthen thy cords, and strengthen thy stakes; For thou shalt break forth on the right hand and on the left. . . .

The words pulsated with holy passion as she imagined Carey preaching on them at the meeting in Nottingham on May 30, 1792. The words of his message became burning coals from the divine altar as though they had been winged her way by seraphim. She visualized not a simple shoe cobbler turned village preacher, but a flaming minister of fire, who with silver sword unsheathed, challenged the slumbering to wakefulness.

"Onward! Outward! Does not His soul thirst for the

thousands, yea millions languishing in Satan's domain, uncontested by His soldiers? Loose the bars, break the chains asunder, proclaim liberty to the captive, offer sight to the spiritually blind; why do you slumber with sword in sheath, and armor set aside? Awake O sleeper!"

For Coral, it was as if God had picked up a quill and began to sketch His will upon her mind. Kingscote sprang up before her, and she saw the hundred Indian children working in the hatcheries.

> *Sing thou barren who bearest not, break forth and cry thou who travailest not, for the unmarried woman hath many more children than she who hath a husband!*

The Scripture verse leaped from the page and demanded her attention.

These, Coral thought, *these children forgotten by all but God are* my *children. It is these that I must go back to Kingscote to save.*

The illusive child she sought in her dream represented more than Gem. The child became many bronze babies; the distant laughter of Gem became the voice of a hundred children calling her to rise up to their need.

Coral's heart pounded. *Oh, Lord, is it possible?* Would He allow her, in the memory of Gem, to reach the untouchables?

But how could I help a hundred children?

Robert Raikes and the Sunday School Movement came to her mind. A school . . . of course. Teach them to read, to write . . . teach them Bible stories and help them to memorize Scripture. What nobler cause is there than this?

Coral remembered how well she had taught Gem. Even though a small child, he had been able to repeat part of John 3:16. If she could teach one, she could teach many. If she could love one child, then God's bountiful love flowing through her could love a hundred, yea a thousand.

Lord, I have prayed so long for guidance . . . is this your Spirit speaking to me? A school? But, how? Coral's pragmatic nature asked.

Her eyes fell on the challenging statement of William Carey that Charles had written across the pamphlet—

"Expect great things from God; Attempt great things for God!"

"Lord, if you make me well enough to go home to Kingscote, I will try to start a school to reach the little children. In your name, I will touch the untouchables."

Late that night, Coral sat at the desk and wrote her mother about William Carey and his work in India. She explained her desire to build a small school on Kingscote and concluded with the verses in Matthew 19:13–14:

Then were there brought unto him little children, that he should put his hands on them, and pray: and the disciples rebuked them. But Jesus said, "Suffer little children, and forbid them not, to come unto me; for of such is the kingdom of heaven."

19

May 17, 1799

Coral's trembling hand held the letter and she slowly sank onto the velvet ottoman in the parlor. Kathleen and Marianna knelt beside her, looking over her shoulder to read the letter for themselves.

Coral struggled to keep her voice calm as she read aloud to her sisters, while Grandmother Victoria stood nearby without moving, her handkerchief knotted in her hand.

Kingscote, October 1798
Daughters,

Circumstances on Kingscote require the three of you to interrupt your stay in London and make arrangements to come home without delay. I will soon be in touch with Seward, who is in Darjeeling. After the death of Michael, he offered his services should I ever need them, and I have no doubt I can depend upon him now. I anticipate his presence in Calcutta to see you safely home by safari. I wrote to Alex in Austria last month. By the time you receive this letter he will have already caught ship and should arrive at Kingscote ahead of you.

Sir Hugo and Margaret are in Calcutta. They will work with Seward to see to your care. I expect you to be there for some weeks until matters are securely arranged for the journey. Aunt Margaret will explain in detail the circumstances requiring you to come home.

> *With deepest love, your father,*
> *Sir Hampton Kendall*

Coral sat there unable to speak. She heard Marianna's voice catch with emotion. "It is Mama! I know it is! Something has happened to her!"

Grandmother came to her swiftly, and Marianna went into her arms. "Child, we do not know that. Oh, drat that Hampton! He should have explained more! He might have known the tumult he would cause!"

"Surely he has written to you, Grandmother, explaining everything," said Coral. "No doubt Father sent both letters at the same time, but yours somehow got delayed." She added quickly, "That *must* be it."

"This means I will never get to work at the Silk House," cried Kathleen. "I do not want to return to India!" She rushed to her grandmother. "Granny V, do something, anything! You promised me! You said Jacques is going to turn me into the finest couturiere!" Her golden-brown eyes pleaded, and Grandmother looked distraught.

Marianna lifted her heart-shaped face, her cheeks wet. "Sissy, how can you even think about yourself at a time like this?" she accused, her tone suggesting that Kathleen was betraying their mother and father.

"We do not know if anything has happened to

Mama!" Kathleen retorted. "You always think the worst."

"Stop it, both of you," ordered Grandmother Victoria. "Heavens! This is no time to be attacking each other like two cats. Simms!" she called, banging her cane on the floor several times. "Simms!"

"Here, Madame!"

"Call Ethan. Tell him to come at once. I do not care what he is doing, tell him I want him now."

"Yes, Madame."

Coral stood slowly to her feet, still clutching the letter, struggling to keep her fears hidden. "Maybe Kathleen is right. We do not know the circumstances behind Father's request for our return. If . . . if anything did happen to Mother, he would have told us."

"Unless it was like you first said," argued Marianna. "That a letter to Granny V giving details has not arrived yet."

"But there could be an entirely different reason why he has sent for us," insisted Coral.

"Then why did Papa not mention Mother in his letter?"

Coral pushed back her alarm. It would be a long voyage to Calcutta. And Marianna's insecurity would not make it easy. "I do not know . . . but Father has written us other letters without mentioning her."

"That is true," said Grandmother hopefully. "And we did receive a letter from Elizabeth only last month."

"Yes, but she wrote it six months ago," whimpered Marianna.

Coral's attention turned from the others to Kathleen. She had walked to the window and stood with her back toward them. Coral could sympathize with her desire to stay and continue her work with Jacques, but what could she expect Grandmother to do? Their father had made his request clear.

Coral walked up behind her sister, noting the familiar stance that announced one of her difficult moods. Kathleen could be stubborn, and when she was, no one could control her except Grandmother.

"I am sorry, Kathleen," she said softly.

Kathleen made a helpless sound and only shook her head, fingering the brocaded drape and reminding Coral that there was nothing she could say to soothe her disappointment. Still, she tried.

"I understand how disappointed you feel—"

Kathleen turned, her emotions breaking like a flood. "No, you do not. No one understands but Grandmother." Her amber eyes flashed. "No one cares anything about who I am. I am simply expected to do whatever I am told . . . and smile prettily."

Ashamed to release her tears in front of them, Kathleen's jaw clamped, and she brushed past Coral and walked swiftly from the room, banging the door behind her.

Grandmother lowered herself into a chair, her own disappointment etched on her face. "India," she breathed. "Cursed place."

Coral looked up from the letter to meet the piercing blue eyes of her grandmother.

"I want to speak to you later this evening in my room," said Grandmother. "Ethan will be here soon. As much as I deplore doing so, we will need to make immediate arrangements for passage to Calcutta."

"Yes, Granny V."

Grandmother Victoria raised herself to her feet with her walking stick. "This is not the end of matters. If necessary, I shall one day journey to India myself to convince Hampton that Kathleen belongs in London with me."

That evening, Coral entered her grandmother's chambers.

"Ethan has arranged everything," said Coral. "We shall set sail Thursday on the *Red Dragon*."

"Oh dear, so it has come to this moment, has it?"

"Do not cry, Grandmother, I will not be able to bear it if you do." Coral swallowed back the ache in her throat as she embraced the strong-willed, but frail elderly woman, and for a moment they clung to each other.

"I shall miss you, Granny V. Know that I have appreciated everything you have done for me. I will always love you, and I will be back someday . . . wait and see. And Kathleen and Marianna too."

"That is not why I asked you here," came the hushed, tearful voice. "I want you to have this."

Coral's eyes widened as Grandmother Victoria removed from her finger the family signet ring, studded with heavy rubies and diamonds.

"Grandmother, I could not—"

"Nonsense, I will see it with no one else but you. There is Kathleen, of course, but I am leaving her some other things. This ring I want you to have. It has been in the Roxbury family for generations. It is worth a king's ransom."

"Grandmother, I—"

"Here, take it. I have also left you a sizable inheritance in my will. Say nothing to the others."

"But Granny V—"

"Hush." Her eyes twinkled mischievously. "I shudder to think of Sir Hugo's reaction, however . . . I am certain you can use this more than the others."

Coral was moved by her grandmother's trust. She enclosed the family ring in her palm, her eyes moist. "Thank you. Perhaps someday I shall bring Gem here to Roxbury House."

Grandmother searched her face, then smiled knowingly. "You went to see Director Rawlings?"

Coral's eyes glimmered with determination. "Yes. I am going to hire someone to search for Gem."

"A word of advice: Say nothing about this to the other members of the family, especially your uncle Hugo."

"I do not intend to."

"Listen, my child, if you change your mind about India, you can always come home to Roxbury House. . . . which reminds me, Ethan is disappointed you are leaving. Do you not think you should settle matters between the two of you first?"

"I—I cannot, Granny V. I have other plans that are more pressing now." Coral hastened, "I'm sure Ethan understands. He has said he is willing to wait."

Grandmother looked dubious. "What plans do you speak of?"

Coral took her grandmother's hand into her own. "A Christian school on Kingscote for the Indian children," she stated quietly.

Grandmother said nothing for a minute and only stared into Coral's eyes. Then a sigh escaped her lips. "In memory of the boy? Well, you will not likely get the family's support, but I can see that the notion means a great deal to you. You are quite independent when it comes to planning your future. But Hampton and Elizabeth will have something to say about it. Tsk! Enough said. If they agree, I too, will support you. And if you find this Indian child—I want to see him."

Coral threw her arms about her, laughing and crying all at once. "I knew I could depend on you! May God make it so, Grandmother."

20

Calcutta, India
October 1799

Jace Buckley strode through the bazaar, ignoring the excuses of his Indian friend and financial partner, Gokul. At the moment it looked as if they were out of business.

Gokul, huffing in order to keep up with the purposeful stride, held palms against his rounded belly protruding beneath his white tunic and hurried along.

"But, sahib," he objected, spreading his hands, "it was not my blame! Would I lease the *Madras* to John Company if knowing what their cargo would be?"

Jace ignored him. His chiseled features were set beneath his trimmed beard—which he still intended to get rid of—and his dark blue eyes reflected a hardness contrary to his age. He wore buckskin trousers and a loose-fitting black Indian tunic, with his prized toledo sword belted comfortably around his hips; it was a blade that belonged, one used with skill.

Jace stopped abruptly and stared down at the little man. "We both know what John Company is. You

273

leased *my* ship to China traders, knowing full well what the cargo would be and the risk to the *Madras*."

"Ah, sahib!" Gokul corrected. "Patience, patience. It is *our* ship. We are partners, you and I, is it not so? We are as they say—'compatriots.' " Gokul gave a placating smile, but it died under Jace's narrowed gaze.

"*Our* ship, unfortunately," Jace relented. "But I am the captain."

"The best captain to ever sail the sea!" Gokul quickly agreed, his white teeth gleaming beneath his gray mustache.

Jace strode forward with Gokul hurrying after him. They owned half of the ship; the rest was debt. Gokul's weakness of taking risks to win the bigger prize was always the thorn between them, but this time Jace was furious. Having sold the Moorish heirloom to Rawlings on his last trip to London, he and Seward had invested the money in Darjeeling, intending to give Michael's share to his younger brother, Alex, though the matter had not yet been worked out. He had not seen the younger Kendall son since sailing with Michael. Seward had told him that Alex was in Vienna.

Gokul winced. "Sahib, what was I to do? We had only a dozen rupees left in fund. Payment from the China traders would buy us clipper."

Jace groaned at the thought. "Another run to London and I would have had the finances to pay her off. You botched up everything, Gokul! I just signed on with the Company to sail. Now? Nothing! We do not even *have* a ship."

He did not want to hear the excuses again. Thanks to Gokul, his hard-earned clipper had been leased to scheming smugglers in the John Company. Jace strode ahead. He had arrived in Calcutta that morning from

Darjeeling expecting to meet Seward and to ready the clipper for the voyage to the Spice Islands. Seward had sent a message from the residence of Sir Hugo Roxbury explaining that he would not be sailing this time. Out of dedication to the Kendall family, he had gone ahead and accepted a temporary position with Sir Hampton to escort his daughters home to Kingscote.

Not that it matters now, Jace thought grimly. *There will be no voyage.* The *Madras* was tied up in harbor at Singapore, impounded by the authorities for carrying a cargo of illegal opium! To free his "first love," Jace had to come up with a great deal of money; money that he and Gokul did not have. Jace feared he may lose the *Madras*.

Gokul scurried after him, nearly colliding with a cart of coconuts. "Wait, sahib!" The golden monkey clinging to his back squealed his displeasure. Goldfish decided to abandon his ride and leap ahead to his master, lightly zipping his way across several carts and onto Jace's back, clutching his black cap.

Gokul stopped breathlessly and threw up his hands, watching until Jace disappeared into the throng. Even Goldfish had turned his back on him. He sighed dejectedly and turned to go back to the small booking office near the harbormaster at the East India dock. Sahib would never forgive him, and did he blame him? It had been a foolish thing to do.

His brows curved downward over eyes the color of midnight. Jace had not yet heard the worst. Burra-sahib Colonel Warbeck had heard about the fate of the *Madras* and was most anxious to use the dilemma to bring his son back under the British military. Warbeck would not be content until his son was back at his side in the uniform of the 21st Light Cavalry. Jace would most likely strangle poor Gokul when he returned to the house they shared in the Chowringhee area and found the letter from Colonel Warbeck.

Gokul sighed. *Nashudani!* he thought of his own actions. Good for nothing!

———

Coral stood with Kathleen and Marianna amid the noisy throng, waiting for Seward to arrive with a dak-ghari. The carriage would bring them to the honorable East India Company, known as Fort William, and to the Roxbury residence of Sir Hugo and Margaret.

The first thing Coral and her sisters did after disembarking the *Red Dragon* was to turn to Seward with worried, questioning faces, their voices interrupting each other:

"Is Mother well?" rushed Coral.

"Is she dead?" quavered Marianna.

"Why did Father not explain why he sent for us?" demanded Kathleen.

"Now, little lassies, of course Miss Elizabeth be alive."

"You see, Miss Pessimist!" Kathleen said to Marianna. "All your fretting during the five-month voyage was a waste."

"But yer dear mother be ill with the fever," continued Seward.

"Oh no," came the echo of alarm.

"Aye, 'tis so. And Mister Hampton, he be wantin' all of his children home on Kingscote."

"Is Alex home now?" asked Coral, hoping her father had her brother's support.

"Aye, he arrived before ye, and he be helping yer father."

The news of her mother coming down with the fever alarmed Coral, and now, as she and her sisters waited for Seward to arrive with the ghari, she wondered just how ill Mother might be. She said nothing to her sisters, but she could not imagine their father insisting they all come home as soon as possible if her health was not seriously deteriorating.

Coral squinted. After growing accustomed to the misty gray of London, the stark white heat and dust of Calcutta was suffocating. The sun glared down, and the crowd of people in the bazaar reminded her of a swarm of locusts. Providing an annoying background hum was the persistent drone of gnats enjoying the overripe mangoes stashed on the cluttered fruit stalls. Everywhere, insects.

Coral smoothed back a stray curl from her face, then felt Marianna's hand on her arm. "Look, Sissy, everything from coconuts to jade and silk." Marianna peered excitedly about the bazaar.

The sight of throngs of people in various costumes identifying their castes was always intriguing to Coral. She was especially interested in the women who covered themselves from head to toe in what was called a *bourka*, a garment with only two slits in the veil to see through.

"At least they do not need to worry about flies," quipped Kathleen, swishing her peacock fan in front of her face. "Oh, where is Seward?" She turned to fix Coral with a scrutinizing look.

Coral saw the apprehension in her sister's face, and guessed that Kathleen noticed the faint shadows reappearing under her eyes. *They must not know how exhausted I feel.*

Kathleen eyed her suspiciously. "How will you manage the safari to Kingscote? Perhaps we should stay in Calcutta with Aunt Margaret until Father himself comes for us."

Coral was not about to delay the journey and forced a bright smile from under her wide-brimmed straw hat.

"Do not worry about me. Why, I could not feel better. Besides, we have several weeks to recuperate before Seward can arrange the safari. I would trust Seward with my life, anywhere."

"And," said Marianna wistfully, "the journey will seem short knowing Mama waits for us."

"It will be dreadful," stated Kathleen wrinkling her nose. "And furthermore—"

Coral was not listening. Her attention was diverted from her sisters to the dusty road where a group of thin walnut-skinned children clothed in soiled loincloths gave up looking for food in the gutters, and gathered near a silver-haired guru seated beneath a large spreading banyan tree.

The bewildered expression on the little faces, the haunted look of hopelessness in their large dark eyes arrested her emotions. The children were listening to the guru's every word, watching his every action.

Coral shielded her eyes and peered across the street. "Look over there. What on earth. . . ?" The guru's cobra now began to sway to the dismal music of its charmer.

There was a cloud of dust, and with it came the sound of squealing children. The squeals were a mixture of fright and pleasure as they gathered closer around the old man and his lethal toy.

"No doubt the guru has convinced them he can talk to animals," said Coral, irritated by the deception.

"Stay out of it, Coral," warned Kathleen. "Seward will be here any minute."

"Wait here," Coral said, her determined voice allowing for no argument.

"Coral Kendall! Come back here this minute!"

Coral ignored Kathleen's warning, pushing her way through the throng.

"Coral!"

Kathleen's protest was buried in the din. Coral stopped before the stall selling *jellabies*, fried sweets made of a honey batter, and handed the man in a dusty white turban several Indian coins, or "pice."

"Jai ram," she greeted the man in Hindi.

He offered a namaste by bringing his palms together to touch his forehead. Coral filled a basket with the goodies and set out toward the children gathered about the guru.

Jace strode purposefully through the bazaar, shouldering his way past the stalls. Somehow he had to come up with the money to free the *Madras*. He would not accept failure.

A black crow swept in front of him and landed uninvited upon a cart of fast-spoiling fruits. With practiced thievery it managed to fly away with a section of juicy mango. Jace's gaze followed the bird to the branch of a large banyan tree across the dirt road. Beneath the branches sat a wrinkled old guru.

The crow promptly dropped its treat into his master's lap.

Jace watched with irony. The guru had trained his crow well—and there were more. At least a dozen perched in the tree. Meanwhile a crowd of children gathered around the holy man. The sight was a familiar one, and Jace was about to walk on when he glimpsed someone passing by that should not have been part of that foul-smelling crowd.

A young English woman, alone. She was wearing a dark blue silk dress with puffed sleeves and white silk ribbons and was holding on to a broad-rimmed straw hat. Her skin was like ivory amidst a sea of black, her mass of golden curls cascading about her shoulders. The vision was balm to a wound, shade from the white-hot sun. And like the tea plantation and his clipper, Jace momentarily savored the thought of possessing the beautiful damsel.

His eyes narrowed a little. Walking to the edge of the street, he lowered his black dusty hat against the glare of heat rising from the ground and strained to see where this vision had evaporated to.

Half-naked children played in the dust, soon joined by an old gray elephant longing for azure waters. Finding none, the lumbering animal contented himself with a shower of dust on his back.

No, the sun had not gotten to his brains, Jace decided. Nor had she melted in the heat. She was real. The woman stood in the midst of the bone-dry road with a basket of goodies on her arm, a fragile contrast to the harsh and brutal background of dust and sweat.

Jace frowned as he followed her gaze to the children. *Do not tell me she is going to hand out treats? She will be mobbed in seconds!*

He glanced about. Where was her father? There was not an Englishman in sight.

By her sympathetic reaction to the children, Jace judged her to have recently arrived from London, fresh from English tea parties. There were many such ladies who came to the Company to join their fathers or to marry. Like the others who came, he supposed that this damsel also felt compelled to hand out treats to the starving children of Calcutta.

Jace smirked. The "blossom" would soon wilt and

retreat to the refuge of the East India Company, sheltering the like-minded wives and daughters of the military. India could not be won so easily.

The old guru sat on a raised earth platform held in place by some stones. His legs were crossed under him, and his rheumy eyes stared ahead, ignoring the sun. His arms lay still at his sides; not a muscle stirred to interrupt his trance, despite the crawling flies. The only clothing he wore was a soiled loincloth, and his bronzed skin was wrinkled, thin, and hardly sufficient to cover his bones. His white hair was long and snarled; a dirty gray beard rested on his sunken chest cavity.

The woman's voice reached Jace through the noisy din about him. He listened intently, for she spoke Bengali as fluently as he did. Strange . . .

"Children, over here! See? Look what miss-sahiba has for you. You would like some, would you not?"

Jace Buckley stood with hands on hips watching. As if she needed to ask! In a moment they would be on her like an army of war ants.

The children had not heard her invitation, so intent were they on the Guru's cobra.

Jace left the stalls and stepped into the road. He moved toward her, pausing a few feet behind.

"Someone needs to warn you that you are asking for trouble."

She whirled. From beneath the large straw hat he felt the impact of bright green eyes under heavy lashes, an alluring face that left little room for his cynical emotions. He paused—

Where have I seen her before? But if he had, she did not recognize him.

He gestured his head toward the basket on her

arm. "Hand out those and you will be mobbed. Where is your father?"

He saw the distinct glimmer of annoyance at the word "father." It amused him.

"I admit the plight of beggars and orphans is unnerving to ladies from London," he continued flatly. Folding his arms across his chest, he scanned her. "But you will get used to it. They all do."

Little of his own feelings at having been an orphan were revealed in his tone. He knew well what it felt like to go days without food. But his armor was in place—where he intended to keep it. Vulnerability was not an asset for survival. He intended to survive, and he was not about to let his guarded emotions suddenly stumble over an alluring face.

Her expression, he noted, suddenly became a mask of anything she might have felt, although a tinge of color had crept into her cheeks. Her eyes tore themselves from his to fix upon Goldfish chattering at her from Jace's shoulder.

"I was born in India, sir. And I do not intend to grow callous to human misery."

He smiled slightly, and a brow shot up. "I stand rebuked for my unsympathetic ways."

She gestured toward the guru. "And he is deceiving the children. They ought to be warned."

Jace realized that there was much more to the fragile blossom than scent. And while the faint dark shadows beneath her eyes said that she might wilt in time, there was something of steel in her convictions. He said calmly, testing her resolve: "Better watch that cobra."

Appearing undisturbed, she turned her head to study the guru. "Obviously," she countered evenly, "it is defanged."

No swooning damsel, this. She also knew the tricks of some of the fakirs. He glanced at her exquisite frock with its ribbons. "You should not wander about alone."

"He is beguiling them. He cannot talk to animals," she said with growing frustration.

"Half the world is deceived."

She stared at him, her lashes narrowing. His mouth moved into a smile. "My apology. Let me put it another way. If you interrupt the guru, you will get nothing for your pains but that trained flock of crows in the tree. See them?"

She glanced up, squinting against the sunlight at a dozen black shadows perched amid the branches of the banyan tree.

"I am not afraid of crows."

Jace did not know what to make of her. He lowered his hat, arched a brow, and unexpectedly turned to walk away, whistling. "Anything you say."

Coral cast a narrowing glance at him over her shoulder as he crossed the street. There was something familiar about him—the way he talked, the way he handled himself. His dress and brash attitude told her that he was an adventurer, but she could not recall having met one while in London, or for that matter, in India. As such, he was a man to avoid.

She noted that he wore an Indian tunic, but an English cap that looked rather arrogant rested jauntily on his dark head. Was he as cynical as he looked? One thing was certain: the man was conceited, she decided. His beard was well-trimmed, and of the latest fashion, and his hair fit the style of a spoiled cavalier. *Like Absalom*, she thought.

Coral watched him stop before one of the stalls, completely ignoring her, and buy some fruit for the golden monkey, which was jumping up and down and doing cartwheels.

Whatever his faults, there was no mistaking the man's knowledge of India. She respected that. So many of those who came from England to serve in the Company knew next to nothing of the heartbeat that belonged to the land and its people.

She dismissed the handsome stranger and turned away. Holding to her hat, Coral walked in the direction of the tree, speaking to the children.

"Stay away from the munshi," she called in Bengali. "He cannot talk to animals. It is a trick."

The children glanced around, puzzled by the voice. "No trick! No, holy man he has ways, you see!"

"It is a trick," she insisted. "The munshi cannot talk to animals."

Coral held out a sweet bread and smiled. Luminous dark eyes widened and grins spread across dirty little faces. A shout went up like the sound of a battle charge, and a surge of midget troops rushed toward her, jumping up and down, pushing at each other to be first, and snatching at the basket. In a moment it was knocked to the dirt at her feet, and they crawled about her like ants. Within seconds the sweet treats were devoured, and the swarming children cried for more.

"Missy-sahiba, missy-sahiba, hungry!"

"No mother! No father!"

Annoyed at losing his audience, the guru raised his head and mumbled something. Suddenly a circle of black crows swooped down from the tree, the breeze from their flapping wings reaching Coral's face. Children's laughter and cries subsided into oppressive silence. Bird claws dug into her hair and pecked at her shoulders. Flapping black wings blinded her vision while deafening caws crashed against her ears. Coral slapped frantically at them, trying to back away.

The vicious whip of a bullet glancing the air scattered the crows as quickly as they had descended.

Coral was still trembling with fright when the adventurer she had shunned propelled her away, leaving the guru with his rheumy eyes fixed north toward the Himalayas.

"Oooh—I feel as if there is bird lice in my hair . . ." Coral reached a trembling hand to straighten her hat. It was missing. She looked back to see the children running off with it. She began plucking the feathers off her silk dress. "He . . . he just made a noise and they came swooping down on me."

"The crows are trained."

"Thank you . . . for shooting your pistol. I . . . ah . . ." she stopped, finding his gaze disconcerting.

"We have met somewhere," he said.

Coral hesitated, reluctant to agree. "I don't believe so," she said, turning away. "Excuse me. I must go now."

"Next time you take on a guru, make sure he does not have a nest of trained cobras instead of crows. They are not always defanged. And you will not have my gallant presence to come to your rescue."

Her eyes dropped to his scabbard, looking for the hidden pistol.

"I will remember that."

"I am certain we have met before. Cadiz?"

"No . . . excuse me . . . I must go—"

"Paris."

She could not help but smile, turning her head away as she did and looking in the direction where she had left her sisters. "I hardly think so. I have never been to Paris."

"A pity. You would fit so well. Where is your father? As I said, you should not be wandering around alone."

"I am not alone, sir."

They were interrupted by an Indian in baggy white trousers who ran up and salaamed.

"I come for you miss-sahiba. Dak-ghari wait now. Follow please? Missies very upset."

"Yes, yes of course." She could imagine how angry Kathleen was. Coral turned to Jace. He watched her, his hat pulled low over his eyes. "Good day, and . . . ah . . . thank you," she said.

"My pleasure."

Jace stood watching until she disappeared with the ghari-wallah into the throng. "Goldfish, I forgot to get her name."

The monkey covered his eyes with his thin furry hands.

"Yes, I quite agree."

21

"Why, being born a silk heiress is positively dangerous," declared Marianna, her strawberry curls bouncing beneath her blue lace bonnet as the ghari jostled down the crowded, dusty street. "Who was that man, Coral? And how could you be so bold as to talk to him like that? If Aunt Margaret finds out, you will be scolded again."

"I do not know his name," admitted Coral, "but he saved me from that pack of crows."

Marianna pressed on. "Granny V said we must be on guard against all manner of fortune-hunting men." Her expression turned dreamy. "We may get as many as a dozen marriage proposals. Just think. We will always wonder whether our husbands married us for love, or silkworms!"

Kathleen made a face. "What a horrid thought . . . competition from a caterpillar . . ."

Marianna sighed wistfully. "I wonder who I shall marry."

"I do not care if I ever marry," announced Kathleen, looking out the ghari window. "In fact, if I were free to do as I wished, I would stay single and be quite content in London working at the Silk House. Granny V has already written Mama and Papa about my return."

Kathleen looked back at her sisters excitedly. "Imagine—Granny V said someday I could oversee the entire Silk House. I may even open a new one in Lyons, France—perhaps I shall go there on my own!"

Marianna's eyes widened. "Why, Sissy, how can you say anything so scandalous? If a girl does not marry and bear children, simply *everyone* gossips about her. How could you endure it?"

"I could bear most anything to oversee the Silk House," said Kathleen, her amber eyes gleaming.

"Your dreams are so strange. All I want is to get married soon, have children, and live happily on Kingscote. But, Sissy—you know Papa will insist that you marry Captain McKay."

"That rogue!"

"He is bound to be at the ball," said Marianna.

"Then I shall avoid him."

Marianna turned an imploring gaze on Coral. "Sissy, what about your ball dress?"

"Hmm?" said Coral absently. She had been wondering why Seward had not showed up with the dak-ghari. The ghari-wallah had explained only that Seward had been intercepted by a sepoy and had gone to see Colonel Warbeck at the garrison.

The mention of the colonel had jarred a memory of something her mother had once told her, that Jace Buckley was the colonel's adopted son. Thinking of him brought a pang of grief as Michael's smiling face flashed across her mind.

"You are not listening!"

Coral turned her head to look at her younger sister. "Can I wear the blue silk ball dress tomorrow night?" begged Marianna. "You said it was a little small for you, and it is so much prettier than my own, and so much more grown-up."

Coral smiled indulgently. "Yes, you can wear it. It will suit you."

"Coral, you spoil Marianna," said Kathleen. "You look so nice in the blue. You are much too generous. I realize Cousin Ethan will not be there, but—"

"But blue is *my* color," pouted Marianna. "And Coral looks good in any color. You said so yourself. So did Jacques."

Coral was no longer listening. Thinking back to their arrival that morning at Diamond Point, she recalled that Seward had manifested little of his usual cheerfulness. She had first thought that his behavior must have something to do with their mother, but now she wondered. Had he been expecting the sepoy? Why would he go to see the colonel?

The ghari turned under the branches of the gold mohur tree at the entrance to the carriageway, and the Roxbury residence came into view.

Double-storied and painted white, it sprawled lazily in the cool shadows of thick trees growing along the bank of the Hooghly River. Coral suddenly felt a rise of pleasure at being back in India.

The familiar cackle of mynahs and the shrill call of peacocks filled the sunny afternoon, flooding her memory with happy thoughts of Kingscote. While in Calcutta, she would see the Indian mercenary about Gem, and in two months or so, Coral would be home on Kingscote, running up the staircase to her mother's bedroom, bringing the needed medication from cousin Ethan.

Between the colonnades on the verandah one could see the harbor and the ships belonging to the traders. Red flagstones encircled the verandah, and purple bougainvillea twined the columns, adding an artist's splash of color against the stark white stone.

The excitement grew as the ghari neared the front entrance. Coral scanned the host of servants who were waiting. Sir Hugo had more servants than good taste allowed, she decided. Each one was dressed in the customary attire: white trousers and long shirts for the male servants, and the women wore their colorful chunnis over straight, ankle-length tunics.

The ghari door opened, and Coral was the first to step down onto the drive. She smiled at the small Indian boy who proudly presented her with a pink parasol. Under her smile, his shy dark eyes faltered downward to gaze at his bare feet.

From the verandah someone called out, "The missy-sahibas have come."

Aunt Margaret and cousin Belinda swept across the lawn in their afternoon dresses, amid the armada of Indian servants carrying parasols. Indian sun was considered the worst of evils to English women. Even their children were not allowed outside without a large hat.

Coral masked her weariness. She felt the familiar wave of the dizziness that continued to plague her. She would not mind staying home tonight and going to bed early, except that she had promised Ann Peddington to deliver a package to Charles, who was now working at Master Carey's mission station. Coral had been told that Charles Peddington would be at the ball because of his brother Franklin's position in Government-House.

Amid embraces and laughter, the barrage of greetings and questions swelled together into a crescendo.

"Did you have a good voyage? Any storms? Oh,

that is quite too bad! But here you are. . . . Coral! How worn you look. I hope this has not been too much for you. . . . Did Ethan see to your medicine before you left? Thank goodness for that. . . ."

Coral walked beside Aunt Margaret as the small entourage made its way toward the shadowed verandah. The heat outdoors was left behind as they entered a hall bordering a colonnade. Water trickled over a fountain, and vines with blossoms trailed over the screened roof. The temperature was surprisingly cooler, reminding Coral of Kingscote with its acres of mulberry trees.

Her sisters and cousin climbed the wide flight of stairs toward the bedrooms, talking of the ball and Belinda's upcoming engagement, but Coral lingered to speak with Margaret alone.

"Girls," Margaret called up the stairs. "I understand you have much to talk about, but lunch will be served in an hour. Then you must separate for the afternoon and nap until the ball tonight." Belinda turned to look down at Coral, her dark eyes flashing with anticipation. "I was explaining that the ball is going to be even more splendid than we thought. Coral! It is going to be a state ball held at Government-House! Father says most everyone is coming, including the military."

As the trio disappeared down the hall, Margaret looked after her daughter, and Coral noticed the troubled expression. Cousin Belinda had written that her engagement to Sir Arlen George was to be publicly announced this Christmas holiday at the round of festivities at Barrackpore, despite her best effort to thwart her father's wishes. And Coral suspected that Aunt Margaret was concerned over Belinda's obvious disinterest in Sir George.

"She cannot wait to get your sisters alone to press them about what Alex is doing," said Margaret wearily.

What Alex may have thought of his cousin, Coral did not know. The one woman he did mention was Katarina Fredricks, the daughter of his music instructor in Vienna.

"Elizabeth wrote me several months ago about Alex's interest in a Miss Fredricks."

"Does Belinda know?"

"Yes. He has written Belinda about her, although Belinda claims Alex thinks of her only as a friend. I admit that I am quite concerned. Her engagement is to be announced this Christmas."

Coral knew little of her brother's romantic life while in Vienna. "He has not mentioned Katarina in his letters to me, but then, Alex is closed when it comes to discussing his feelings about marriage."

"I wish Belinda were a little more like you," said Margaret as they climbed slowly up the staircase. "You have always been sober-minded, so much like Elizabeth. I am afraid Belinda takes after me. I, too, was a trifle frivolous at her age."

"I cannot imagine you ever being flirtatious," said Coral in surprise.

"Not exactly flirtatious, but I thought I knew what I wanted in a man, and was determined to have my way, until . . ."

Until what? Coral wondered, but did not press when her aunt said nothing more. Had there been someone else other than Sir Hugo? She reminded herself again that she would exercise great caution when it came to her own marriage.

"She is young," said Coral graciously. "Belinda will settle down once she marries Sir George."

Margaret smiled ruefully. "Belinda is only six months younger than you are. If Alex was not at Kingscote, I could wish to send her home with you."

"I am sure Belinda would find my life unexciting," said Coral with a little smile, thinking of her cousin's busy social life.

"I am not so sure about that. You will stir up a hornets' nest if you insist on your idea of a school for the untouchables."

Coral looked at her with surprise. "Who told you about the school?"

"Elizabeth mentioned it in her recent letter."

"Mother has not even responded to my request yet. I am surprised she would write you about it. What did she say?"

"Very little. I do not think she has told Hampton yet. And now that she is so ill, she is not likely to. I must say, however, that your uncle is upset about the idea of the mission school."

That did not surprise Coral. He had opposed the adoption of Gem and had manifested little sorrow over his abduction. She knew that she must move with caution.

"Granny V thought there were possibilities for the school," said Coral. "I discussed it with her before I left."

Margaret smiled. "Mother would, of course. She has always encouraged young women with conviction. But she is limited in her understanding of India. Especially of the risks involved to the silk enterprise should the natives become offended with the English presence. Hugo is convinced we must keep our religious beliefs to ourselves."

Margaret's brown eyes flickered with uneasiness and she paused on the stairs. "I hope you will reconsider bringing the matter up, especially with Elizabeth so ill, not to mention your own health. I doubt if Ethan will approve of putting yourself at risk."

Coral drew in a breath. Now did not seem the appropriate time to promote her cause. "At the moment, all I want is to get home to Kingscote."

"Yes, I understand your concern for Elizabeth. But your uncle thinks the school is the reason for your return. I told him that he must not be too hasty, but you know Hugo."

Yes, she did know him. Coral tried to smile. "I did not realize my arrival had caused such a stir. One would think my plans for a school would put an end to the East India Company itself."

Margaret smiled. "At times it does appear a tempest in a teapot, as they say, but after the fire on Kingscote the night Gem was abducted, you can understand the family concern. Sericulture is a family enterprise, and anything you wish to do on your own, such as starting a Christian school, will require approval from all of us." She looked at Coral with sympathy. "I understand your loss over Gem. But a school will not fill that void. Marriage, and your own children, will." She laid a hand on Coral's arm. "I hope you will not upset your uncle. He has been difficult to get along with recently. All that trouble in the north with Burma has him on edge."

Coral chose not to reply, although she disagreed with Uncle Hugo's views. Kingscote was owned by the Kendall family, and if her parents permitted her to build a school, Sir Hugo had no right to throw obstacles in her path. *I must leave all this to the Lord,* she thought. *Only He can make a way.*

"I have been thinking about that fire, Aunt Margaret. I believe it was merely a diversion and not intended to destroy the silk hatcheries."

Margaret hesitated. "I thought of that."

Coral looked at her in surprise. Aunt Margaret had never talked much about that night on Kingscote.

"But, Coral, it is best to forget the entire matter. Why stir up more trouble? Anyway, dear, Hugo is concerned that teaching Christianity may bring down a mutiny upon our heads. He fears that even the Company may be put at risk to the zealots if we give them cause to resent our presence."

"Nonsense, Aunt Margaret. He is overreacting."

Margaret chuckled. "Oh, dear. Do not say that to your uncle. He claims the zealots wish to expel the English from India. And after all we have done for India, too."

A slight flush crept up Coral's cheeks. "Some would say that the Company has done precious little except to use the culture to support its financial pursuits."

"Missionaries would say that, of course. The Company insists they are meddlesome extremists. I have not formed an opinion either way."

Coral made no comment as they made their way up the last round of steps, lifting their skirts as they went. The silence grew awkward. The bearer named Pandy—back and head erect, his blue turban spotless—led the way, making certain that he did not outdistance their slow procession. At the landing he turned to wait for them.

"I understand Charles Peddington will be at the ball tonight," Coral said, intentionally changing the subject.

"Peddington? Oh, the young music instructor you had in London."

"I promised to deliver him a package from his sister."

"Perhaps Pandy can deliver it for you."

"I would rather give it to Charles myself. I thought perhaps he might attend the ball, since he has an older brother who works for the governor-general. A Mister Franklin Peddington."

"Franklin! Of course! I had forgotten Charles was his brother. The two men are so different. Then yes, I suppose he will come. Franklin is secretary to the governor-general. An important position. Too bad about Charles," Margaret said as they reached the landing. "I would think that an industrious man like Franklin would speak to his brother about supporting William Carey's work."

"Oh! Then you know of Master Carey?"

"Only indirectly. The Company is concerned about his printing press, although he does have a friend in Governor-General Wellesley, who appointed him to the staff of Fort William College. But most in the Company oppose missionaries. The other day there was a near riot by brahmins because of some sort of leaflet being distributed on the streets of Calcutta. Do you know this missionary?"

"I have read his work on evangelizing the heathen. Charles is supporting his work. But, honestly, I cannot imagine Master Carey deliberately affronting the brahmins. There must be a mistake."

Coral hoped to visit Master Carey and see his work before returning to Kingscote. From Aunt Margaret's reaction, she could see that this would prove difficult without upsetting the family.

"I am certain Master Carey would be wise enough to not hand out printed matter attacking the Hindus," continued Coral. "He has a genuine respect and love for the people and understands the grave difficulties of introducing Christianity in this culture."

"There are those in the Company who say he and the other missionaries should be deported to London."

"Deported! The East India Company has no right to do that."

Margaret gave her a measured look.

"I mean," said Coral, hesitating, "it would not be a just action. William Carey is a Bible translator. As such, he would not be out stirring up the Hindus. That is not his purpose. I know this, because there are a number of Hindus working with him on the Bengali language. They do not feel threatened by his beliefs. Why should the Company?"

"Well, I know little about the translation of the Scriptures, dear, but your uncle insists that it is bound to stir up trouble eventually. And he is not alone in his belief."

Coral said no more. Neither the Kendalls nor the Roxburys were known for their Christian zeal, although they did attend the Anglican church on holidays, at births, and at funerals. The need for the translation of the Scriptures into the Indian languages was not an important priority on their minds. If she had anyone to turn to in the immediate family, it would be her mother. Coral felt tense. Just how ill was her mother?

As they reached the door to Coral's room, Pandy left them. Through the open doorway, the mahogany floor gleamed with polish, and lace curtains fluttered beneath the ceiling fan called a *punkah*. Made of canvas stretched on a wooden frame, it was pulled vigorously by a small shirtless boy in short white pants to make a breeze. She recognized him as the child who had handed her a parasol upon leaving the ghari.

"You can go now, Jay," said Margaret.

Coral smiled at him as he grinned, salaamed, and ran out.

"They are all darlings. Another untouchable . . . they are everywhere." Margaret sighed. "I will send one of the girls to fill the tub and lay out your ball dress." She scanned Coral's face, evidently noticing the fatigue. "I will have your lunch sent up. That way you will have several hours to nap."

"I would like that. I am tired."

Pandy reappeared with a tray bearing a tall glass of cool lemon water. "For Missy," he said.

Coral smiled. "Marvelous, Pandy, thank you."

When he had gone, Margaret lingered at the door. Coral began removing her gloves, anxious for a cool bath.

"Coral, forgive me for having put this on you the moment you arrive, but . . ." She cast her niece a nervous glance.

"No need to apologize," Coral insisted.

"Hugo and I think a great deal of you."

"Oh, Margaret, I know that. You need not explain." Margaret continued to linger as though feeling the need to convince her about Hugo.

"Your uncle has always had an ongoing interest in your education and future. More so than for Kathleen. It may seem we intrude a little too much." She smiled, and the inner tension showed. "He is so hopeful of your marriage to Ethan. That would almost make you his daughter-in-law."

"I realize Uncle Hugo looks on him as a son, but I would rather not discuss my involvement with Ethan now."

"Yes. And Coral, you will not upset your uncle by mentioning your interest in a school for the untouchables? At the moment, politics in India are unsettling; more so than when you left. You will be careful?"

Coral was weary and anxious to rest. She smiled and gave her aunt a kiss on the cheek. "Do not worry. I shall be discreet. For your sake."

Margaret gently touched Coral's cheek with her palm. "I knew I could depend on you. Hugo and I are already strained over Belinda's upcoming engagement. I should hate to make more tension between us by needing to defend your school."

Coral felt uneasy. The last thing she wanted was to cause more trouble in the family.

"Better get some rest now. With such a pretty face there will be a dozen soldiers wishing to dance with you."

Margaret opened the door, but Coral's question stopped her.

"The ghari-wallah told me that Seward went to see Colonel Warbeck. Do you know why?"

Margaret hesitated. "I did not wish to alarm you so soon after the war with Burma, but one of the military wives mentioned that her husband had news of several sepoys arriving last night from the military outpost at Jorhat."

Jorhat was not too many miles from Kingscote.

"Seward went to see the colonel to discover what information the sepoys may have brought."

Coral was suspicious. "I was told that it was the colonel who called for Seward."

"Yes, that may be. John—" she stopped and a tint of color came to her cheeks. "Ah, the colonel will want to make sure the area is safe for your travel. But I would not worry. The ball is still scheduled, so I suspect the news cannot be all that serious. Perhaps another border skirmish with Burma."

Coral had grown up on the northern frontier amid the tension with Burma. It was not unusual to be seated at the breakfast table and hear her father discussing the fighting between soldiers of the Maharajah of Assam and Burmese infiltrators. War had broken out in 1792, and the East India Company had signed a treaty with Assam to protect them. The war was mostly over now, but there were, as her aunt had said, incidents along the border. It was true that life on the silk plantation was a pleasant one; but the Kendalls were under no illusions. Their subculture in India could crumble with slight provocation. She must not allow anything to keep her from getting home.

The door closed behind her. Coral fell across the cool white sheet and sipped the lemon water while listening to the Indian girl fill the tub.

There came a tap on the door, and Marianna tiptoed in. Her strawberry curls framed her small face, now flushed with excitement. She looked around for Coral's trunk.

"Coral, you promised I could wear the indigo."

Coral smiled wearily and pointed toward her trunk. "Yes, you had better hang it up."

"Oh, Coral, thank you. You *are* going, aren't you?"

Coral yawned. "Yes . . . I need to bring Anne's package to Charles Peddington."

"What will you wear?"

"Oh, I do not know . . . maybe the jade."

"You look good in green. It matches your eyes. You can wear my jade earbobs and combs if you like."

Under Marianna's prodding, the Indian girl had opened the trunk, and the shimmering indigo silk was brought out. Marianna embraced the multitude of folds to her cheek.

300

"I am going to waltz and waltz until the sun comes up!"

Coral watched her younger sister leave the room, anxious to show off her prize.

She swallowed a teaspoon of the bitter medicine that Ethan had prescribed and quickly took a mouthful of the cool lemon drink.

"And you, Miss Coral? So many pretty dresses!"

The girl carefully emptied the trunk, hanging the frocks in the wardrobe.

"Um . . ." said Coral sleepily, setting her glass down on the rattan table beside the bed. "Silk . . . and from a humble caterpillar . . . the ways of God are mysterious and breathtaking." She could hardly keep her eyes open. "I will wear the green."

"Oh, very pretty!"

As the girl shook out the dress and hung it up, Coral watched the breeze from the verandah lift the yards of the skirt and billow it outward. Jacques' design would be lovely, the jade-green reminding her of the soft richness of the tropics. Coral's eyes closed while she imagined hearing the songfest of birds in bright plumage in the jungle around Kingscote . . . she could almost hear the distant rumble of a Bengal tiger . . . and that made her think of a certain golden monkey that she had seen dangling on the back of the handsome adventurer at the bazaar.

22

Stars were white against the ebony sky. The heat remained oppressive even though a light breeze from off the Hooghly River touched his face. Jace was in a reflective mood. He would have his first meeting in almost seven years with the man who had raised him after his father's death—Colonel John Sebastian Warbeck. It promised to be uncomfortable.

"Ye be lookin' like ye did in the old days," Seward commented as they climbed into the rickshaw that would take them to the East India Company. He cocked his head to scan Jace approvingly. "Maybe not quite. Ye be lackin' the uniform."

Having shed his worn buckskin trousers, Jace felt a stranger in the black broadcloth, the spotless white frilled shirt that tightened at the wrists, and the blue sash. His boots were polished, his sword gleamed, and as Seward said, he looked again like the prized son of the burra-sahib, the colonel. Jace had even shaved his beard and cut his hair.

"I will not be staying for the ball," Jace stated, as though Seward intended to chain him there for the night. "I do not like these gatherings. I never did. I am to meet with the colonel. That is all."

Ahead, Jace could see the familiar outline of Fort William, which housed the Company and its large contingency of workers, families, and soldiers. It was built on the river's bank, surrounded by a strong wall with gates. He had been a boy when he first arrived here with Warbeck. The Company had ended up being his home until after his graduation from military school.

As the rickshaw left the outlying districts of Calcutta and entered the fort, the houses of the English and other Europeans came into view—some of them very fine, even extravagant, and boasting lush botanical gardens.

"Old memories stir like ghosts, do they not, lad?" remarked Seward. "I be thinkin' of the time we served together on the frontier under the colonel."

Jace smiled grimly as he followed Seward's gaze. The lamps outside the quarter guard of the 19th Bengal Native Infantry were bright; the sepoy sentries stood guard in red coats and shakos. His own regiment, the 21st Light Cavalry, was still on duty at the outpost in Jorhat on the northern frontier.

The court buildings and jail loomed ominously against the night sky. At the north end of Maidan Square, the lights burned brightly in Government-House and fell softly across the grass and shrubs of the garden. Near the gate pillars, a half-dozen sepoys stood guard, swords at their sides.

Jace watched the affluent symbols of the honorable East India Company pass by, as though regiments on parade. As the adopted son of Colonel Warbeck, he was an heir to its spirit and ambitions, but Jace had shed his uniform and allegiance to the Company to forge his own way. Now, that gate of freedom, through Gokul's rash actions, had been barred shut.

Jace had been born in and of that empire, but still he was not sure that he agreed with the power created by the Company, which had made itself lord of the maharajas. Two centuries had passed since the first envoys had come to Agra and convinced the great Moghul king to let them build a small trading post beside the Bay of Bengal. Now the Company's authority over India had so expanded that the presidency of Bengal alone ran from Calcutta to Assam.

Someday, thought Jace, English control would most likely sweep across Burma and Afghanistan. Today there were independent provinces yet remaining to the rajas; however, most of these states were forbidden to make treaties with each other or with any foreign power.

The Company, which had begun as a humble trading corporation, was now a colonial lord. The governor-general made treaties with maharajas, enforced the peace, sent out its own tax gatherers—and made war from the Bay of Bengal to the borders of Sikkim. The trouble that brought Jace here tonight was in the region of the northeast, and the man who was England's chief representative in India, the governor-general, had unlimited power in India. Jace knew that when he spoke, a formidable army would move in obedience to the supreme authority in England, His Majesty King George.

In fact, the governor-general controlled the troops of the presidencies in Calcutta and Bombay in the south. Some 200,000 Indian sepoys and sowars serving under British officers in regiments controlled by the East India Company moved at his command, as did the king's 15,000 all-British troops.

Jace found his resentment toward the Company an odd thing to define. He owed his survival as a boy

305

to Colonel Warbeck. His military education, his success in the Company—all had been made possible by the colonel. In return, the colonel demanded his dedication to the cause of the Company. For a time Jace had cooperated; he had even told himself that he wanted nothing else but to serve the Company's ambitions. But later he found himself at odds with many of England's goals in India. When he could no longer follow the leadership, he shed his uniform to chart his own course. Now Jace was once again under the colonel's command.

"I see the Government-House be still in the process of completion. A wee bit like Kedleston Hall in Derbyshire, England, do ye not think, lad?"

"It is the habit of an Englishman," said Jace dryly, "to take their home with them wherever they go."

Seward chuckled. "One would think your blood be less than pure English, talkin' that way. Don't forget, I was a friend of yer father when you was still in knee pants. A truer Englishman ye'll not be findin' anywhere, not even in Oxford."

Jace might have smiled at that bit of rhetoric. However infamous his father's reputation as a China trader in John Company, he was said to have been the younger son of a renowned Buckley family in London. Jace had often tried to recall memories of England; yet he could remember only the rough deck of the ship beneath his feet, the smell of tea, spices, and the dialects of strange ports like Cadiz in Spain, or Malaysia in the East. When a boy, Seward had once suggested to him that his mother had been the deceased Lady Anne Wimbleton, whose father had been stationed at the Company in Bombay. At the time Jace had been naive enough to believe it.

Jace turned toward the Hooghly River. In the dark

were the shadowed hulls of ships and the sound of water lapping against wood.

"No use thinkin' of the clipper, lad. Unless ye go along with the colonel and put yer uniform back on, ye won't likely be seein' the beauty again."

Jace knew that. His stepfather was not a man known to be given over to sentiment, even when it came to his son. Colonel Warbeck was as tough and demanding as the empire he helped to rule. He wanted his son back in uniform beside him, and he would not give up until Jace relented.

He would not relent.

Jace interlocked his fingers behind his head and continued to gaze up at a black sky laced with white pearls. "I was remembering the feel of the deck of the *Madras* beneath my feet; the cool foamy spray wetting my face, the salty taste touching my lips, the sound of gulls—"

Seward moaned. "Hush, lad, the sea still pounds its waves in me own blood."

Both the clipper and the lush cool tea plantation in Darjeeling were fast slipping through Jace's fingers. Like the sands in an hourglass filling its world with tiny grains of white, he too would soon find himself buried in the grip of the Company.

Jace fingered the letter from the colonel beneath his jacket. Seward jumped down from the rickshaw, a ruddy man in a battered tricorn hat and buckskin coat, his even white teeth showing in a grin beneath the wide bushy mustache. "Good luck, lad. I be leavin' ye here. I've business with Sir Hugo Roxbury aboot the trek to Kingscote."

Jace watched Seward disappear through the shadows in the direction of the commissioner's office, then he turned his attention back to the great hall of

Government-House. The state ball was under way. He sighed again, and his boots crunched across the gravel. Chinese lanterns were brightly lit along the front verandah, and orchestra music drifted through the open doors and windows. Jace would not stay long; he was in no mood for festivity.

He went up the steps and entered the wide hall. Through the arch he could look into the huge ballroom, its floor recently polished to a glassy sheen. Lights dazzled from the ceiling, chains of flowers and greenery were strung for decoration along the high walls, giving a palatial effect. The guests were already waltzing, and for a moment he watched the blur of swirling ball dresses amid a floral garden of colors, mingling with the spotless dress-uniforms of familiar regiments and fine civilian clothing of the men serving in the governor-general's council. Indian servants, in white turbans and knee-length coats with red sashes, walked about with silver trays. Across the large ballroom, an orchestra sat on an elevated platform and played the popular waltzes from Vienna.

" . . . I say! Our safari after tiger—"

A voice blurred with the drone of others about the room as Jace began to maneuver slowly through the guests. Colonel Warbeck was nowhere in sight. A woman was coming toward him, and he recognized her as the granddaughter of retired officer Henry Tilliton.

"Why, it is Major Buckley, isn't it?" said Mrs. Marcia Tilliton, swishing her fan, her eyes suggesting they waltz. "Conway was remiss in letting us know you were back in Calcutta," she said, her smile turning to a demure pout.

Bowing a little, Jace acknowledged her greeting, all the while wondering how he could escape. At the same time he met the gaze of Miss Cynthia Daws, who flushed with pleasure. She leaned toward the dowager who sat beside her and said something. Immediately, the dowager looked at Jace and beamed, then struggled to her feet.

Jace turned to flee only to find Marcia Tilliton still at his elbow. Just then a young man in the white and scarlet uniform of the 88th came up, tapped his program, and said cheerfully, "By golly! Number three—this waltz is mine, I do believe, Mrs. Tilliton?"

"Oh my, yes, so it is, I had nearly forgotten!" She turned to Jace apologetically.

"My loss," murmured Jace gravely.

He disliked dancing and moved quickly toward the verandah where he could avoid the guests but safely spot the colonel.

It was sultry for October. Usually the weather had begun to cool by now. Not even the light breeze coming through the windows brought much relief. He stepped aside as a couple left the darkened verandah and passed by him on their way toward the dance floor.

His gaze swept the ballroom, searching for the colonel. Then Jace saw her, and paused. Her expression appeared oblivious to the festivities about her. She stood alone, midway up the winding staircase, while ladies made their way up to refresh themselves in one of the guest rooms. She was holding a package, and glancing about as if expecting someone. But of course, she would be.

She was wearing shimmering silk the color of jade, over an enormous billow of crinoline, with three deep flounces at the left side gathered up with white lace. Her golden tresses were swept up into a mass of French curls and decorated with jade combs, and exquisite jade ornaments dangled from dainty ears.

Ah ... the beautiful damsel he had seen at the bazaar ... the woman rattled off Bengali like a native and was not shy about confronting a guru and his crows.

Jace studied her appreciatively for a moment, then as her eyes made a full sweep of the ballroom, they passed him, paused, then quickly looked away, only to come back to him with surprise.

Obviously she remembered him from the bazaar, he thought. But no, he had shaved and cut his hair ... then—? He, too, hesitated. All at once something in her demeanor opened a door from the past, and he remembered.

Kingscote. So, this was the girl of the monsoon who had carried an Indian baby off to the Kendall mansion so many years ago ... that boy was now dead. How had she accepted the tragedy?

As they stared at each other, remembering, neither making any approach, he thought of the letter she had written to him about Michael. *She believes me guilty of his death.* He noticed an unexpected stiffening of her stance, and a look of coolness masked her features as she quickly turned her head away.

Just then, a young man, slender and somewhat unassuming, walked toward her from the other side of the room.

"Coral! How grand to see you here in Calcutta!"

"Charles!"

Jace watched her talking to the young man she had addressed as Charles, then Jace glanced about for a form he could pretend was his program. He saw a slip of paper on a table and picked it up. Recklessly he filled in her name for the evening. He was bound to get one of them. She was too polite to refuse him a waltz. After all, they had something in common to talk about. Michael was a good beginning.

An Indian servant appeared at his side and whispered, "Captain-sahib? Colonel Warbeck waits for you in the billiard room."

23

Colonel Warbeck stood in spotless black and white, the golden braid of his jacket reflecting the light of a chandelier. With concentrated precision, he leaned over the far end of the billiard table and made a smooth shot. Jace's entrance coincided with the loud smack of the billiard balls that rolled successfully into the various pockets.

"By the cock's eye!" blared General Basil, his shaggy white brows jerking together. His stubby hand, fitted with too many Indian rings, patted his portly belly. "A lucky shot, Colonel!"

Smiling, the colonel looked up to see his adopted son. "Not at all, General. A matter of calculation."

Jace wondered how much calculation had gone into his summons to see the colonel.

The colonel straightened. For an awkward moment, neither of them spoke. Jace was unreadable and tried to ignore the tug within.

A major, whom Jace did not recognize, left his place near the billiard table and came up behind him and closed the doors, shutting out the strains of the waltz.

"Jace," the colonel greeted, and gestured him with a wave of his hand to a winged chair near the open verandah.

He spoke with the voice of an oracle, a tone which Jace had automatically rebelled against in his youth after the easy rearing of his blood father. After military academy, however, he had come to expect the strong and clear commands of the British army.

Jace crossed the faded red carpet toward the cooler verandah, but did not sit. He scanned his father, noting that the years had not changed him, but then why should they? The colonel was too disciplined to change, or to grow flabby and indolent in India's heat.

Looking at his stepfather, Jace shielded his emotions. He could almost believe that they had never parted company, that the time span which had passed between them had not been years, but merely the length of a waltz about the dance floor at one of the many balls or dinners. The only thing missing for Jace was his own uniform.

Colonel John Sebastian Warbeck was a strong, handsome figure in his early forties, taller than Jace and pounds heavier, but solidly built and able to move with alert grace. His eyes were ice blue and glinted as keenly as sunlight on a frozen lake. Jace felt his eyes flicker over him, but they showed nothing.

His own words were abrupt but appropriate to the meeting. "You asked to see me?"

Colonel Warbeck said nothing for a moment, then set his game piece down and walked out onto the verandah. Jace followed, but remained in the shadows behind him. The colonel, holding the rail with large strong hands, gazed across the spacious courtyard where the colored-glass lanterns cast their light through the leaves of the golden mohur trees. Along the Hooghly River the breeze was a trifle more pleasant. Boats wound their way in both directions, their lights shining upon the water to warn of crocodiles. Palms grew thick along the bank, and the music from the orchestra filtered up to them from the ballroom below.

"A tea plantation," he mused. "You are serious about this?"

Jace was somewhat surprised, but he should not have been. Gokul had told him that his father kept informed of his ventures.

"Gokul was born in the area of Darjeeling. His claim of tea growing wild proved accurate. It can be cultivated and looks to be equal to anything grown in China. I intend to make Darjeeling tea a name known in London."

The colonel remained silent for a moment. "Too bad about your partner. A Kendall son, was it not?"

"Yes. Michael. Who told you?"

"Sir Hugo Roxbury. He did not mince words."

Jace gave him a measured look. "Meaning?"

"Only that as Michael's uncle, he finds it disturbing that he was lost aboard your ship."

Jace found his anger rising. He thought again of the letter that the Kendall daughter had written to him before he sailed from London. Had it been Roxbury who suggested to her that he had been drunk?

"Michael was like a brother. I explained what happened to the Kendall family. They have accepted my explanation. Who is Roxbury to question me?"

"It is best if you do not confront him now. He is a powerful man in Calcutta. A friend of the governor-general. There is a younger brother who Roxbury says is bitter toward you."

Jace thought of Alex. *Does he believe me responsible?*

"If Roxbury has anything to say of my behavior as captain of the *Madras*, he can say it to me."

"I did not call you here to question your behavior as captain, any more than I questioned your leadership when you were in the military. I suspect they are both above reproach."

"Thank you," Jace said flatly.

The colonel said nothing for a minute and Jace walked over to the rail.

"Roxbury insists the Kendalls have no interest beyond silk. Why would Michael have been interested in tea?"

"Sir Hampton is a born master of the regal caterpillar, but Michael wanted to branch out on his own."

"It is the way of sons to disown the paths of their fathers. As though disdain wins them their accolade."

Jace knew that he did not speak only of Michael but of himself. "You know how I feel about the Company. We debated the subject before I left, and came to no understanding." He folded his arms. "Why should I not be interested in a tea plantation? The trading routes into the East may become less rich and fat. Instead of the port of Canton, the Company's ships could be loaded with tea grown here in India. Our beloved King George is screaming for new markets."

The colonel smiled unexpectedly. "We will not argue. Tea it is, and I wish you luck."

Jace was taken off guard. Again, he measured his father, who continued to smile. He offered Jace a cheroot. Jace shook his head, and watched the colonel take out his pipe.

"I have a proposition for you," said the colonel.

Caution . . . He is laying a trap, thought Jace.

His father faced him squarely as his hand played with the hilt of his saber.

"I will be brief. Burma is a smoldering coal on a bed of dry wood. The war went well enough for us, but it is my opinion Assam will never be at rest until we enter Rangoon. A recent raid was made on the outpost near Jorhat."

Jace tensed a little. His friend Major Selwyn was now the commander of his old 21st Light Cavalry. Jace also knew the royal family of the King Gaurianath Singh, in Sibsagar, who had ruled Assam during the Burmese war of 1792. Assam was now a princely state. The raja had long been in disagreement with Burma over who owned the territory and had signed a treaty with the Company. Further trouble in the north could also affect Jace's holdings in Darjeeling, a mountainous region near the Himalayas. His personal treaty with the king of Sikkim giving rights to the hill of Darjeeling hung in delicate balance. The colonel was clever enough to understand that.

The colonel bit on the empty pipe. "You knew Major Selwyn?"

Jace's concern mounted. He did. They had gone to military school in London at the same time. The colonel's use of the past tense prepared the way for dark news. "Selwyn took my position when I left the outpost."

"Hmm . . ." the colonel sucked on the pipe. "A good man. Not as precise as you, but dependable for the sensitive position of Jorhat. Matters with Burma have quieted. You understand what could happen if Burmese are to blame for the attack on the outpost?"

War could begin again. "You do not sound as if you think they were involved."

"The dewan insists they were Burmese."

A *dewan* was the chief Indian minister. This one, Jace assumed, served the Maharaja of Assam.

"Roxbury backs him up," said the colonel. "And Major Selwyn was assassinated in the raid. Sorry."

The colonel turned away for a moment. "Roxbury blames Burma. I doubt it. They have denied it. You have friends in Rangoon who serve the ruling warlord. Have you heard anything about an attack on the British?"

"No. And I am inclined to agree with you. Burma is not ready to begin the war again."

"Selwyn's assassination could not have been instigated by Burma."

"That leaves the maharaja . . . or members of his family. Not all agree with his treaty with the Company."

His father's features hardened, and he glanced toward the billiard room. "Or someone closer to home. The question is, for what reason?"

Jace considered. He would not put anything past certain ambitious men in the Company in Calcutta. But what would they gain?

The colonel bit his pipe. "It is the motive that bewilders me. Why would anyone from headquarters want renewed trouble in the north?"

"To further personal aims perhaps."

"Before I can go to the governor-general, I need something I can get my hands on." He looked at him. "I think Major Selwyn discovered something and was silenced for it. I want you to find out what it was. How well do you know the royal family at Sibsagar?"

Jace hesitated. Selwyn's death prompted his interest in the incident, but he remained cautious. He knew his father was determined to involve him.

"The present raja is a clever ruler and a cunning warrior," said Jace. He thought of Rajiv, the husband of Jemani . . . "I knew his nephew. He is dead now. But he has another nephew, a prince—the Rajkumar Sunil."

Jace was not anxious to run into Rajiv's brother, Sunil. It was said by spies that Sunil intended to use a scimitar on his head. Jace had no doubt that he could protect himself, but he was far from desirous to do battle with him.

"Sunil blames me for a raid on a Hindu temple. A jeweled idol of Kali was stolen before I left the outpost. It was my name that was brought to the maharaja," explained Jace.

The colonel appeared alert, as though he might know something that he was not willing to share with Jace at the moment.

"You have heard of the stolen idol?" Jace prodded.

"Hmm . . . word of such matters travels swiftly. One of the soldiers involved in the raid on the outpost was captured. He is Burmese but has suggested the men he fought with were mercenaries, that they did not serve the warlord in Rangoon."

"Paid mercenaries. Interesting. Did he mention anyone hiring them from the Company?"

The colonel measured him. "No. That is why I called for you. He has asked to speak with you about it. He will not cooperate with anyone there."

Jace arched a brow. "He knows me?"

"He said only that he has heard of you in Rangoon."

Jace was silent. He had secret contacts in Burma.

The colonel passed over his silence and went on smoothly, "I expect your friendship with both the royal family and the Burmese warlord may be able to get to the bottom of what is going on. Your Indian shipping partner, Gokul, should also prove helpful since he is from the area. I want this ugly business swept clean before it erupts into another war. We cannot have our outpost attacked at whim and have the murder of our commanding officers go unpunished. If others see that we do nothing, it will open the door for any who wish to see the British out of Bengal."

"Now wait a minute. I did not agree to become involved—"

The colonel interrupted with a smile and a wave of his hand. "There is one other small matter . . . your clipper—the *Madras,* isn't it? You will be pleasantly surprised to learn that she will soon be at anchor in Diamond Harbor."

In Calcutta? My ship?

"Go to Jorhat. Discover the answer to what is going on, and the clipper is yours. Debt free. You will go, of course, in uniform. You will be reinstated as Major."

. . . *Debt free* . . . Jace stared at his father, then said flatly, "This is no less than extortion."

The colonel was undisturbed. He replaced his pipe inside his jacket. "I prefer to call it something different. Say—*confidence* in your military abilities. You have contacts in the Indian world that I do not. Find out what is going on, deliver the culprit behind this plot, and the clipper is yours. You shall soon be raising tea in Darjeeling."

As Jace watched, surprised, the colonel reached inside his jacket, producing a white envelope. He smiled. "The bill of sale. The impound fee is paid, and the charges of opium smuggling have been dropped."

Jace groaned within. He heard the prison bars of military life clanging about him.

The colonel would never be satisfied until his son

made the army his career, and Jace knew it. It was on the tip of his tongue to turn down the offer and walk out.

He bit back the words and for a moment was silent, not trusting his speech. He tried to remind himself that there was a man behind the spotless uniform, his adoptive father, and that the colonel's game of high stakes, however unfair from his vantage point, were played not in a spirit of revenge for his son leaving the military, but to bring him back.

"Major Selwyn was your friend. I would think you would want to discover his assassin and bring him to justice."

The colonel had touched a second chord of response. Along with the *Madras*, the death of Major Selwyn had all but sealed him back in uniform. The colonel's own plot was progressing as planned.

"I do not need to wear the Company's uniform to find out who killed Selwyn. I can do that on my own. In fact, I could do it better."

The colonel affected indifference. "Ah yes, I nearly forgot . . . there is one other small matter. You will also take up command of the post for two years. Use your discretion to execute the governor-general's policy at Jorhat. The arrangements for your travel are already in force. Papers authorizing you to take command of the prisoner will be given to you. Take the Infantry Company of the 16th with you."

So, his father had risked everything on the gamble that he would not be able to resist.

The colonel tapped the white envelope against his palm. There was a slight smile on the bronzed face and a melting of the hard blue glint. "Welcome back, Jace."

Jace looked from his father's face to the white envelope, and in his mind's eye he saw instead the white canvas of the *Madras* billowing in the warm trade winds. He could pay off Gokul for his small share of the clipper. No more John Company, no more hiring her out to pay bills. He envisioned the fair ship docked in the Calcutta harbor, all his own, and ready to haul Darjeeling tea. . . .

Colonel John Warbeck quietly laid the envelope on the rattan table and walked away.

Jace watched the breeze lift the edge of the white envelope. He sighed. *Major Jace Buckley Warbeck, reporting for duty.*

24

Coral was seated on a teakwood ottoman near the entrance of the verandah with her yards of jade silk gathered about her slippers. She sipped from a tall glass of sweet lemon sharbat, finding it cool and tangy. Across from her, Charles Peddington sat in a chair, exuberant over the Scripture commentary that his sister Anne had sent through Coral.

They sat away from the festivities, and Coral hardly noticed the glittering chandelier and the array of waltzing couples moving across the wide polished floor. The strains of the orchestra danced on the warm night air, and mingled with laughter and voices, but it was the surprise of seeing Jace Buckley that still held her attention.

He was in Calcutta! Did she dare question him about Michael? He had not answered her letter, and she could only conclude that he was ashamed.

God demands we forgive others as He forgives us, she thought, troubled. How could she find the strength to forgive a man responsible for her brother's death? *His grace is sufficient,* she told herself, but continued to wrestle with her emotions.

Another thought raced through her mind. Did he know about the abduction of Gem? Questions whizzed like passing arrows in the night. It was inconceivable that Seward had not told him. Her heart thumped. Would he be able to tell her anything about where Gem might be held? But that would mean forgetting about Michael. . . .

Coral had watched the Indian servant call Captain Buckley away from the ballroom where he had entered the billiard room. A discreet inquiry by Charles had given her the information that Colonel Warbeck was meeting there with some military friends. She sat now with a subtle eye on that closed door. Had he recognized her? He must have. Jace Buckley masked his thoughts too well. One thing was certain. He did not look guilty about the past.

"Coral? Are you feeling well? The journey must have been trying for you," said Charles.

Coral rebuked herself for not paying attention, for she really was interested in what he was telling her.

"Yes, you were describing William Carey's translation work at the compound in Serampore." She also noted that Charles looked ill. He had told her that he was leaving to join his brother Franklin in working for Government-House. *He does not look well at all*, she thought.

"I have been battling this wretched disease for two years now . . . and Mister Carey buried a colleague not long ago."

"From the fever?" inquired Coral worriedly, thinking of her mother.

"Afraid so. His name was John Fountain."

"Oh no, not John!"

Charles turned to her with surprise. "You knew him?"

"Not well enough, but he was an acquaintance. A fine man. He was to marry Miss Tibbs. I met him at the Mission Society in London. I knew he was going to join Mister Carey. Does Miss Tibbs know?"

"Yes. She arrived with the Marshmans and Mr. Ward, the printer. Mr. Grant also passed away . . . the fever, I think."

"This is sad news for the mission work. Mr. Carey needs every man he can get."

Charles fumbled with his napkin. "Yes. Well, the ways of the Lord are oft past finding out. But I find myself wondering. Are these trials from the Lord that we might learn to trust Him in hard circumstances, or attacks from Satan?"

Coral shivered. "The powers of darkness cannot take the lives of Christians."

"But the warfare can be oppressive. I should tell you the work is not going as well as William expected. So far there are no converts and a great deal of opposition from unlikely sources." Charles lowered his voice. "I speak of the East India Company, even though Governor-General Wellesley is a fair man. But when he retires, the mission will be in a strait. And Mrs. Carey is having a time of it. Her mind hangs in a delicate balance."

Coral saw his strain. She could not help but notice how much he had changed. No longer was he the gentle, boyish music instructor, but nervous and thin. His hand jerked now and then, nearly spilling his glass of sharbat.

"Mrs. Carey was ill again when I left the mission station at Serampore," he said.

"She grows worse?"

"It grows worse indeed. Lack of finances, food, and shelter have all taken their toll."

"But how did it happen? They say she appeared well enough when they left London with her sister Kitty and Doctor Thomas."

"There may have been something troubling her mind all along, and coming to face the tribulations here in India only brought the matter to the surface."

Coral wondered . . . she remembered something her father had once said about "druggings that permanently affect the mind."

"The death of little Peter did not help, and she was ill in the jungle near the Sunderbans before they came to Serampore."

"Peter? A child?" she repeated.

"He died of fever and dysentery . . . he was the brightest of the Carey children. Even at five he could speak very good Bengali. Mrs. Carey's mental faculties broke with his death, and Master Carey was sick then, too. They could not find anyone to bury Peter."

Coral knew that the Hindus would not break caste.

"Mrs. Carey must be kept in her room. Her meals have to be sent up. There are times when the poor woman rants and raves so that nothing can be done to still her."

"How dreadful."

"It is yet another trial for William, but the work goes on."

Mrs. Carey's loss of Peter brought Coral's mind to Gem. Gem had been just three when he was taken from her. She knew the familiar pang in her heart.

"She did not want to come to India," said Charles.

"No wonder she is ill. She's been through so much. How has Master Carey managed?"

"He is a noble man, Coral. Very dedicated to his work, and to India. While his wife is ill in the next room, William is bent busily over his desk laboring on the Bengali translation. It is the sufficient grace of Christ; what else could it be? He is but flesh and blood as we are, yet he plods ahead doggedly."

Charles lifted his glass to drink, and his hand was shaking.

"Is not Serampore a Danish settlement?" Coral asked.

"Yes, and an open door from the Lord. The move down the Hooghly River has secured our lot. Thankfully, William was able to buy two acres of land from the funds he had earned while running the indigo farm in Mudnabutty. Matters have much improved, but new problems arise from the East India Company."

Coral remembered what Aunt Margaret had told her about the Company's resentment of the missionaries.

Charles hesitated as if he did not care to discuss the opposition now that he was to begin working for the Company. "The British authorities are opposed to missionary work of any sort, fearful of offending the brahmins, although Lord Wellesley has allowed some open-air preaching in Calcutta."

"What of the translation work?"

"It proceeds well, now that Mr. Ward has arrived from London, and we have a printing press. It is by the grace of God that Mr. Bie, governor of Serampore, shows favor toward the task, and even attends the Sunday preaching, bringing other friends of the European community. But the British authorities threatened to send the Marshmans and Mr. Ward back to London when they arrived to work with William. It was Governor Bie's intervention that saved them in the end. Thank God for Denmark!"

"I dare say the Company would hinder the work

in the district altogether if they could get by with it,"
Coral agreed, feeling troubled. "But they cannot do
that, can they, Charles?"

"Carey fears anything might happen after the
governor-general retires. They have already threatened to close down the printing press."

"But they cannot do that," she insisted.

"They can, indeed. The East India Company is the
law in India. They have no jurisdiction in Serampore;
it is Dutch controlled. But if they side with France in
the war, that will give the Company reason to enter
Serampore and claim control over the mission station
and what it prints."

"Let us pray that it does not happen."

He looked unhappy. "My work with Franklin will
prevent me from helping Master Carey. But Mr. Ward
is doing a splendid job, and he has a wonderful relationship with Mr. Carey's boys, especially Felix. He is
like a second father." He hesitated. "I should say, I am
not working for Franklin but for your uncle, Sir Hugo
Roxbury."

Surprised, she said nothing. No wonder Charles
appeared so tense. He walked a tightrope, and Indian
crocodiles swam the river beneath.

There was silence. Suddenly the festive color of
the evening turned drab, the tang of her lemon refreshment tasted flat, a mosquito buzzing about her ear
became loud. Seeing Charles give up his work in exchange for a position with Sir Hugo—even if it was
for health reasons—was discouraging. No, disappoint-
ing. Charles no longer looked like the zealous young
man to whom she had waved goodbye when his ship
sailed from London. He was sick and defeated. It
seemed that the spiritual enemy had won the first battle.

What would the Company's opposition to the mission work mean for William Carey? And what of Sir Hugo's antagonism toward her plans on Kingscote? How could she possibly think that she could stand?

"You look a bit tired, Charles. Maybe you should retire early this evening."

"Yes, so I was thinking." He smiled. "Perhaps we could discuss the work another time. How long will you be staying with your uncle?"

"Not long. Perhaps only two or three weeks. It is important I return home to Kingscote as soon as possible. My mother, as well, is ill. And I wish to see my father."

"About the mission school?"

"Yes . . . and other matters. I have been away for nearly four years, and I am anxious to see my family." Charles's eyes brightened. "Two to three weeks will give you time to visit Master Carey at Serampore. I can show you about before I go, and Mrs. Marshman can give you some sound advice on your school. She runs the Carey school very well indeed."

Coral measured the consequences of Sir Hugo's displeasure against her desire to visit, and decided his scowl must be risked. She hoped to receive portions of Scripture in Hindi to use with the children, especially the Christmas story.

"I would like that, Charles. I will try to arrange it. In a day or two?"

"Let me know. I will send a ghari to pick you up. You will need to take a small boat up the Hooghly to reach us." He stood. "I have not been the best of company tonight, I fear."

"You will feel better in the morning. Just exactly what is your new post in Calcutta?"

"I shall aid my brother Franklin as secretary to

the governor-general. Sir Hugo convinced me that with my health as it is, I was not using my talents to the fullest at Serampore."

"I dare say, any investment in the work of Master Carey is hardly a waste."

"Yes . . . well, we agree there. As for the Company, it is against making proselytes from the religious sects in India. My work will be strictly business."

"Any uprising would threaten the success of trade," said Coral with a trace of sarcasm.

"I am sorry to admit it, but that is exactly the Company's motive. With my health failing at times due to the climate, I decided to accept Sir Hugo's offer. At least I shall work with my brother. In time, when the Carey school grows, I am hoping to teach music there." He paused. "I thought I had made my plans so well. How soon the wind sends them scurrying like dead leaves."

"You sound weary, Charles. Surely the Lord knows the end from the beginning. Our plans are always on hold for His approval. Once you get well again you can always go back to Serampore."

"Your faith encourages me. You are so much like Anne."

"You have done your best, and you are a champion. But me? I have only begun. How can I turn back before I start?" said Coral.

"You will not. I can see the determination in your eyes. Whatever God has for you, Coral, He will see it through to the end. You believe in what you are going to do. That is half the battle."

Charles Peddington was ill, a wounded soldier on the battlefield of the Lord. And Mr. Carey? Even wounded, he continued to plod his course.

"The merchants of London have turned into

greedy lords, caring not for the souls of men but their access to Indian treasure!" she said.

"Do you speak of Kingscote silk when you speak of Indian treasure, my dear?" came the well-modulated voice from behind her.

She saw Charles Peddington flush beneath his tanned cheeks, his gaze fixed on the man who had spoken.

Coral gathered up her skirts and stood, turning to face her uncle.

Sir Hugo Roxbury, swarthy of face and stern of eye, nevertheless smiled down at her. For a moment she thought he would say more, but he changed the subject. "Well, little niece, how pleasant to have you with us in Calcutta!"

"Hello, Uncle."

He gestured his head, with bushy black locks, toward the embarrassed Charles Peddington. "I am pleased to see you two have renewed old friendships. Did I hear you discussing Carey?"

Coral spoke first to alleviate Charles's predicament. "Is it true that translation of the Scriptures into Bengali is not permitted in Calcutta?"

"You need not concern yourself, my dear. I understand Carey is doing well at Serampore under the protective cloak of Governor Bie. I have nothing against the distribution of Scripture to the heathen, but the Company is not here to legislate Western beliefs upon the brahmin."

Western beliefs. . . . Coral wanted to wince.

"The Company is here to trade. We make no apology for that. It is good for England; it is good for the merchants and shippers."

Coral felt affronted. "But is it good for the people?"

He laughed. "The rulers of India want us here. If they did not, they would send us packing. They outnumber us at least ten to one." He placed a strong arm about her shoulders as though he were the protective, indulgent uncle. Even though he was smiling, she found his dark gaze troubling.

"I hope your concern for the Indians does not goad Hampton into risking the silk production. You are quite a young politician, Coral. One would think you would be on the floor waltzing, sending the hearts of young soldiers pounding. Instead you debate Company policy with Charles!"

His veiled attempt to make light of her concerns was typical, and she tried not to let his mockery embarrass her.

"There is such a thing as the practical side to any matter," he went on. "All Europe praises the quality of silk that Hampton is now producing. Soon we shall clothe Napoleon himself!"

Sir Hugo gave a pinch to her chin as though she were a child engaging herself in matters too adult for her reasoning powers. Coral was furious, but only turned her head away.

"My dear, remember, meddling with the beliefs of the Indian people will cause nothing but dissension and riot."

Charles Peddington quickly gathered his books under his arm, looking troubled. "I regret that I must leave early. Good night, Miss Kendall, Sir Hugo." But before he could get away, they were interrupted by Margaret and Belinda.

"There you are, Coral," Margaret said, smiling. "I wondered who had swept you away. Was that not Captain Buckley who arrived a few minutes ago? Why, hullo Charles. Is Franklin about? I do believe he has forgotten his number," she suggested, looking at Belinda's program.

Belinda looked bored, and swished her peacock-feather fan, obviously not thinking of Franklin Peddington, or Sir Arlen George, who was engaged in a discussion with several military gentlemen across the room.

"Good evening, Lady Margaret, Miss Roxbury," Charles acknowledged politely, blushing as Belinda scanned him. "How good to see you both again. Franklin is across the room talking to Dr. Harvey. If you will excuse me, ladies, I shall remind him of his remiss."

Belinda pursed her lips and looked unhappy, but not so much so that she failed to cast a smile at one of the officers walking past. She leaned toward Coral and whispered behind her fan, "Where did Jace go?"

Jace? Was Belinda on a first-name basis with him? Coral recalled how her mother had told her that the colonel and his son were often guests in the Roxbury home. "I do not know," said Coral tonelessly, and turned in time to see Sir Hugo walk toward the handsome figure in uniform who had just entered from the billiard room. The man with a touch of silver at his temples was watching Margaret Roxbury escort her daughter into the ballroom.

"Evening, Colonel," said Sir Hugo. "You have enjoyed your success in getting your son back into the military, I hope?"

The colonel smiled faintly, taking a glass from off a tray as an Indian servant strolled past. "One of my more difficult tasks, Hugo."

So this is the colonel . . . thought Coral curiously, watching him intently from a distance.

"Miss Kendall, I believe this next waltz is mine."

At the resonant voice coming from behind her, Coral turned, surprised. Her gaze confronted the deep blue eyes of Jace Buckley studying her intently.

25

"Good evening, Captain Buckley," she said politely. But as Michael rushed to mind, she felt her cheeks grow warm and was about to excuse herself.

"Your servant, Miss Kendall."

She doubted that, but his words were the pinnacle of chivalry. He offered a precise bow. "I was certain we had met when I saw you at the bazaar . . . but then, it has been over five years."

For a confused moment her mind darted back to that afternoon. The man before her was not the cocky young adventurer whom she had met; and yet . . . beneath the proper bearing, perhaps he was. She recalled the beard, the long hair, the wild, rugged demeanor. No wonder she had not recognized him. He appeared once again as she remembered him at Kingscote: disciplined, a gentleman of the highest order. All that was missing was the silver and black uniform, the impenetrable militaristic facade that shielded—what? A derelict sea captain? It hardly became him and seemed impossible. The words came before she could think to hold them back.

"What other masquerades do you have stored

away in your sea chest, Captain?"

"Surely your imagination can come up with a few things, Miss Kendall. A uniform, the trappings of an Indian guru, a pirate's cudgel, a bottle of rum, perhaps?"

"No. But I did think the monkey on your shoulder rather cute. If you will excuse me—" she tried to brush past.

"I left him with Gokul, much to his displeasure. He was having a tantrum when I left. By the way, you might offer a finishing-school smile. We are being observed by many curious eyes."

Coral gave a casual glance about her. "I doubt if it matters to you what others think."

"It matters to me what you think. I also doubt that you will walk off and leave me standing on the floor alone. You are much too cultured for that, even without Lady Anne's Finishing School."

Yes, he was still the brash young man that she had met years earlier . . . "Perhaps. But I think you are mistaken," she replied demurely.

"About what?"

Coral looked pointedly at the program in his hand. "This waltz. My aunt thought I would be too weary after the journey, so she did not sign me up."

He smiled slightly and tossed the paper aside, meeting her gaze evenly. "What luck. Then I need not share the evening with any other officers."

Coral did everything she could to keep her poise. What good was a finishing school? All *savoir-faire* failed the moment you needed it. "I . . . ah . . . thought I might retire early after a long day's travel."

"I was not drunk the day Michael was lost."

His bluntness took her off guard. Her eyes came reluctantly back to his.

"I will not let you walk away until I explain," he stated.

The waltz was beginning, and Jace offered his hand, his eyes flickering with amused challenge. "You would not refuse, would you? A precocious young lady who fears neither guru nor crows? Whereas, I am completely harmless—and sober. You believe in fairness, of course?"

She *did* want to waltz with him, perhaps a bit more than she would admit even to herself. "Well . . . I suppose . . ."

The lilting strains of the waltz filled the elegant ballroom of Government-House.

If I miss a step I will feel a fool, she thought as they began to move about the dance floor.

"Somehow I thought better of you," he said, one hand gently resting on her back, the other encircling her own petite hand.

Thought better of *her*! Coral's eyes lifted to his. No, there was no amusement to be found in their depths, only challenge. "A change of opinion regarding character is supposed to be my prerogative," she said.

"You wrote me an accusatory letter. A very *nasty* one, actually. Then you refused to see me to let me defend my honor. That is hardly the epitome of fairness. And it is not the memory I had of you from Kingscote."

"But, sir, I did not refuse to see you."

"But, *madam*, you did not respond to my letter."

Letter? Coral lifted her head, then looked away again. "What letter, Captain Buckley?"

"The letter, Miss Kendall, that I sent in reply to yours. I gave it to Seward to deliver to Roxbury House, and he assured me that he did."

"You answered my letter?"

"Of course."

"But—I did not receive it," she said in a small voice. "I was waiting for it, I hoped—" she stopped. Then what had happened to it? And what had happened to Jan-Lee's letter?

"I asked to see you before the *Madras* sailed, to explain about Michael. I do not know where you came up with the idea that I was derelict in my duty, but I find it offensive to everything I believe in."

Coral's step fumbled, her shock showing through in her lack of concentration. "Oh! Excuse me. Did I step on your foot?"

"Think nothing of it. Then you did not receive my letter?"

Coral drew in a small breath as they swirled about the ballroom. Two letters were missing. One from Jan-Lee, the other from Jace. But she was hesitant to tell him so, for fear he would confront her uncle. *I cannot risk Uncle Hugo's wrath, yet.*

"I was ill for some months . . . my grandmother has a faltering memory, and perhaps she forgot to tell me about it."

His expression displayed obvious disbelief. "Let us not fault your grandmother. I think we both know with whom the blame rests. But for the moment, I will let it slip by. I would like to tell you about Michael. We hit a storm off England. One of the worst I have been in. I had him in my grasp . . . but a wave tore us apart. I will never forgive myself for what happened, but I can assure you of one thing. I did not lose him because I was drunk in my cabin. I cannot understand why you would think I was!"

Coral kept her gaze averted. He had tried to save Michael! But naturally he would, since he was with him, and evidently he had not been in his cabin. Her own guilt was sharp. Why had she believed Uncle Hugo? The truth was, she had doubted him, and that was what had motivated her to write the letter. But when he did not answer . . .

She glanced across the ballroom floor toward her uncle. He was still in conversation with Colonel Warbeck. *Why would he benefit from deceiving me?*

Coral tried to remember back to what had happened after the episode in the library with her uncle and could not recall the details clearly. She had vague recollections of the carriage ride to the summer house on the London Strand, followed by weeks of illness away from the family. She stopped—was it not then, after her mind had cleared, that she discovered the letter from Jan-Lee was gone? Had the entire stay at the summer house simply afforded her uncle opportunity to destroy the letter and gain her cooperation in altering her plans to see Director Rawlings?

Coral wrestled with gnawing doubt. She wanted to trust her uncle, despite their differences. And yet, Coral found her trust shifting to the man before her.

She said a trifle breathlessly, "The waltz is so lovely, Captain. And I do not think Michael would approve of our ruining the entire evening by mourning his death. Oh, please! Will you forget what I said in my letter? I see now that I was wrong. Can you forgive me?"

Was his grave expression a pretense?

"Well . . ."

"Oh, please!"

"I will give serious consideration to your request, say, during the next five waltzes?"

Coral laughed. "Anything to make up for my rudeness." *And to keep you away from Uncle,* she thought, and hurriedly went on: "It was inexcusable of me to jump to such odious conclusions."

He smiled a little and his eyes twinkled merrily. "You will need to be exceptionally nice to me all evening to make up for your trespass. Otherwise, I may need to speak to Sir Hugo about what happened to the letter I sent you."

Coral's eyes swiftly met his. *He must not incur my uncle's wrath!* "Uncle Hugo would have nothing to do with the letter not reaching me."

"No?"

"I am sure it was my grandmother, Lady Victoria. She forgets matters very easily. No doubt she merely mislaid the letter. . . ."

The flecks of black hardened in his eyes. "Perhaps. But she did not tell you the captain of the *Madras* was drunk in his cabin. And I do not believe you would come to that conclusion unless someone suggested it. Which leads me to believe that your uncle filled your mind with deliberate lies about me."

His eyes held hers, and Coral spoke quietly, "Please, will you not forget all that?"

"Yes, as long as you no longer believe it."

"I do not," she said quickly, noting the humor behind his eyes. *He looks as though he is enjoying this,* Coral thought, a bit flustered.

"Good." He smiled. "Then shall we put the past behind us and enjoy the evening?"

"Yes, I think so, Captain. And the waltz has stopped."

"Ah, but the next is just beginning."

EPILOGUE

Coral awoke to the sounds of birds cooing, whistling, and scolding. Half asleep under the satin coverlet with a film of mosquito netting drawn around the bed, her brain, dull from lack of sleep, wondered if Aunt Margaret had erected a bird aviary beneath the window. . . .

Suddenly, images of last night's ball burst like daylight into her subconscious. *Jace Buckley* . . . Coral's eyes flew open.

She smiled, having thoroughly enjoyed the evening. There was an energy, an excitement about him, and because she found him so, Coral reminded herself that she must regard him with caution. Ethan would not like the adventurous sea captain. However, in fairness to Captain Buckley, he had behaved the gallant gentleman—or at least, he had gone out of his way to don the role.

Coral only now realized that she had learned very little about him or his plans, whereas he had managed to learn a great deal about her stay in London, her illness, and Ethan. What they had not discussed was her plans to start the school for the untouchables, and

Gem. Somehow the gaiety of the ball and the whirling waltzes had not permitted serious subjects. All that would come later.

Coral seized the pearl-handled mirror from the nightstand and gazed critically at her face. Despite the late hour she had gone to bed, she felt only a little tired, and a closer inspection showed that the faint shadows beneath her eyes had not darkened.

She threw aside the coverlet and slipped into the ankle-length peignoir lying across the foot of the bed. Pushing aside the veil, Coral crossed the room to the window with its drawn-up bamboo sunshade. The early morning still held the night's whisper of coolness. Along the bank of the Hooghly River, the trees were teeming with a rainbow of color as parakeets fought for landing space.

Coral's thoughts jumped ahead to the upcoming safari that would bring her home to Kingscote. Remembering what Margaret had told her about Jorhat, she frowned a little. "I should have used the opportunity last night to ask Captain Buckley about the trouble at the outpost," she murmured aloud. There was Seward to ask of course, and she intended to speak with him today if possible and discuss the journey. Nothing must be allowed to delay her travel plans, not even political unrest. Yet even the safari home must wait a few weeks—there was something more critical she must do while in Calcutta.

A surge of expectation sent her heartbeat racing. Staying in Calcutta permitted her to pursue the clandestine meeting between her and the Indian mercenary who would search for Gem!

But how could she slip away unseen? She must plan painstakingly.

From downstairs came the morning sounds of the

servants preparing the Roxbury household for the main breakfast in the dining room, and a steaming urn of tea and platters of fresh fruit arrived at her bedroom by a servant and the small Indian child she had met the day before. Jay smiled shyly as he arranged the platter on Coral's rattan table, then lingered. She followed his gaze to a white ceramic dog with a rhinestone collar. The servant gave him a stern look and the boy turned and hurried out.

As Coral chose a wedge of orange mango, she heard Aunt Margaret coming down the hallway. Her aunt looked in through the open doorway, already dressed, her thick dark hair plaited and a smile on her attractive face. But Coral noted a certain tenseness in her eyes, as though other thoughts were troubling her.

"Good morning." She smiled at Coral. "You are looking well. I was afraid Captain Buckley kept you up too late."

Coral smiled in return and took a sip from her teacup. It seemed every woman at the ball had noticed that Jace had not troubled to waltz with anyone else. In a way, she had found it embarrassing, but at the same time she was flattered that he had even stayed at the ball, for she knew that he hadn't intended to. He danced well, and his looks were indisputably intriguing. She recalled the envious glances from Cousin Belinda.

"You do not have much time before breakfast. We have a rule: no one is permitted to straggle in for meals. We eat as a family, and everyone is to be fully dressed. You have thirty minutes."

The door shut, leaving her alone. *Thirty minutes!* If she wanted to send a message to her contact, there was no time to waste.

Coral waited until the sound of her aunt's footsteps died away, then she hurried to the desk. She wrote quickly in Bengali on a sheet of paper:

Saturday, October 13
Huzoor! Javed Kasam:
    I am willing to pay a worthy price for important information. Needless to say, our meeting must be kept in the strictest confidence. My ghari will be parked by the Armenian church in the Chowringhee district next Saturday, October 20.

        Signed,

Coral paused, tapping the end of the pen with uncertainty. Suppose he sent an inquiry to Sir Hugo? Uncle would then put a guard on her for the rest of her stay in Calcutta. Quickly she signed, *Ayub Khan.*

Coral slipped from her room into the hall, her heart racing. If Sir Hugo saw her . . .

The hallway remained empty while the others busied themselves dressing. She sped to the banister and leaned over. The Indian child was carrying a jug of water up the stairs. She waited for him, then motioned for him to follow her into her chamber. Coral shut the door without a sound and, kneeling, took hold of his tiny shoulders. She smiled to ease the curiosity in his large brown eyes, and whispered in Bengali: "Find me a big boy. One who can deliver a secret message. I will pay him a fistful of rupees. If you do this quickly, unseen, missy-sahiba will have a present for you."

Coral pointed to the ceramic dog she had bought in London.

Jay grinned, caught on swiftly, and whispered, "Big brother, he go, he go for fistful rupees!"

"Hurry then. Find him. Tell your brother what I said. If he agrees, come back to my room."

344

The boy darted out and, moving as silently as a cat, disappeared.

Coral paced, keeping the door open a crack to watch for his return. Within ten minutes he was back, casting a glance over his shoulder. She drew him inside. "Yes?"

"Big brother in yard behind kitchen. He will go now, missy-sahiba."

"Good boy, Jay." Coral stuffed the sealed envelope inside his tunic, then handed him the dog. He grinned, salaamed, and backed out into the hall.

With relief, Coral sank against the door.

The way was now open to gain the precious information she needed to locate Gem's whereabouts. She would get the money to pay the mercenary, and if her son was alive as she suspected, somehow she would buy Gem's release from his captor.

As Coral hurried to dress for breakfast, she hummed the refrain of a waltz she had danced in the arms of Jace Buckley.

Yes, she was going to enjoy the brief stay in Calcutta. . . .

She reached a hand to touch her Bible on the dressing table, opening it to the presentation page. In her mother's hand was written:

It is never so dark that God cannot deliver.

Hope beat strong in her heart, for she believed the Lord had already heard her prayers, and in His timing, in His own way, He would return the joy of her heart. Coral smiled and left her room to go downstairs, still humming.

GLOSSARY

AYAH: A child's nurse.

ASSAM: Northeast India, location of Kingscote.

BRAHMIN: Highest Hindu caste.

BOURKA: A one-piece garment, usually white cotton, covering the female from head to foot, with a small square of coarse net or slits to see through.

BURRA-SAHIB: A great man.

CHUNNI: A light head-covering; a scarf.

DAK: A resting house for travelers.

DEWAN: The chief minister of an Indian ruler.

GHAT: Steps or a platform on the river; also where the Hindu dead are cremated.

GHARI: A horse-drawn vehicle; a carriage.

GHAZI: A fanatic; usually with religious overtones, but also referring to political beliefs.

HOOKAH: A water pipe for tobacco; also used for smoking other types of drugs.

JAI RAM: A Hindu greeting.

JOHN COMPANY: Another name for the East India Company, usually hinting at its clandestine activities (i.e., opium running).

KANSAMAH: A cook.

347

KOTWAL: A headman.

MAHARAJA: A Hindu king.

MAHOUT: An elephant driver.

MANJI: A boatman.

MAIDAN: A large expanse of lawn; a parade ground.

NAMASTE: A respectful gesture of fingers to the forehead with palms together.

NAUKER-LOG: Servants.

PUGGARI: A turban.

PUNKAH: A fan made of heavy matting or canvas, sometimes wet, and pulled by a rope to make a breeze.

RAJA: A king.

RANI: A queen.

RAJPUTS: A warrior caste of the Hindus, a rank below the *brahmins*.

SEPOY: An infantry soldier.

SHARBAT: Iced lemonade

SOWAR: A cavalry trooper.

UNTOUCHABLE: One that is below the Hindu caste system, condemned as unclean in this life.

VEDAS: Ancient Hindu sacred writings; their orthodox scriptures.